Praise for Leah Hager Cohen's
Heart, You Bully, You Punk

"*Heart, You Bully, You Punk* describes the mysterious, unpredictable, even mutinous ways people's hearts mess with their lives . . . packed with detail . . . *Heart, You Bully, You Punk* is a lively, thoughtful pleasure."
—*The New York Times Book Review*

"Attraction is a slippery concept . . . but [Cohen] is a good author, not just filling her characters with feelings, love among them, but lavishing care on everything from the food . . . to the minute details of rooms. . . . The single window that the science and math departments share says as much about Cohen's fine eye as it does about the dismal architecture of school buildings."   —*The Washington Post Book World*

"Esker is the kind of broken soul you root for, and Cohen's wistful novel evokes the intense vulnerability of love and the shattering pain of loss. B+"
—*Entertainment Weekly*

"Insightful, charming, quirky, beautifully written . . . it's a testament to Cohen's skill that the novel—despite the stubborn and seemingly self-defeating will of the protagonists—delivers a dessert course in emotional truth that will leave the reader longing for more. Cohen is a writer to watch."   —*The Tampa Tribune*

"Lovingly crafted. . . . Small gestures carry great weight, and images and details reverberate throughout, as tension builds, not organically from situations, but from Cohen's descriptive layering."
—*Publishers Weekly*

"Rigorous and accomplished."
—*Kirkus Reviews*

"Beguilingly cheerful and alive to the nuances of pain . . . *Heart, You Bully, You Punk* has enormous emotional scope and frequent astonishing insights."   —Andrew Solomon, author of *The Noonday Demon*

ABOUT THE AUTHOR

Leah Hager Cohen is the author of the novel *Heat Lighting* and of three acclaimed works of nonfiction, *Train Go Sorry; Glass, Paper, Beans;* and *The Stuff of Dreams.* She lives with her three children near Boston, Massachusetts.

heart, you bully, you punk

LEAH HAGER COHEN

PENGUIN BOOKS

PENGUIN BOOKS
Published by the Penguin Group
Penguin Group (USA) Inc. 375 Hudson Street, New York, New York 10014, U.S.A.
Penguin Books Ltd, 80 Strand, London WC2R 0RL, England
Penguin Books Australia Ltd, 250 Camberwell Road, Camberwell, Victoria 3124, Australia
Penguin Books Canada Ltd, 10 Alcorn Avenue, Toronto, Ontario, Canada M4V 3B2
Penguin Books India (P) Ltd, 11 Community Centre,
Panchsheel Park, New Delhi – 110 017, India
Penguin Books (N.Z.) Ltd, Cnr Rosedale and Airborne Roads,
Albany, Auckland, New Zealand
Penguin Books (South Africa) (Pty) Ltd, 24 Sturdee Avenue,
Rosebank, Johannesburg 2196, South Africa

Penguin Books Ltd, Registered Offices:
80 Strand, London WC2R 0RL, England

First published in the United States of America by Viking 2003
Published in Penguin Books 2004

1   3   5   7   9   10   8   6   4   2

"Heart, You Bully, You Punk" is from the poem "One is One" by Marie Ponsot.
Grateful acknowledgment is made for permission to reprint "One is One"
from *The Bird Catcher* by Marie Ponsot. Copyright © 1998 by Marie Ponsot.
Used by permission of Alfred A. Knopf, a division of Random House, Inc.

PUBLISHER'S NOTE
This is a work of fiction. Names, characters, places, and incidents either are the product
of the author's imagination or are used fictitiously, and any resemblance to actual persons,
living or dead, business establishments, events, or locales is entirely coincidental.

THE LIBRARY OF CONGRESS HAS CATALOGED THE HARDCOVER EDITION AS FOLLOWS:
Cohen, Leah Hager.
Heart, you bully, you punk / Leah Hager Cohen
p.   cm.
ISBN 0-670-03167-4 (hc.)
ISBN 0 14 20.0432 4 (pbk.)
1. Teenage girls—Fiction.   2. Teacher-student relationships—Fiction.
3. Fathers and daughters—Fiction.   4. Mathematics teachers—Fiction.   I. Title.
PS3553.O42445 H69 2003
813'.54—dc21   2002069191

Printed in the United States of America
Set in Adobe Garamond
Designed by Erin Benach

To
Barney Karpfinger
and
Betsy Lerner

ONE IS ONE

Heart, you bully, you punk, I'm wrecked, I'm shocked
stiff. You? you still try to rule the world—though
I've got you: identified, starving, locked
in a cage you will not leave alive, no
matter how you hate it, pound its walls,
& thrill its corridors with messages.

Brute. Spy. I trusted you. Now you reel & brawl
in your cell but I'm deaf to your rages,
your greed to go solo, your eloquent
threats of worse things you (knowing me) could do.
You scare me, bragging you're a double agent

since jailers are prisoners' prisoners too.
Think! Reform! Make us one. Join the rest of us,
and joy may come, and make its test of us.

—Marie Ponsot

heart, you bully, you punk

1.

Says Esker, "I'll do it," when Ann James winds up with casts on both legs and needs home tutoring. She says it resignedly, as if, being department chair, only she might be expected to assume this extra burden; she also says it pre-emptively, denying the other two math teachers an opportunity to volunteer. Either of them might; what with open classrooms and team teaching, no one instructor is more responsible for a particular student than another. And Ann James is the sort of student any teacher might volunteer to tutor at home, even if she weren't also gifted in math. Esker can tell by the look on his face that Larry might like to; there go his sandy eyebrows tilting toward each other in an offering sort of way.

But Rhada, the quicker, speaks first. "No, me. I'll do it." And Esker feels a flare of annoyance until Rhada adds, "That's time and a half for overtime, right?," making obvious to Esker what she ordinarily would have realized immediately, that Rhada's being sarcastic, of course. Esker moves briskly to the next item (the lack of a single freshman on Math Team), and the matter remains settled.

The radiator in the math office makes slurpy, digestive noises, and the narrow window (whose other half belongs to the science office, behind the particleboard partition) grows reflective with early dusk. Esker, never a lingerer, progresses with her usual efficiency through the agenda, adjourning just before five. Then, amid brief, amiable bustle—Larry stuffing algebra quizzes into his nylon briefcase, Rhada sliding mustard-stockinged feet into black chunk-heeled boots—the subject of Ann James returns.

"How long is she going to be out, do they know?" asks Larry. It happened last Friday; this is Monday. Word of the accident has gotten round, but few details.

Esker peers at the memo Florence, the headmistress, left in her box this morning. "Through the holiday, it sounds like."

"Poor kid."

"But, really, home tutoring?" says Rhada. "What happened to Florence's boundary issues?"

"What do you mean?" Larry zips his bag shut.

"You know." She strikes a pose, hand on hip, high-pitched attitude. Rhada is young, only three years out of Hunter College and still at the clubs every weekend. "All that 'no student-staff socializing' she's always going on about."

Esker, listening at her desk, keeps her eyes on paperwork. A hefty series of memos and policy statements, clarifications and initiatives, all that sort of thing, did clog their faculty mailboxes for a while when Florence came on as headmistress last year, but Esker suspects Rhada was spoken to individually as well. Sort of abruptly in October, she stopped hanging out on the building's wide front stoop with the hip-hop kids during lunch.

"Well," says Larry, considering. "Still, I guess she wants to please the customers."

"The customers!" Rhada makes a derisive sound as she slides her coat off the hanger. It is burnt-orange and has a hood rimmed in burnt-orange fake fur. "How'd Ann do it anyway, anybody hear?"

Esker shakes her head; the note, in Florence's aggressively professional cadences, only says something about a bilateral fracture incurred on school grounds.

Larry says, "Fell off the bleachers, apparently," and Rhada says, "Ouch. *Ow.* Jeez," and leaves, characteristically abrupt. Esker is glad to have it end at that; she's aware of feeling an unaccountable protectiveness—no, possessiveness—around the subject.

Larry slings on his embarrassing leather jacket—too tough for his wispy blondness—and says to wish Ann a speedy recovery. He doesn't close the door behind him, and Esker listens to the clomp of his boots on the stairs, his pace as headlong and galumphing as a student's. Then, in the empty office, she smooths the headmistress's note and dials the number given.

"Hello?" Ann answers, sounding as if she were expecting the punchline to a joke.

"Ann? Esker from The Prospect School here." Teachers at The Prospect School are generally known by first name to students and colleagues alike, but Esker only ever goes by her last. Her first and middle names are Iphigenia and Julia, which she long ago found too preposterously romantic to use. On forms she is I. J. Esker.

"Oh. Hey!"

"You sound too chipper to've broken both ankles. How are you feeling?"

"Not my ankles," says Ann, "my heels," and, with some boastfulness, "I have bilateral calcaneal fractures. And I'm not really chipper. I'm on drugs."

"Oh."

"They gave me codeine. I feel excellent."

Esker smiles a smile located mostly in the movement of her throat and speaks crisply into the receiver. "I'm calling to arrange a tutoring plan for you while you're out. Your father, I guess, spoke with Florence."

"Yeah. He's not home right now."

"Would you like me to call back and speak with him?"

"No, that's all right. I can. What's the plan?"

"The plan," says Esker, "so far as I know, is to set up a time for me to come over and help you stay caught up with your math work."

"Okay."

"What would be a good day for you?"

"Any. I'm not exactly going anywhere." Ann is the sort of student who, codeine or no, speaks to a teacher with the same frank confidence as she would a peer. There is something unwittingly flirtatious in this. They agree on the following afternoon. Esker copies Ann's address into her engagement book with green pencil. Then she hangs up and gets her coat.

It is December already. No snow yet, but a cold vagueness hangs in the air, fumes of things burning, thinks Esker as she stands for a moment tying her scarf under the spread iron wings of the beast of indeterminate species that hovers over the school entrance. Some kind of predator, with its hooked beak and claw feet; Esker finds it macabre. She hurries toward

Grand Army Plaza, weaving in and out of the flow of other pedestrians, dodging a stooped woman towing a metal cart of groceries. Her train is already there when she reaches the platform. Esker slips in, claims with efficiency the last empty seat. She's been making this commute for nine years.

The Prospect School is a small alternative high school housed off Prospect Park in a beguiling and dilapidated formerly private estate. The elaborately mosaicked floor in the lobby is minus a large portion of its intricate marble tesserae; the crystal chandelier hangs too high for anyone to bother replacing the burnt-out bulbs; the basement classrooms not only stink of mildew but sport bluish-greenish pointillistic growths on their walls; tiny mounds of fine, crumbled plaster collect in the coffin turns and on the wainscoting and the sills; and on and on; the Renovation Committee, inaugurated by Florence, compiled an exhaustive list last spring for fund-raising purposes.

Most of the 180-odd students come from Park Slope or Brooklyn Heights; most of the faculty do not. Esker finds teaching at The Prospect School to be rewarding in almost every way but monetary. She rents an apartment in lower Manhattan, on an anonymous block of Greenwich Street. The building is unusually old and tiny: three stories high and only thirteen feet wide; its immediate neighbors are warehouses, garages, and a nameless corner bar with a slow-blinking neon shamrock hung over the entrance. She's lived in the same apartment since she began teaching at age twenty-two. She doesn't remember when she ceased thinking of it as a temporary abode.

She'd moved in on a miserable dog-breathy day in August. Each crate and carton she'd lifted from the whitish van had seemed twice its weight: the very force of gravity that day had seemed unnatural, heavy as grief, and she lay, afterward, as if pinned to the bare mattress, damp-skinned, dry-eyed, taking in the ceiling. It was a splendid ceiling, actually, tin, stamped with a pineapple-y box design, and as evening sifted gradually into the room, the heaviness lifted and the shadows went bluish and soft. Esker rose then and walked two blocks west to the river, the breeze sweeping along her muscles, which were still shaky from exertion. She had drifted, a porous, untethered body, between the West Side Highway and the chain-link fence that ran along the docks, where the soft figures of coupling men moved together and apart in darkening indistinguishability. Radiant heat came at her from the asphalt, and headlights careened behind her back, and in her exquisite insignificance she'd found a measure of freedom that was almost like peace.

Esker gets off now at Chambers Street, ten blocks from home, and ascends into a light, cold rain. She puts on her hat. Taxis beckon along the avenue; she passes them by. Mastery over her own unhappiness has given her a clean, forceful gait.

2.

What she told Buddy, the art teacher, was that she slipped. She told her friends she jumped. The truth, Ann knows, is not quite either. Her body was *lifted* off the top bleacher at school last Friday, propelled by a morphous desire with invisible hands. Morphous (she is studying for the SAT's): having a specified shape or form. Examples: Cone, cylinder, snowflake, egg. Coral reef. Chicken bone. Desire. This desire had clear fingers, which cupped her heart the way a magician cups a dove before flinging it into the air. It scares her a little, even now, four days later; that's how much she had no control. It was like all those times you're looking out over the edge of a balcony thinking, "What if I can't fight the urge to jump?" and of course you never do jump, some little primitive, vestigial switch inside your body prevents you from ever doing so—only last Friday hers malfunctioned. But, oh, it was exhilarating. For a moment (this is her gorgeous, frightening secret), she was airborne, she is certain: the air held her up. Like a lover in a black-and-white movie. A lover's arms and zero gravity. She really believes this happened.

Then she was crumpled on the hardwood floor of what had been a hundred years earlier a ballroom and was now the Big Room, a sort of gymnasium-cum-auditorium, and Malcolm Choy was looping an arm around her back and between the soft part of her arm and her breast. Malcolm is a senior, beautiful and remote, and everyone Ann knows has a crush on him. He is lean, the color of a Heath Bar, with forearms and cheekbones as unrealistically defined as if inked in a comic book. He is part Chinese and part Trinidadian. He wears his heavy black hair parted in the middle, sometimes tucked behind his ears, and an elephant's-hair bracelet on his right wrist. He is swoon material, and utterly tranquil.

Last year, the great fad among a certain highly charged and visible group of Prospect School students had been bisexuality, the Prospect School version of which had mostly boiled down, among the girls, to wearing lots of Hanes underwear for men and kissing one another on the mouth upon arrival at school every morning. Among the boys, the most lasting and surprising by-product had been the forging of several intimate and platonic relationships with girls. But this year, the new height of hipness is asexuality, as exemplified by no one better than Malcolm Choy, with his kindly smile and smooth muscles and maddening monk's air. He exudes the absence of need. He makes Ann pant.

It was his entrance into the Big Room that ignited the urge that propelled Ann off the bleachers, where she'd been dangling her legs sideways off the edge of the uppermost level, waiting for Winter Concert auditions to begin. He'd come in the doorway, a drum under each arm, and, glancing around, met her gaze. Her heart had gone off like a cap gun. All she could do then was fly, so she did. For one extended unclocked moment, she sprung aloft, and then Denise Escobar shrieked and two dozen pairs of eyes looked up, buoying her, a miraculous Anna-bird with straight hair streaming, and then she landed much too hard on both heels, and was saying, *"Shit. Ahh—shit,"* her face pink with excitement and shock and her eyes wet and bright with pain.

But, miracle of miracles, it was Malcolm Choy who helped her rise, and Malcolm Choy's hard Heath Bar (bare!) arm against which she, finding she could not put weight on her feet, fell. It would have been nice if Malcolm Choy had then swooped her up, one arm below her shoulder blades, the other under the bend of her knees, and transported her, pressed against his warm black T-shirt, to the office, and waited there with her while the ambulance was called. In fact it was Buddy, the faculty member in charge of Winter Concert, who interceded at this point. Buddy is small of stature and has a famously bad back; he sent a freshman into the art room for his padded swivel chair, and in this Ann was wheeled, haphazardly, to the office, while Malcolm, no doubt, set up his conga drums.

Now the phone rings, and it's the doorman saying her teacher is in the lobby. Her teacher! Ann forgot. She is wearing her Curious George pajamas and has Peppermint Blues nail polish on all twenty nails, and her hair is still in the braids she made last night, which is to say wisps sticking out in every direction. Around her on the red couch are strewn books, magazines, sections of the paper, manicure things, a virtually empty tube of Pringles, a sports bottle of water, the remote, the phone, a set of feminist Tarot cards and accompanying instruction book, a toy periscope, a Discman, a plate with a crust of grilled cheese on it, a magnifying mirror, tweezers, a bag of Tootsie Rolls and corresponding candy wrappers, and Killycot, the stuffed camel she's had since she was one. "Send her up, please," says Ann. She buries Killycot beneath the afghan.

The Jameses' apartment, except for bedrooms and bathroom, is entirely open space, with a series of red-painted posts where walls have been knocked down. It hasn't rooms so much as areas. When the door opens, Ann says, "I'm over here," and waves Esker toward the living area, which is arranged before the French doors leading onto the balcony. This is the system for letting people in, because she can't get up. She's in not one but two non-weight-bearing casts. The wheelchair is parked by the couch like some mute, shiny houseguest, super-polite and oppressive, along with the slide board she's supposed to use for maneuvering herself in and out, but Ann is so far fearful of attempting this operation alone.

Esker nears, her mouth set disapprovingly. "Your doorman gives out the key?" she says by way of greeting, holding up the item in question. It glints.

"He has to. I can't get up, and it's better than leaving it unlocked."

Esker takes in couch-ridden Ann. Both feet are done up in bright-blue air casts like express-mail parcels. "I don't think it's a good idea, though. How does he know I'm who I say?"

Ann considers this delightedly. Intrigue! "Maybe we should have a password." Then all she wants to do is think up a good password—"Leg-o' mutton . . . Gilgamesh . . . Hamper . . ."—but Esker is standing there with her slight frown, and her briefcase, and her coat on, glistening a little with rain or melted snow. Ann never realized how small Esker is. She looks grimly out of place, like someone in a Magritte painting. "Oh," says Ann. "Sit anywhere. Hello."

"Hello," says Esker, setting her briefcase on the cherry coffee table. "What do I do with this?" The key.

"You have to keep it so you can bring it back downstairs. You can't forget. Don't let me let you forget."

Esker takes off her coat and sits on the leather ottoman. She surveys hastily the large, unconventional apartment, drags her briefcase into her lap, cocks her chin at Ann. "So what did you do to yourself, anyway?"

Ann shuffles the versions in her head. There is something in Esker's tea-brown gaze that looks so perceptive Ann gets flustered, more so than when she explained it to Buddy, or the emergency-room people, or her friends, or even her father, and what comes out is, "I got pushed off the bleachers in the Big Room."

"Pushed?"

"Accidentally. Nudged."

Something passes over Esker's face.

"I was kind of nudged from the inside. I mean, pretty stupid, I know, forget it," she says, suddenly overcome by embarrassment. Besieged by embarrassment. This has been happening lately: moments of high self-consciousness, an absurd, almost paralyzing sense of detail. Moments when she wants to dodge under the covers and be seven. Her neck is heating, and her cheeks. Ann picks up *Seventeen* and actually holds it in front of her face for a minute.

"Hello," says Esker.

Ann says something that sounds a lot like "Whew!" and fans herself with the magazine and throws it back into the heap. Outside the French doors the world is gray, too gray to see Governors Island or even the East River; it's all gray pea soup out there. Graypea. Grapey. Shut up, brain. Water clanks in the pipes. Esker is doing the absurd thing of waiting patiently for Ann to return. Not quizzical, not frowning, not smiling. She just waits.

"It's funny for you to make a house call," says Ann brightly. "I feel like in *Little Women* or something."

"Why *Little Women*?"

"Oh, I don't know, I never read it. Just—you know, *Jane Eyre* or something."

Esker smiles a little and sips an audible portion of air, as if about to pursue something, but then she only opens a small hinged case and slides her glasses on. They have rather heavy black frames. Ann has more than once had the impression that Esker doesn't really need them to see. Her hair, indifferently cut, not long, not short, suggests the color and texture of a paper bag. Her mouth is soft, her chin sharp. Her neck is a surprisingly elegant column. "Have you had any other teachers by yet?"

"No. I think only you're coming."

"Really! Why?"

"That's all I wanted."

Eyebrows up. "Why?"

"I mean, not you, but math."

Esker nods, still inquiring.

"Well, because. The SCEEs are at the end of January, and I registered for the math one."

SCEEs are Special College Entrance Exams, an elite national testing service designed—as Rhada once put it, with a somewhat lewd lip-licking gesture—to extract the creamiest of the cream of the crop. Esker is more than a little repulsed by it, this increasing pressure on students to subject themselves to ever more tests, whittling themselves down to rows of tight black integers upon a transcript, all ready to goose-step straight into a computer. Uses like these give numbers a bad name. Still, The Prospect School gives no grades, only written evaluations, so its college-bound students (99 to 100 percent of any given year's graduating class, as Florence is wont to stress at every opportunity) feel particular pressure to rack up actual numerical scores.

"I see," says Esker. Of course Ann would want to take the mathski (mathski, litski, chemski, bioski—they're known among the students by their Iron Curtain–sounding pet names). Esker wouldn't call Ann James a math prodigy, but that's because she doesn't use the word "prodigy." She's had students whose work has been cleaner, quicker, more precise and direct than Ann's, but she's never had anyone with Ann's capacity to *play* with math, with Ann's understanding of math as something creative, amusing, unpredictable. She regards this student, perched sort of luminously on the red couch with her ratty pigtails and chicly childish pajamas and big blue clown-shoe air casts, and she is struck, as she has been before, on several occasions at school, but more so now, here in Ann's own apartment, by an alarming and unprovoked wave of tender feeling. She pulls her engagement calendar from her briefcase, appears to consult it. "I can come once a week, if you like, until you're better. Or until the SCEE. Will you be on your feet by then?"

Ann squinches her face, shrugs. The resident in the emergency room had been very festive, prattling charmingly in his Brazilian accent as he fit the braces (which she wore for twenty-four hours, before getting the casts), very gently, onto her swollen feet and ankles, informing her that most people who incurred bilateral calcaneal fractures were petty burglars who, surprised in the act, had jumped out of windows trying to flee. "It's very ironic!" he'd declared. "Society then gets that person off their feet for at least three or four weeks!" Ann had wondered whether this qualified as irony. Irony: incongruity between what might be expected and what actually occurs. Falling instead of fleeing. Flying instead of falling. Flying into Malcolm Choy's arms. That would have been ironic. What she'd said to the resident was, "Three or four weeks—is that how long I'll have to wear casts?" and he had assured her, festively, "At least!"

"I hope so," she tells Esker now. "With crutches if nothing else."

"Okay, lady. Let's work, then." Esker hauls a fat textbook out of her briefcase. "By the way, what are we listening to?"

Amahl and the Night Visitors has been looping all afternoon on the stereo, and the shepherds have just begun joyously calling to one another.

Ann beams and says the title. It is her happy music. But Esker freely grimaces. "Can we kill it? I can't work with noise in the background." Ann isn't offended. Esker's rudeness—is that the right word?—has a certain purity, is kind of exquisite, so that Ann finds herself stimulated by it, alert to see where it might lead. She aims the remote and halts the music.

The silence that zooms into the room triggers for Ann a new wave of high, singing embarrassment. There's nothing untoward here—is there? She checks: nothing to be embarrassed about (except the stupid leap that landed her here in the first place). Yet, in this moment, every little thing stands out unbearably: the flat planes of Esker's forearms emerging from her pushed-up sleeves, the tooth-dented colored pencils she's laid on the coffee table, the lump of Killycot against Ann's hip, oh, everything—the red-painted posts holding up the stupid ceiling, the slow-milling dust motes, the feel of air going back and forth through her nostrils. It's as if the dull pretense of ordinariness that normally coats and tempers each object has been stripped. Everything is gigantic and exposed, a throbbing signpost of itself.

She hasn't tried to tell anybody about these moments, doesn't know whether they're shared by others, whether they're visible on her face. Esker is regarding her closely, the tea eyes keen and unreadable.

"Ready to work?" Esker flips open the textbook. A word problem about surface area and regularity accompanied by an etching of a coral reef.

The room grows very dark as they work; neither one notices. They scratch fast, messy equations and plot graphs. On the ottoman, a woman with paper-bag hair and long clean fingers, eyes bright behind their lenses with the task at hand. On the couch, Curious Georged and Peppermint Bluesed, a hobbled and forthright girl, grateful at this moment to be so difficultly consumed.

3.

The restaurant is busy for a Tuesday night. Come January, it won't even be open Tuesdays. But it's bustling tonight. The holidays will do it, and the snow. It's the first snow of the year and it's a light snow, entrancing, every flake twirling, slow motion, six points intact, to the ground, and there vanishing as if by sleight of hand, lending the asphalt a satiny sheen, a tuxedo-and-top-hat luster. All over the West Village, people sift out of brownstones and wander along the convoluted streets and alleyways. They stick out their tongues, blink wet eyelashes at each other. "Careful," people tell each other, "it's slippery," and they hold hands.

In a month or less, a snowy night will hurt business. People will be sick of it by then, the dirty crusted humps of it blocking the curb, the slushy brown ponds of it endlessly sopping their skin. In a month or less, they'll be sending out for pizzas and Chinese and Indian and Cuban and eating at home, alone, in their overheated apartments, sock-feet up on coffee tables, sitcoms on their TVs. Like last year. But tonight nobody remembers any of this.

"Wally. Number seven never got the rabbit appetizer. Can you take it off?" Justine, the new waitress, hands over the check and flits off to take a drink order, and Wally James turns from the window and the streetlamp-lit flakes. This is the first night he's come in to work since Ann's fall, and he's more appreciative than usual of the restaurant's rhythms and tempos.

Tiny, textured dramas play themselves out in the corners of his eyes, in the weave of dialogue around him. Now he goes to the register and vanishes the rabbit. Only he and Nuncio, his maître d' and manager, can delete an item since the system's been computerized. He delivers the new check to table seven himself.

"How was dinner?" He's a comfortably compact man. His stomach protrudes firmly under his beet-colored wool sweater, and a neat laurel of gray-brown curls frames an otherwise smooth pate.

"Very good."

"Excellent. The woodcock was excellent. I never tasted it before."

"Thank you." People say it often, that they've never before tasted an item on his menu. "I'll tell the cook." Wally himself had never tasted game until they began developing the menu. The restaurant's specialty is also its name: Game. It had been Alice's idea. Seven years ago, when Ann was nine. "We can hang old rifles on the walls," Alice had said, remembering the Maine fishing-and-hunting camp of her childhood. "We can have daisies and clover in paper cups on the tables. Everything can be unfinished pine. Knotty. Hand-hewn." Game had been Alice's idea, but she'd meant it as a gift to him, a way to liberate him from his job in city planning. They'd paid for it with her sudden inheritance, which they always referred to as her sudden inheritance, like a plot device in a drawing-room comedy.

The bells on the door ching, and three more people flock inside with a gust of sparkling air and a shaking out of scarves. Glowy faces and eye-glasses steaming up. The restaurant is romantically lit by the fire in the big stone hearth, by oil lanterns on each table and mounted on the walls, and by scores of tiny pomegranate-colored lights strung in the storefront windows. Nuncio, with his long sideburns and pistachio ruffled tuxedo shirt, greets and seats. The door opens again. Nuncio tells them there's a wait. A moment later, he catches Wally's eye and smiles: he's having fun. There is in Nuncio something of the perpetual fourteen-year-old. He even looks fourteen, sort of, when he smiles: full of an innocent's cockiness. They appreciate the momentum and moods of the restaurant jointly, Wally and Nuncio: it's theater as much as supper.

Game is small; it's on the crooked part of West Fourth, the little scorpion-tail end of it, where it rears up like an avenue and starts intersecting other streets. On either side of the storefront windows hangs a swag of red velvet, something Wally only recently added. Alice would never have approved; it doesn't fit the original conceit, but to Wally it feels right, framing the world inside the restaurant as something apart, something created.

Wally goes back behind the bar and fills Justine's drink order. Lamplight polishes the beer he pours, and pools in the amber scotch. Plates of roast pheasant in pancetta are borne out of the kitchen high on Peter's palms. Peter is the other waiter working tonight. A ballet dancer, he walks like a very suave duck. Justine laughs her raucous laugh with table eleven. Faintly, on the stereo, French horns. Game, though it should make him sad, its tenuous theatricality never quite enough to erase Alice's absence, almost never does. Wally picks up the phone and dials home.

"Hello?" Ann sounds groggy.

"Hi. It's Dad. How are you feeling?"

"Okay."

"Did I wake you?"

"No. It's snowing."

"I know. Pretty." She would be seeing it in the light off their balcony. "Okay, you were sleeping, weren't you? Go back to bed."

"No, it's okay. My math teacher was here today."

Peter comes to the bar and says, "A Bass and a cranberry with seltzer and lime," and Wally nods and gets out two pint glasses and says into the phone, "Good. Was that good?"

"Yeah. She's coming back next Wednesday. Are you crowded?"

"We are, actually. A little crowded."

"That's nice." A yawn distorts the second word.

"Okay, Anatevka." A nickname from when she was five and decided her name was too short. "I'm just calling to say hi. I'll be home late."

"Okay."

"You okay?"

"Yeah, Dad. I'm fine."

He hangs up, picturing her alone on the debris-strewn red couch, her increasingly blighted kingdom these past few days. The visiting nurse will have been by since he left for work, and Willette and Emil, two of his oldest friends, will have brought Ann supper and shared it with her, and Carla, their neighbor down the hall with the pit bulls and heart of gold, will have checked in on her way back from walking the dogs. He tells himself all this. It would be untruthful not to admit that he's also relieved to be back at work tonight. Ann's accident has thrust him and his daughter into closer and more continuous proximity than they've shared since she was in diapers. Well. He immediately pictures the look Alice would give him upon hearing that claim. All right: closer and more continuous proximity than they've shared ever. He bows mentally. But a certain amount of distance is good between a father and daughter. Especially with no mother at home. Wally has perhaps never been as angry at Alice's being gone as he has been these past four days.

He delivers the beer and the cranberry spritzer and stands schmoozing a few minutes with table one, a ruddy couple from South Africa, it turns out, who are eager to know whether he's ever tried ostrich on the menu, whether he's ever hunted at a game park, whether he's ever tasted grubs. Yes, no, and no. They're clearly disappointed he's not going to engage in some blustery one-upmanship with them (Well, have you ever wrestled an alligator? Ever shot a charging elephant? Here, let me show you my scar . . .), but then he draws them out, lets them regale him with a couple of their own escapades, which is what they wanted anyway, and leaves them to their drinks diffused and charmed.

Nuncio, who has been eavesdropping, gives Wally a private salute—two fingers curling an imaginary handlebar mustache—then swivels to hold open the door for some exiting customers. Whatever he says elicits a laugh and a retort, and then he laughs, appreciatively, and waves goodbye. He is a gentle and laconic flirt. Sometimes he shakes hands with customers as they're leaving. Later tonight, when the last people are finishing dessert, Justine will climb on a bar stool and massage his shoulders. Later still, when Justine and Peter have totaled out and the cook has gone home to his wife and new baby in Washington Heights and the dishwasher is taking out the garbage and mopping the kitchen and putting the mats back down, Wally and Nuncio will sit at their back table with cocoa and scotch, respectively, and talk for a while in the closed restaurant. They've had little manly crushes on each other for seven years; they always will.

Now a trio of young women comes in, chatting animatedly while Nuncio swats snow off their shoulders. One of them is holding a flute case, and one is holding an armload of blue delphiniums. Justine leads with her hip through the kitchen door, plates of venison burgers balanced up her arms. "Hot stuff, hot stuff!" she whispers to herself like a mini-circus barker. Outside the window, framed by Game's velvet drapes, a couple across the street breaks into a momentary tango, and a sloe-eyed greyhound lifts its pale, elegant leg to urinate against a tree trunk. Everything—he has resolved to believe this—conspires to make Wally James happy.

4.

*E*sker sticks her sock-feet up on the trunk she uses as a coffee table. Around her shoulders is draped an afghan, one of several her mother crocheted a long time ago. In her lap she cradles a pot holder and a pot of Top Ramen. It makes a warm weight against her stomach, almost like a cat, but she has never been a cat person; more to the point, she has never liked the idea of being a cat person. On her way home from work she often stops at the Korean grocery, and there seems always to be someone buying a head of lettuce, a pint of Ben & Jerry's, and a half-dozen tins of some deluxe brand of cat food, Sultan or Infanta or whatever it's called: lamb and veal and mackerel entrées. She isn't cut out for that kind of doting.

Outside her windows snow falls: white, then green, white, then green, in the blinking light of the no-name shamrock bar. Hers is the bottom floor of this skinny old house rife with charm and defects. The top two are inhabited by the owners, a pink-nosed, Birkenstocked, gray-haired couple who still get arrested now and then, for demonstrating in front of one embassy or another. They are gentle landlords, who think Esker shy and dependable, and shower her with zucchini and radishes from their little vegetable plot out back every summer. For her part, she never complains about the swaybacked floors, the peeling paint, the cracked windowpanes. In nine years, she has never asked them to fix the faulty toilet, just bought herself a plunger and a snake; she uses paper clips to fasten the chain inside the tank; when one rusts through, she fits a new one.

Albert's ghost is back in town. She felt him this morning before she opened her eyes, felt him lurking bedside, relentlessly silent. Then she spied him on the train, first in the nape of some man in a suit, then in the shin of another. An exposed band of skin between pant leg and sock. Sometimes she is gladdened by such glimpses, more often burdened. Sometimes she wills him, but not today. He just came. He bowed out when she went to tutor Ann James, but fell into step beside her again outside the apartment building. Accompanied her heavily to the subway entrance. There left her with a scuffing up of gutter leaves.

Soup done, Esker sets her pot in the huge enamel sink, gray with abrasions, and runs a bath. For privacy, when she first moved in, she'd taped over the single, handkerchief-sized bathroom window a laminated photocopy of a Mandelbrot–Peano–von Koch snowflake, and there it remains, buckled from years of moisture: her beauty. She first encountered the snowflake by accident, on the seventh floor of the NYU library, during the autumn of her freshman year, back when she thought she'd be an English major. Esker always studied in the library, or the Cozy Soup & Burger, or sometimes even in the lobby of the gym, any busily populated place; something about the proximal hum of lots of bodies and voices calmed her. It was as if she, who had opted for so much anonymity, so much colorless complacency in her outward manner, required a giant matrix in which to locate herself, something definite and solid enough that she couldn't disappear entirely.

On this day, someone had left a science magazine in her preferred carrel, and it was too ready a tool for procrastination to pass up; she'd leafed through it and found herself bewitched by an article with the forbidding title "Fractals: A New Kind of Geometry." The accompanying images, with their strange captions, dazzled: Mandelbrot and Julia sets, the Sierpinski carpet, the Menger sponge. Tesselating shapes like paisleys on acid, crisp and swirly color-drenched diagrams like the drawings she'd made in childhood with her Spirograph set, and then actual photographs of the equations played out in nature, as moodily theosophical as the Ansel Adams calendar everybody in the dorms seemed to have that year: a page of trees in black and white, complex in their winter nudity on the page, and then kelp, and cliffs, and frost against a pane, and a cross-section of human bronchia. What the hell was this? Her heart knocking. Looking

up and around at the other students, all locked in concentration, bent
over texts in all their finery—for they wore finery, the other students, or
so it always seemed to Esker, whose unvarying wardrobe consisted of
turtlenecks and jeans and her old suede jacket that matched her eyes. She
wore small gold posts in her ears and transported her books in a green
army knapsack. In comparison, the other students seemed virtually cos-
tumed, in their mishmash assortments of uptown chic and downtown
tongue-in-cheek, and all of them, all the time, even when apparently im-
mersed in studying, as those students around her now gave every impression of being, were artfully poised for romance.

This much she could perceive: her fellow students everywhere—in
cafeterias and classrooms, in lounges and laundry rooms, playing Hacky-
sack in Washington Square Park, standing on line at the bursar's office,
giving blood at Student Health Services, *everywhere*—were alert primarily
for romance, or, alternatively, sex. Everyone except her seemed bathed in
it, steeped in it, this ineffable aura, this singular purpose. It permeated
the campus like a fine mist. And they all seemed so *easy* in it, moving
through the air with a kind of charged grace, a blinding awareness of
undercurrents which dwarfed everything else. Esker, apart, was mystified
and unnerved. It was as though she'd been admitted to an advanced class
without anyone's checking to see that she met the prerequisites.

That day in the library, she had looked up from the pages of the
serendipitously abandoned magazine and seen, briefly, in a dizzying haze,
an application of the theories within the article in the way the students
had randomly selected to seat themselves around the stacks, clumped here,
spread apart there, as if plotted points on a complex plane, repeated with
variation throughout the building, which was designed in a horseshoe
shape with open flooring so that she could actually see people, progressively smaller and farther away, playing out the pattern on descending lev-
els all the way down to the lobby, which bottomed out in geometrically
interesting black and white tiles (whose pattern, she'd heard, was supposed to discourage suicidal jumps). To think that there was something
mappable, something graphable and ultimately therefore *graspable,* about
the way people chose to distribute themselves in relationship to each
other! *Me, too,* were the words she had thought then: *Me too.*

And although in the next instant all semblance of logic slipped from
that thought and she could not have explained what she meant by it, she

was left with a hopeful residue: the possibility of a formula into which everyone fit regardless of will or intent or ability, but somehow binding them, embracing them all, even, improbably, her. Some years later, when she first heard the term "unified field theory," it triggered a memory of the excitement she'd felt that day. It had been like stumbling across an actual mile marker for a destination she'd feared was only mythical. Although the words of the article made little sense to her, she'd put ten cents in the copy machine and brought the Mandelbrot–Peano–von Koch snowflake back to her dorm room.

Now, in the bath, she traces it with her eyes. Not the original copy— that one traveled with her through four years of college and eventually succumbed to one-too-many masking tape scars—but a nicer one she'd blown up and darkened and laminated to withstand the steaminess of this little room. She can articulate its charm a little better now than the day she first spied it: an infinitely long line surrounding a finite area. But having the language doesn't dispel the magic. On the contrary. Higher math is her higher power, her cathedral, and her prayer all in one. She relaxes her eyes against it, the simultaneous openness of its center and delicate impenetrability of its crimped edges, the comforting repetition of the same shape, same shape, radiating throughout. Behind the snowflake, beyond the pane, real snowflakes fall. Ann looms. Behind her, Albert's ghost.

It had seemed an impropriety, going to Ann James's apartment today. Nothing to do with Florence's purported boundary issues (she'd gone at Florence's bidding, after all), but an impropriety all the same, to bring herself into Ann's world. Esker is well acquainted with the inverse: students presenting themselves in her own (and Larry's and Rhada's) little office, asking for help or advice, sometimes wanting only to schmooze, to glean, it seems, information about Esker: picking up objects from her desk, inquiring about her past, her family, her first and middle initials, swiveling themselves round in her chair, commenting on the state of her clutter. Esker is not the faculty member most set upon in such fashion— her manner hardly encourages it—but Prospect School students are a quirky bunch, and every year one or two gravitate explicitly toward Esker, as if seeking confirmation for something they sense about themselves. Whether or not they find it she never knows, but she has often been touched and bemused by their presence.

This is not Ann, though. Ann James neither idles in Esker's office nor seems to ask anything of her—other, of course, than math instruction— yet there is some kind of connection, something sharp and almost famil- iar, something anomalous, too, in the quality of their exchanges, even before today. Esker leans her head against the hard, curved enamel of the tub. There was something bothersome today in Ann's account of how she broke her heels. What had she said? She was pushed? Nudged? By a friend? Horsing around? Something hadn't been right. Esker can't put her finger on it, but she sees Ann now in her mind, blushing, holding a magazine over her face. Ann is pretty in a rather plain way: hazelish eyes, baby-brown hair, slightly lopsided lips, and skin so translucent it is like a lightbulb, broadcasting every change of heart or mind with an immediate roseate pulse. Was that it? Ann had changed her mind partway through telling Esker what had happened? But what had she told her? Nothing, really. Esker chides herself for seeing intrigue in a teenager's sudden blush. And of course she likes teaching Ann James, as who wouldn't? Teachers are wild about her, with her huge, unfettered appetite and her straight- forward confidence. She's one of those students who remind them of why they chose teaching. Still, Albert's ghost, lurking somewhere in the vicin- ity of the shower head, hints there is more to it.

"Well, go away, Albert," says Esker, sitting up and plucking the stop- per from the drain, and the weariness in her tone surprises even her. Then she grips the cool, slick side of the tub and lays her cheek on it, suddenly dizzy. It's the heat, and sitting up too fast. Her view is the bathmat close- up, its weave for an instant elaborate and swirly and as ordered as snow- flakes. She has flashes of missing him so densely, so wholly; the missing is like an injection of poison through her blood, a dye staining her tissues. And then it subsides, and so does his ghost, and mechanically she licks a tear from the side of her mouth and rises, and wraps herself in a large rough towel.

It is later, in bed, that the worrisome phrase resurfaces: *nudged from the inside.* Esker stares at the tin ceiling, hearing the words repeat them- selves, spiraling on and on inscrutably.

5.

Ann decides Esker is poignant. Poignant: profoundly moving, touching; also agreeably intense, stimulating; also keenly distressing, sharp; from *poindre,* to prick. Esker pricks. She is prickly (prickly pear, thinks Ann), but also she pricks, and it is the opposite of when Sleeping Beauty pricks her finger on a spinning wheel and is cast into sleep. Spinner. Spinster. Ann lies on the couch, clad in her casts, relentlessly awake at 2:00 and 3:00 and 4:00 A.M., and her mind goes to Esker.

Esker is poignant because (a) she always sits on the ottoman, (b) whenever she does break into a smile it's always as though she's lost a little internal struggle, (c) she whistles Beethoven's Ninth while plotting parabolas, and (d) she does *so* nothing with her hair. This doesn't exactly say it, but it's the closest Ann can come to pinpointing it.

She had tried conveying this to Denise Escobar earlier in the week. Ann had been—where else?—on the red couch, doing butt exercises before her entire ass atrophied, and Denise, who had dropped by after school with a history assignment and the prize from a box of Cracker Jacks (a rub-on dinosaur tattoo), had been in the wheelchair, trying to figure out how to steer ("I can't believe people play fucking basketball in these things!"). Denise didn't get it. "Poignant like what?"

Ann ran through her little compiled list of Esker's poignant traits, but Denise remained unconvinced. "She's just eerie." "Eerie" is a big word this year at The Prospect School, where its connotation is not derogatory; it's a catch-all for anything enigmatic or unplumbed. "What kind of a name is Esker, anyway?" asked Denise, bumping squarely into the coffee table.

"German? Finnish? How the hell should I know?"

"No, fool." Denise laughed. "I mean is there any more to it or what? You think that's the name she was born with: Esker?"

That dissolved Ann so thoroughly she couldn't speak.

"What? What's your problem?"

"You're not *born* with a name, idiot."

Denise coughed. "You're the idiot, moron."

"Ahhh . . ." Ann wiped her eyes and picked at the stegosaurus on her arm. "Anyway, it's her last name."

"So what's her first name?"

"Oh, do I look like the FBI?"

"Oh, snap—I don't even think you want to be asking me to *tell* you what you look like. Anyway, she's . . . she's . . ." Denise searched for the precise adjective and drove the wheelchair lightly into a post. "You know what it is?" she said, with the energy of sudden insight. "She's got a little Malcolm Choy thing going on. Without the physique."

"Ow," said Ann.

"What?"

"Nothing, I bit my lip."

Naturally, her mind goes to Malcolm Choy, too, in the middle of the night, the small of the morning. Everyone on earth but her will be deep into rehearsals for Winter Concert by now. Ann and three other girls were to have performed a modern dance using a variety of fans as props; Malcolm had agreed to accompany them. The dance was incredibly cool (at one point, Ann had a *pas de deux* with an electric box fan), and she is disappointed not to be doing it now, but she is more disappointed to be missing rehearsals with Malcolm Choy. She had looked forward to the idea of spending all that nonverbal time together; that, she had decided, would be the key to their connection: proximity and oblique collaboration. Now it'll just be the other three girls twirling and arcing in their leotards to the rhythm of his hands on skins. Denise, one of them, has reported back uneventfully on rehearsals thus far. "He's in his own world. I'm telling you, the guy's a monk. Friar Choy." Ann recalls the hot sprouting in her chest that had levitated her off the bleachers, and says nothing.

As for Denise's observation about Esker, Ann finds herself unnerved. Obviously, Esker couldn't be more unlike Malcolm Choy. And yet. Despite her initial offer, Esker has come three times in the past week and a half. She says Ann could use the extra help. This is doubtless true, but Ann notices she has been able to distract Esker from mathwork a little more each time. By now she has been able to compile a short compendium of random assorted facts about her teacher: she doesn't like to dance, has never broken a bone, has no siblings, no pets, no car, no subscriptions, doesn't play an instrument, doesn't like talking on the telephone. She keeps, surprisingly, a tin of crystallized ginger in her briefcase, which explains why her breath always smells distinctive, and what that distinction is. She misses canoeing. She knows which birds sing which songs, and what kinds of plants were on earth when the dinosaurs were around. And she worked one summer as a maid and wore a pink dress uniform. All of which adds up, Ann thinks, to surprisingly little: that much more evidence of Esker's essential eeriness.

Ann knows she has been, increasingly, a brat the past few weeks—which she has every reason to be, her father keeps saying every time she apologizes for having snarled at him again, until she is so irritated with his understandingness and patience that she stops apologizing altogether, and still he is tolerant and kind, although perhaps a little more than usually detached. And then she resents him for *that*. But the thing is, Esker is the one person these days who doesn't annoy her. Maybe it's because Esker herself is such a prickly pear. If Ann snaps, Esker snaps back, and then they are off sparring, up-tempo, and it's fun, and Ann's on her toes craning her neck to see what's around the next bend. In any case, Ann finds herself anticipating tutoring sessions impatiently. During them she never thinks about her stupid lame feet. And for a long time after Esker leaves, she remains on edge in a glittery, trembling way, like an October leaf grown gold and loose on its stem.

So, by Friday afternoon, day fifteen of Ann's fractured calcaneas or whatever their stupid plural is, when Esker has failed to arrive forty minutes past the appointed time of their scheduled session, Ann is feeling foul-tempered, foolish, and self-pitying. The apartment this day is unneglected-looking. Ann's junk no longer dominates the red couch like evidence of invalidism; she's adapted to the wheelchair and no longer requires all of her important possessions to reside in a single heap. Lovely old Carla came by yesterday and washed Ann's hair in a basin, and today it's gathered in a single silver barrette, the rest of it hanging shiny down past her shoulders. The building won't allow Christmas trees (fire hazard), but Ann's father has hung the potted grapefruit tree by the center post with ornaments and white lights. The area lamps have been switched on, the rugs vacuumed, the woven metal garbage cans emptied. Ute Lemper is singing Kurt Weill in German on the stereo.

But the wall clock cuckoos the half-hour: forty-five minutes late, and Ann feels ready to machete something. She wheels herself over to the kitchen table, cuts a blondie from the pan Carla brought over, and crams the whole thing into her mouth. The phone rings: the doorman: her teacher is here.

"Shend her up, pleash." Then she has to chew fast to get it all down by the time the elevator arrives.

"Did you get mugged?" greets Ann, opening the door herself, wheeling backward as she speaks.

Esker stamps in smelling like the cold and the subway. "There was the faculty party, and a last-minute makeup test, and the train stopped between stations, blah-blah-blah, sorry." She unwinds a dun scarf from her neck, removes her tan coat.

"Oh yeah, today was the last day." The Prospect School always closes a full three weeks for the winter holiday. Ann feels a little pang hearing about the party, which is stupid, since she wouldn't have been there anyway, nor would she have wanted to. But she pictures, for a moment, Esker animated and flushed, cup of punch in hand (all faculty parties serve punch, don't they?), being scintillating. Like a sparkler. Ann hasn't had one of those since she was a child, one Fourth of July out at her parents' friends Willette and Emil's house in Amagansett. Anyway, this is stupid, too: Esker is undoubtedly as much of a pill at the faculty holiday party as she is the rest of the time. Ann threads herself a little recklessly around red posts toward the living area. "So does that mean you're not coming anymore after this?"

"Not necessarily." Esker pulls off a dun knitted hat, stuffs it down the sleeve of her coat, and hangs everything on the cherry coat-stand. Her hair statics out like a burry electron cloud, and she flattens it absently. The potted grapefruit tree twinkles, and she peruses it as she passes, taking in the homemade walnut-shell-and-cotton-ball Santas, the clove oranges, the Popsicle-stick-and-yarn God's eyes. "Did you make these?"

"Some I did," says Ann. "Some my mother." And she glances at the rectangle over the bricked-up fireplace. Esker's eyes travel with her.

The canvas is large, maybe three by four feet, lit today by a small light affixed to the bottom of the frame. It is a portrait, but not the sort a person might commission. Up close it looks like a collage of fabric swatches and oil paint. Ten feet away, these meld into a not entirely flattering likeness of a nevertheless unmistakably beautiful woman's face. Strong mouth, navy eyes. Wide cheekbones, wide brow, freckles. Honey-brown widow's peak: a blonder version of Ann's. "Is that her?" Esker, noticing it for the first time, takes it in at length.

"My mother's friend did it. I mean, a friend of my father's, too."

"You're a lot like her."

Ann has heard this before; she shrugs. She sees Esker puzzling; people who know always think it's odd that her father still has the portrait up. People who don't know automatically assume her mother dead because of it; what man keeps a portrait of his deserting wife over the mantel? "It's just that he still loves her," Ann imagines explaining. "It's just that he loves her better now in absentia." Absence: the state of being away. A want, a lack. A hole filled by a ghost. Instead, she forestalls any questions Esker might put (Esker, being Esker, would probably ask outright) with an act of physical bravado: she flings herself out of the wheelchair and pitches forward onto the couch, all hands and knees and a tidal wave of red velvet, and then, with dexterity and cockiness, flips around into sitting, the bulky blue parcels of her feet propped on the coffee table. She is wearing plaid boxers and a giant pink fleece thing.

Esker squints. "Is that part of your physical-therapy regimen?"

Ann flashes a cereal-box smile. The distraction has been successful. "I can do a pop-a-wheelie." She indicates the wheelchair. "Want to see?"

"Some other time." Esker draws up the ottoman and extracts textbook and graph paper from her briefcase. "What's with the guttural ranting?"

Ute on the stereo is in full swing: *"Du hast kein Herz, Johnny, und ich liebe dich so!"* Ann snatches the remote and cuts her off. The silence comes back at them. "You never like my music," she complains.

Esker contradicts her lightly. "No, I told you, I can't listen while I work." She pulls out a pencil, a straightedge, a calculator.

"Limited."

Esker gives her a look. "Testy." Removes a final pink rhomboid eraser and tucks the briefcase away with a certain briskness.

Ann, meanwhile, is blushing because of the word's similarity to "testes." It's a terrible thing being sixteen and having everything sound like sex. Of course, then she has to think of Malcolm Choy, and then Denise's remark about Esker. "Can I ask you something?" she says, amid the heat.

Esker exhales. Her face is a calmly impregnable fortress.

"Can I?"

"Shoot."

"What's your first name?"

"Iphigenia," she says flatly. "Today we're going to do some graphing."

"Are you putting me on?"

Esker looks at her.

"No way. Is that, like, a family name?"

"No. Are you interested in passing the mathski?"

"It's beautiful."

"Glad you think so. Today we're going to do some graphing."

"God. That's the name I always wanted."

Another look.

"Not necessarily that exact one, but that kind."

A little smile is rising. Ann can see it tremble in Esker's throat.

"I hate my name. Ann. Ann. Not even an 'e' at the end. *Ann.*" She squeezes it out of her throat like a flat beige crumb. "You'd think my parents were stockbrokers."

Esker's eyes crinkle. "Ann James," she intones, making a megaphone of her hands. "Today we're going to work on graphs." And then, differently, "What's the matter?," because Ann's eyes have welled up.

"Nothing, I'm just sick of graphs." Ann croaks a laugh at that, and a tear falls to her cheek. She swipes it, and her face goes sad again, and Esker is patient, but Ann says nothing. Outside, it is dark. No snow is falling. The streetlights make the dark look dull, incomplete.

Esker says, "Do you remember when you told me how you broke your ankles?"

"Heels."

"Do you remember what you said?"

"No."

"You said you felt nudged from the inside. I asked Buddy, and he told me you just said you fell. But when you told me, you said something else. Do you know what I'm talking about?" Ann, looking at her boxer shorts, nods. "Do you think it's something to worry about?"

Ann looks up and looks Esker in the face and says, "No." The tea eyes hold hers. "I'm just bratty right now because I'm sick of staying in, I'm sick of not walking. That's normal. Plus hormones. Did you want to graph?"

Esker, without letting her feel off the hook, slowly opens her book.

They graph word problems for close to an hour, mutually swallowed in the peace afforded by the discipline. When the clock cuckoos half past six, instead of promptly gathering her things Esker gives Ann a little present: she shows her how to make a Cantor dust. Start with a line, remove the middle third. Remove the middle thirds of the two resulting lines. And so on. Eventually yielding a dusting of clumped points, infinitely many yet infinitely sparse. Esker watches Ann closely, sees her face goes soft with excitement. She gets it.

"What's it for, though?"

"Nothing," says Esker, a little more harshly than she intended. "It was devised by a nineteenth-century mathematician named Georg Cantor. It's an abstract construction." She begins to repack her pad of graph paper, pencils, straightedge, eraser.

"You mean it's for fun."

"Well, all right."

"Are there any more like it?"

Esker gives a considered nod.

"Can you show me?"

"Next time."

"Are you coming again even though now it's the holiday?"

"I could. What would you like to do?"

"Yes. I mean, keep studying."

Esker closes the clasp on her briefcase and stands. "You know you're going to do well on the mathski," she says.

"You think so?"

Esker nods.

"Yay."

Esker smiles a smile composed of pressing her lips together so that the ends of her mouth actually dip down; on paper it would be a frown.

She takes such pains, thinks Ann. "But you can still help me study?"

Esker shrugs. "I can."

They make a date for the following week. Ann hoists herself into the wheelchair, rolls to the kitchen, and cuts another blondie, which she insists Esker take "for the subway," and then Esker gets her scarf and coat and hat and briefcase and goes home, leaving her appointment book behind on the Jameses' cherry coffee table.

6.

Wally James snaps the broadsheet crisply and attempts to fold it back and into the flat, narrow quadrants that a crowded subway car dictates— even though it is ten o'clock on Saturday morning and the car is nearly empty—and as usual ends up with a bulky, mangled sort of tetrahedron. He will never perfect the art of fitting neatly into modest spaces. A vestige of his childhood in the more rural expanses of Dutchess County. Alice used to tease him about this. At dinner parties she actually used to do an impression of him folding the newspaper. She was always very clever with physical comedy. And back when she'd loved him, he'd loved her doing him. The impression itself had seemed a most intimate expression of love, partly because it verged on cruel: if she could afford this public display of unkindness, what depths of counterbalancing love that implied!

He gives up on the paper and looks about the subway car. Another giveaway that he's not native to this city: his habit of drinking in un- guardedly the presence of people around him. This morning these in- clude two women with pink plastic shopping bags, a generation apart, speaking Mandarin and eating yogurt; a young white man in a Yankees cap with a baby strapped to his chest; a teenage couple, the boy lying with his head in the girl's lap, both dressed in last night's club gear; a person of indeterminate sex and age inert under a heap of gray blanket. The train rocks them all along in its crashing, heedless way. Wally feels good this morning, which is to say wistful and awake.

Beneath this, though, something nags: Ann. He has not quite admitted to himself that he is concerned. Not about her heels: X-rays have determined that both fractures are minor and healing quickly, and she has adapted to the wheelchair, slideboard, and commode they rented from a medical-supply company with almost arrogant finesse. It is Ann's account of how it happened that bothers him. He cannot really see it: someone falling spontaneously off bleachers. There would have to be a cause, Wally believes. Either horseplay, which Ann flatly denied, or something medical, which is too preposterous and scary to consider (also, Ann scoffed at inquiries about dizziness or blacking out). Then there is what the resident in the emergency room called as they were leaving: "Promise you do not jump more off high things!" He'd had a strong accent, and Ann's claim that he misunderstood her had seemed perfectly plausible, but Wally has not forgotten these words. Perhaps he would have if Ann hadn't been so oddly moody these past few weeks, not so much bored or depressed, which he would understand, as brightly, rawly on edge.

But, then, fathers are supposed not to understand their teenage daughters, aren't they? What if this is all routine stuff, and only *looks* alarming because of the coincidence of broken bones? Surely coincidence is all it is, happenstance, unfortunate but meaningless—what, for example, if there *was* some horseplay and Ann's covering up for the friend who jostled? Ordinary adolescence, that: both the horseplay and the denial. Wally's own youth is a litany of this kind of thing: cherry bombs thrown at passing cars on the Taconic; illicit trips downriver in a "borrowed" canoe; sneaking into the abandoned breading factory, which had once manufactured the coating for fishsticks and chicken patties, and hand-cranking the rusted-out gears into life. None of the escapades, even this last, which had resulted in Chris Petroni's losing his right ring finger after the first knuckle, had ever been revealed fully to adults (certainly not the fact that Chris's brother had dared him to climb the moving machinery). Nor had any of the escapades (even given what now, in adulthood, strikes Wally as the frighteningly stupid games they played inside the breading factory) ultimately seemed at a remove from the generally wholesome task of growing up.

If Alice were here, she would know whether or not to be worried about Ann. But is that true? Perhaps it's the inverse: if Alice really knew such a thing, she would be here. Awful, to doubt what you once knew you *knew*. He wishes there were someone else he could ask.

Ann was still asleep this morning when he left. The wheelchair won't fit through the bedroom doorway, so she continues to sleep on the red velvet couch, which is shorter and narrower than her bed; she invariably appears each morning less tucked in than flung open: one or both blue casts dangling over the side, an arm as well, pillow bunched or canted or slipped entirely off. She has always slept in fierce, exhausted postures. When she was little, she used to insist that she slept with her eyes open, that she could see around her room even as she dreamed. Two worlds at once. This morning she'd been sleeping with a slightly furrowed brow. Wally had smoothed her forehead lightly with three fingers, and the frown had only deepened.

He's going in early today for a couple of reasons: One, since Ann's accident, he hasn't been putting in the hours at Game that he should. He's behind on payroll and ordering. Two, Ann's teacher left her engagement calendar at their apartment last night. She'd been apologetic on the phone when he'd called this morning, as though it had been blocking their way around the room or something, and she nearly took his head off when he offered to drop it by. Maybe not quite his head, but she really insisted, "Please don't," in the tone his high-school teachers might have used to insist, "No talking during the test." But Ann had been equally insistent last night, when he got home from work, that he do it. "You can do it on your way in tomorrow. Please?" And she'd added almost shyly, "I want you to meet her."

Esker's name has cropped up often in the past few weeks, and Wally is curious to meet her himself. Probably he has met her, at a school event, but he cannot for the life of him picture her face. So on the phone he did his affable thing, what Alice used to call his "innkeeper dance," and simply informed Esker, quietly so as not to wake Ann, that it was no trouble and he'd drop it off on his way to work.

"We should do something for her," Ann had proposed, "for all this tutoring." It seems clear, though no one has spoken of it, that Esker is more than meeting the expectations of a teacher, even of a department head, even at the special request of the headmistress and the father of one of the best math students at The Prospect School. "Invite her to dinner," suggested Ann, when Wally had gone to kiss the top of her head good night. She sat up brightly, bumping his mouth. "Not at the restaurant!"

Wally, with the natural vanity of a parent, is not surprised that Esker has elected to tutor Ann into the winter holiday, but he is struck by Ann's enthusiasm for Esker, and feels slightly anxious about meeting the woman. Putting away his mangled paper, he notices the top of her engagement calendar protruding from her bag. He pulls it out.

It is a plain thing, brown and inexpensive, spiral-bound. It is of course wrong to look, but also human nature. Nine out of ten people probably would. Wally turns it over, turns it back, fans the pages with his thumb. He looks around the subway car. The Chinese women got out at Wall Street; a stooped man in a tie has got on, and a girl with a safety pin through her lip. Fellow travelers. Wally turns again to the book. After all, they are going to be friends. Hasn't Ann practically ordained it? He opens the book.

It's all mundane or indecipherable. Faculty meetings, assignments due, a phone number or street address jotted here and there, and most of the o'clocks are during business hours. The handwriting is plain, brusque, ballpoint. He looks in a choppy, fleeting manner, as though that cancels any crime, pausing only when he comes across his own familiar address and phone number in green pencil, and then, recurrently on the next several pages, "ANN 4:30."

A jarring sensation, to come across one's own personal information in a stranger's book, in a stranger's hand. It's his not entirely unpleasant comeuppance for trespassing. Wally rubs his nose and shuts the book, wedges it firmly back inside his bag.

At Chambers Street he leaves the subway car, along with the safety-pin girl and, surprisingly, the person (still of indeterminate age and gender) who'd been wrapped prostrate under a blanket, and rises into a morning suddenly bright, suddenly yellow. A sweet, un-December-like smell of mud hovers in cracks between the dull, stolid smells of buildings and street. Wally stops into a greengrocer's and buys two mangoes. He is thinking of Ann's decree, "We should do something for her, for all this tutoring," but the truth is, Wally gives gifts all the time, at the drop of a hat, little, odd ones. The gift not so much in the item itself as in the transaction, the act of passing something along.

"Another tchotchke," Alice used to say, to *deliver*, when he presented something to her. Even when it wasn't a tchotchke, even when it was im-permanent, a Gerbera daisy or a length of licorice, she'd tease him. "You don't always have to bring me things. You don't have to woo me." He wasn't wooing her. It wasn't even mostly about her, it was mostly about the daisy or the licorice, the good thing he'd found and, having found it, needed to pass on. Tucking the flower behind her ear, biting into the candy, she'd wrinkle her nose at him. Or once she'd quoted, " 'She prizes not such trifles as these are: the gifts she looks from me are pack'd and lock'd up in my heart.' " "One and the same," he'd protested, but she missed it, kissing his shoulder and laughing, and then plucking some fuzz from her mouth. He recalls this with that mixture of fondness and annoyance—is there such a thing as fond annoyance?—that always informs his thoughts of Alice. But no. "Fondness" and "annoyance" are only code for something else. The words he chooses are as always too mild.

Wally is surprised when he locates Esker's address. It's more like a tall wood-frame house than an apartment building, incongruous somehow, the wrong scale or city or century, maybe. He's not even sure what neighborhood this is, not Tribeca, not the West Village, not even the meat-packing district, really. At first he thinks it's depressing, and then he thinks it's lovely. There is no buzzer, so he knocks on the door. It makes a soft, dull noise, ineffectual on this street of big warehouses. He raps again, this time on one of the glass quadrants at the top of the door, and shatters it.

In almost comical slow motion, one jagged segment of the pane sways out and drops at his feet; more tinkle to the floor inside. Then a crunching glass sound, and the door opens. Esker is wearing leggings, and a giant gray confusing thing, a pilly, fleecy kind of sweater or tunic or jacket (or bathrobe?), and (fortunately) sneakers, and whatever look of petulance she wore on coming to the door is quickly mixed with something like confusion now, as she takes in the bits of glass on the floor. "Oh. Did that happen just now?"

"Yes. I'm Wally James, Ann's father. I won't offer my hand."

They both look down to see blood dripping from his knuckles.

"I'm sorry," says Esker.

"What? No, I'm sorry, I broke your door."

"Don't be ridiculous. Does it hurt?"

"No."

"Well, come wash it."

In this way they manage to avoid ceremony completely, and Wally finds himself standing over the bathroom sink with his hand under a cold waterfall while Esker rummages unsuccessfully in a linen closet for first-aid cream and bandages.

"It's all right," he says, drying his knuckles and examining them. Crisscrosses of blood well again immediately.

"Anyway, wrap it in this." She sticks out a dish towel, pale yellow with purple starfish all over it. "I use it as a rag," she says, when he hesitates. "I mean, but it's clean."

He winds the pretty cloth tightly around his hand and feels embarrassed. "I feel like I'm getting ready to box," he says.

"Now, after all that, you have to stay and have a cup of tea," says Esker, surprising him. "Do you drink tea?"

So they go back out into the main room, where Esker puts the kettle on in the galley kitchen, and Wally remembers the bag of mangoes and extends it, and she looks inside (suspiciously, he thinks) and then laughs, a sudden, free sound that he wouldn't have expected from her. "How tropical." She considers them, one in each hand. "Oh. You have a restaurant," she says, as though arriving at an explanation.

"Yes. But the mangoes are different." What is he saying? "I mean I might've brought them anyway."

"Thank you." She takes out little dense-walled mugs. "Now is when I should be reciting the list of fifteen teas you could choose from. However . . ." and she completes the sentence by holding up a box of Tetley and shrugging.

Is she making fun of him for having a restaurant? "I'm not picky," he says. "I used to clothespin tea bags to the light pull to save them for the next time. When I first moved to New York."

"Where from?"

"Upstate."

"Me, too. Where?"

He gestures vaguely with his starfish-bound hand. "Grange Hill. A tiny place kind of near Rhinebeck. You?"

"Delos. A tiny place kind of near Lake Placid."

"Huh." This feels like a coincidence, although he's not sure the relative proximity of their upbringings is rare enough to occasion the label. The city is rife with emigrants from upstate. On the other hand, the city is rife with emigrants from everywhere.

"Huh," says Esker, too.

Coincidence or no, it feels significant.

She places the mangoes on the sill over the sink. She looks quite grave, and for some reason this pleases him.

They wait, in considerable silence, for the water to boil.

7.

"I don't get it," ventures Ann, a while into the conversation. "Wouldn't that kind of hurt?"

The others regard her, her tentative squint, her cloddish blue feet sticking way out on the coffee table like an unusual centerpiece. Hannah Stolarik sprawls in the easy chair, her combat boots on what Ann has come to think of as Esker's ottoman. Denise Escobar sits cross-legged at the other end of the red couch, leaning forward so her dangly earrings swing, working on a Slim Jim. Saturday afternoon, and the meanest specks of snow are blowing about in brilliant sunlight beyond the French doors.

The older girls, both seniors, look at her. They are having one of their marathon sex talks, and Denise has been relating information from some cable talk show, on which the expert recommended that one practice going down on a banana.

"Well," Denise enunciates in a way that manages to be not unkind while making perfectly clear her incredulity at sharing the same planet with someone on this level of dimwittedness, "you *peel* it first."

The clouds do not lift from Ann's face. Her lip curls. "Okay . . . wouldn't that be a little messy?"

Denise squints back, equally uncomprehending. "What?" She looks to Hannah for help.

Hannah is large, with white skin and dyed jet hair and garnet-painted lips: all white and black and red, hard. She looks tough on the street, with her size and her boots and her sardonic jaw and stare, but this all masks the surprising heart of a judge: dispassionate, protective, fair. Now she inclines her head toward the ceiling, so when she looks at Ann it's through her heavily blackened lashes. "You know you don't actually *blow* . . . ?"

"What are you talking about?"

"A blow job."

"Going down on a man is a blow job?"

"What did you think it was?"

The couch shakes with Ann's laughter, and her answer gets gasped out between what could pass for sobs. "Going *down* on a man—what it sounds like—you know, the woman lowering herself *down* onto the guy—like not missionary position."

There is nothing girlish about their laughter. It's cacophonous—ice in a blender, pig in the mud, rusty bellows on a windy day—and as one dies down the others swell anew, so that even after the big laughter is spent smaller waves of sound continue to lap and overlap at finally greater and greater intervals, and then they float in the after-silence for a while, their bodies still transformed by all that extra oxygen. Ann basks in the glow of her ignorance, her cherished little-sister status that affords so much amusement to the others and provides such an island of safety to herself.

"Shit," Denise sighs on a residual breath of mirth, and she rests her well-gnawed Slim Jim on the coffee table. When she sits up, it's with renewed energy: a remembered scrap of news. "Speaking of which—"

"Speaking of shit?" queries Hannah.

"Hardy-har-har. No, speaking of not the missionary position, guess who asked for your number?" To Ann.

"Malcolm Choy," she says, to be funny.

Denise gives her Saturday-morning-cartoon grin and nods.

"Get the fuck out." Ann can't catch her breath.

"No, I swear to God."

"What did he say?"

"He said, Do you have Ann's number?"

"That's it?"

"Yeah."

Hannah looks mysterious, but only smiles.

"Oh my god." Ann does some yoga-breathing. There are her big blue air casts in front of her. "I can't believe I still have these fucking things on."

It is sweet to curse with her friends. The "shit"s and "fuck"s tumble from their mouths like pastel sugared almonds, as perfect and frivolous. They wear their expletives like body glitter, a cheerful and audacious accouterment of adolescent femininity. Ann is the only one of the three who's never had sex. Denise, in what Ann believes has to be the most wholesome loss-of-virginity story ever, had sex at age thirteen after a big snowball fight with her boyfriend in Prospect Park, after which they went back to her apartment, where her unsuspecting mother made them hot chocolate. For her part, Hannah reeks of experience: for the first half of last year, she had a boyfriend from Bronx Science, and for the second half a girlfriend from Cooper Union.

Ann is neither jealous nor intimidated by her friends' comparatively extensive activities. It's somehow reassuring to know actual people, peers, who have sex and emerge without wounds and scary secrets and broken hearts, with their senses of humor supremely intact. It is a wholly different possibility than what she has garnered from movies and books, and one in which she still does not really believe.

The only movie she ever saw that endorsed the strangely, implausibly weightless version of sex that Denise and Hannah seem to practice was a porno film, or actually a string of porno shorts, rented and viewed in a fit of curiosity one night when the three of them were house-sitting Hannah's half-sister's apartment. For once, Ann was not the only one for whom the experience was new, and they were each shocked and offended: Hannah politically, by the simultaneous penetration of a woman by two men; Denise aesthetically, by the meager, stubby bands of pubic hair on the women ("If you're going to shave that much, why not the whole thing?" she'd wanted to know; as it was, she pointed out, they all looked like Hitler); and Ann personally, and most profoundly, by the absence of plot.

She could not stomach the idea of sex devoid of story, and the story-less acts shown in the movie were strangely unsexy, so much senseless, bland, rabbit activity. It was depressing and also boring, and she'd quit after two segments to remove her nail polish and flip through Hannah's sister's back issues of *Ms.* and *Elle* in the bedroom. But why, she'd wondered, wiping Copper Penny off her nails and alternating between news briefs about women's rights in Ireland and Zimbabwe and articles on getting along with your boss and the best way to remove facial hair, why does she feel comforted and even protected by Hannah and Denise's brand of casual wit and affection regarding their own sex lives, when she herself cannot conceive of sex except as something devastating, apocalyptic, and utterly unfunny?

Now Denise pops up from the red couch and her knees crack. "Where are the bananas? I want to try."

"For real?" asks Ann.

"Spare us," says Hannah.

"Oh, go wait in the car," shoots Denise, and Hannah laughs appreciatively. They are on a continual mission to coin new insults.

"Go wax poetic," suggests Hannah.

Denise comes back with, "Go pee in a cup." She is the quickest draw, and blows on the tip of her index-finger gun before reholstering it. Now she turns to Ann. "I'm serious. Where, on the counter?"

"If we have any." As Denise recedes into the kitchen area, Ann turns to Hannah and asks softly, "What were you going to say about Malcolm?" She suspects Hannah of being unusually wise, even prescient, although, like most people, unable to apply her wisdom to herself.

"Nothing."

"Then what were you thinking?"

Hannah smiles, caught out. "Birds of a feather."

"Who? Me and Malcolm Choy?"

"Peas in a pod."

"What are you talking about?"

She shrugs and smiles and cocks her head contemplatively.

"Yo, Confucius. What the hell are you saying?"

"On the other hand, two magnets, both set to repel."

Ann throws Killycot at Hannah and actually nails her on the cheek. "Oh, go choke on a fortune cookie!"

Hannah raises an eyebrow, holds up an imaginary scorecard. "The Polish judge gives it a six."

"Oh, go scour the sink."

New scorecard. "Four and a half." Then, without warning, Hannah turns serious. "What I think, Anna Panna Banana, is that Malcolm Choy finds you intriguing and that, if you and he managed to get together, you might teach each other a thing or two." She holds Ann's gaze as though she knows something, her broad, impassive face all white and black and red, like a deck of cards, every suit at her disposal. Alarm crashes through Ann's chest. She is again on the bleachers, filled with a volatile, dangerous faith in her own heart, in her ability to sprout wings, defy gravity, exist in midair. She cools her cheeks with the backs of her hands. "You don't look good," declares Hannah brightly. "We need to get you out."

"Yeah, you'll get scurvy," says Denise, coming back and flourishing her banana. She has sculpted it into an excellent likeness of a penis.

"You already are scurvy," Hannah tells her.

"No, that thing sailors get from lack of fresh air."

This dissolves Ann. "Idiot! They're *in* fresh air! Lack of fresh fruit."

"Oh yeah, citrus." Denise snaps her fingers. "So why are you saying Ann'll get scurvy?"

"I didn't. You did."

"I did?"

"Yeah. Shut up and go down on a banana. So"—Hannah turns back to Ann—"does your wheelchair fit in the elevator? Seriously, can we take you out? Push you along the promenade?"

Ann glances over her shoulder at the French doors and the balcony. Bits of snow are still flitting in the sharp winter glare. It's a day out of an adventure story: fake and thrilling. "It fits."

"Then let's go meet Malcolm."

"Now? What, you think he's just going to be strolling by?"

"There's this thing called a telephone."

Ann protests, but without any vehemence. No one knows Malcolm's father's name, but Hannah knows he lives on Joralemon, and Denise dials information and gets the number. She starts to write it on one of Ann's casts. Ann slaps the back of her head. Denise smiles and applies the pen to her own palm instead.

"You're going to wash that shit off before we see him," avers Ann, whose heart is meanwhile rattling the bars of its hot, sealed chamber.

Denise extends the phone to her. "Go, girl." Her felt-tipped palm is flexed to face Ann with the number.

The phone rings. They all jump. Denise emits a shrill of laughter, then claps her hand over her mouth.

"Hello?" A freaked-out tremolo. A pause. "Oh, hello, Alice," says Ann. The others see her face adjust. It's like watching a sheet of paper fold crisply in half.

8.

*E*sker's not a social kisser. The convention has always struck her as unlikely. It seems as random and farfetched a thing to do as tugging earlobes or knocking wrists or something—a contrived, codified gesture, not springing from natural impulse.

So she is deeply surprised when she kisses Ann's father. It wrecks the whole rest of her Saturday; she can't put it down. It rides her shoulder like a sharp-taloned bird and won't be shooed away.

It wasn't, at any rate, a *kiss* kiss. It was a brief, quiet thing on the cheek before he left, a warm little baked good of a kiss, neat: a beginning and end unto itself. Still, most unlike her. And even more unlike her to be remembering it now, remembering the actual sensual detail of the kiss, the curving, unused plushness of her own lips against the smooth, slightly cooler plane of his cheek. She even remembers a sensation of taste, in an olfactory sort of way: some subtle mixture of shaving cream, tea, and clay mug.

The details come to her unbidden in the bath at the end of the day. Baths are her addiction. Albert started that. She bathes in plain water, as hot as she can stand.

He'd looked so startled when she'd answered the door, so abashed, bits of glass winking and crunching underfoot. She'll have to replace the pane; her landlords never will. Putty? she thinks. Buy the rectangle of glass and then stick it in with putty? That doesn't sound right. Cardboard in the meantime. But he'd looked so abashed, and it was her fault, really; she'd heard him knock the first two times but didn't answer. She had actually contemplated pretending she wasn't there. How pushy of him to insist on coming after she'd assured him she could do without her calendar until next time she tutored Ann. And underneath that, how mortifying, how mortified she'd been, to have left something of hers behind in their apartment. The Freudian-slipness of it! He'd worn an orange sweater, and drunk two cups of tea, with milk *and* sugar (she'd had to hunt to find sugar, and then spooned it straight from the sack). When they finally began to ease into conversation, it hadn't been about Ann at all, not until the end, but first there'd been the better part of an hour talking about, of all things, food: mangoes first, and then his restaurant, and game cooking, and unusual things they'd tasted while traveling (Wally had had a single bite of whale in Japan, which led them to think of other items they'd tasted once and no more. Esker: grits. Wally: Marmite. Esker: Raisinets. "Raisinets?" "I had them once as a kid: there were maggots in the box"), which segued into a discussion of the annual entomophagous banquet in New York (Wally knew a food critic who'd been), and then more loosely into talk of water chestnuts, cherries, rice pudding, kale. Esker gave Wally her grandmother's latkes recipe ("Take a couple potatoes the size of your fist . . ."), and Wally gave Esker his secret for a perfect pie crust ("Rub the chilled butter into the dry ingredients with your fingertips").

"But that's my PIN!" cried Esker. "PIES, 7435."

"No. Really?"

She nodded, a little sadly. "But you're never supposed to tell anyone your PIN."

The tea had vanished from the pot and the minutes from the clock, and then they noticed the time and both were disconcerted, and Ann's father had been on his feet, bringing his mug to the sink, retrieving his bag and his coat there on the peg by the door, and Esker kissed him.

Upon which he said, "I've been wondering whether I should be worried about Ann," and Esker didn't know whether to take this as a rebuke, meant to remind her of who she was in relationship to him, or as his parallel descent into a new level of intimacy. Unmoored by her action, and further so by his quick shifting of gears, she failed to respond with her like concerns, or even to come back with an inviting comment about what a pleasure it was having Ann as a student. She said lamely, "Oh?"

and left him to dismiss his own statement with a deprecating wave of his hand. "Your visits have been really nice for her," he said. And then, all but slapping his forehead, "Oh! I'm supposed to invite you for supper!" They picked a time, Monday, seven, then shook hands goodbye.

But it's the kiss she recalls in the tub. Whatever possessed her? It's because he's short, she thinks doubtfully. After all, she's short, and not ordinarily near anyone's cheek; a kiss in most cases would involve tiptoes for her and stooping for the other party, a little series of contortions and accommodations, and all for the sake of what? A social nicety she's never appreciated, never liked.

Unbidden, sensory elements flood back: his orange wool shoulder briefly under her palm, the arresting firmness of his cheek, the tiny click her lips made pushing off his skin, like the tight golden clasp on a change purse. She is thoroughly vexed, and tunnels her scowl into the infinite black center of her snowflake.

In another apartment, Albert had sat on the toilet and read aloud to her while she bathed, his eyes on the page. He'd read her the quirky human-interest pieces from the front page of *The Wall Street Journal*, and then Isaac Bashevis Singer stories over a series of weeks. Back then she'd used bath salts, but never bubbles; the water was always clear, and still he would keep his eyes on the page, even when she rose, eventually, and stood towelless and dripping on the mat, even when she came over and dripped right on the page, the drops spreading dark across the print. Only when she shrugged and turned away did he clap the book shut and grab her slippery wrist, twirl her back around, laughing, so that she lost her balance and skidded, and he caught her very fast then, like the sportsman he wasn't remotely.

But that was only at the very end, when they'd both known he was leaving in twelve weeks, eight weeks, six weeks, five days. . . . Only in that last summer had she let herself go, let herself fall and be caught. And who knows if it counted, when they'd both known it wouldn't last? Not a real fall. Only a pratfall, after all.

And now, nine years later, she cannot buy *The Wall Street Journal* and she will never read anything else by Singer. And she does not care for kissing.

Monday, seven.

It's her student's father, she argues silently.

You kissed him.

Just a freak attack of social graces, she scoffs, and searches her mind for some reason to dismiss him: falsely conspiratory, she thinks; hadn't he been a little falsely conspiratory about his pie-crust tip?

Across from the tub, soaking in the stoppered sink, floats a yellow-and-purple-starfish towel with his blood on it.

In fact, Esker has to admit, he had not sounded conspiratory; it had simply been a startling suggestion, oddly graphic, and surprising coming from a man, but he had offered it in an appealingly matter-of-fact way. For just a second she fails to prevent herself from imagining him working butter into the dry ingredients with his fingers.

Do the math, Albert whispers in her mind.

"Albert," she whispers, shutting her eyes.

It is her deep shame to be haunted by the ghost of a living person.

9.

The last thing Albert Rose said to Esker, nine years ago, when both were twenty-two, was, "I don't know about this." It was his afterthought, his loose thread, his pale, anxious face turning back once more after they'd said goodbye and not kissed, after he'd climbed back into his whitish van from which all of her belongings had just been cleared on that torpid August day down on Greenwich Street. She hadn't even known if he was referring to everything they'd just done or everything he was setting off to do. He'd simply left her with that thought, that dangling addendum, that disastrous question mark to hover like a vacuum, expectant, enduring, over the entrance to her new apartment. Then he'd driven off to Baltimore to get married as planned.

In the second grade, Esker had grasped—intuited, more accurately—the arbitrariness of math. She and her teacher nearly drove each other wild that year, each with her positive insistence that the other was wrong. Here is Iphigenia, called Genie, kneesocked and pigtailed, holding a sweaty fistful of Cuisenaire rods, and here is Miss De Witt, cropped gray hair and Peter Pan collars and heavy breath that somehow makes Genie think of cooked carrots-and-peas, holding her pristine, corrective length of chalk like an extra digit.

"All right, Genie." She sighs. "Can you count out a bundle of ten?"

And Genie, not an imbecile, after all, does it: ten white cubes, tinier than sugar cubes, tinier than dice, they are baby teeth to Genie. The one-units are baby teeth.

"Yes," says Miss De Witt, holding out her hand for Genie to deposit the bits of wood. "And here is a ten for you," handing over an orange rod, ten whites long. She writes it on the board as evidence: nothing in the ones column, a one in the tens column. "You see!" Triumphant and relieved.

Genie looks at the orange rod: a carrot stick, like Miss De Witt's carrots-and-peas breath. "But why isn't there just another number for it? Why does the ten stick have to have a different column?"

"Because there's *one* ten." Miss De Witt traces firmly over the number, then underlines it for further clarity.

Genie's voice gets a little high-pitched now, in the way that grates so on her teacher. "But it doesn't *have* to change at ten, does it? Really? Like it could have been at eleven or seventy or something? Someone just decided ten, right? It's that way because someone said so."

"It isn't that way because someone said so. It's that way because it *is* so!"

Miss De Witt stares. Genie stares back, unmoved. She bites the button on her collar.

"Get that out of your mouth," says Miss De Witt. Obviously a behavior problem: after all, the child tests bright. "Oppositional," she puts on the report home.

Later, in junior high, when they talked about base-ten, Esker felt as much affirmation as vindication. It was ten because people had ten fingers; it was ten because it was convenient; it was ten because people agreed to go along with it. Esker found it reassuring to confirm that math was a human conceit, a humble and lofty approximation. That somewhere beyond the boundaries of mathematical rules lay a place where the rules held no sway. You see, Miss De Witt! What a comfort, queer comfort, but comforting nonetheless. Up in her slope-ceilinged room after school, the winter she turned twelve, Esker filled composition books with sequences of strange numbers, counting to a thousand over and over again in base-one, base-two, base-three, base-four. . . .

And then, in her eleventh-grade math teacher's classroom, a poster of Einstein with his shrunken-apple countenance and leonine wisps bore this quote (she has searched for and been unable to find this poster ever since she became a math teacher herself): "The series of integers is obviously an invention of the human mind, a self-created tool." You err, Miss De Witt! Miss De Witless. A great comfort, and Einstein's background in the poster was black space and a bit of Milky Way, starry and shifting, finally out of everyone's reach, even his. Finally unsusceptible.

And then, in college, in the library that day, the aggressively geometrical library with its oddly beguiling antisuicide tiles in the lobby, its peekaboo floor plan like a cross-section of some vast multileveled organism, she'd chanced upon a magazine and been thrown for a loop, thrown back into the world of Miss De Witt's absolute, pre-existing hierarchy of numbers, orders, operations. If it was all an invention of man, how did man's humble equations come to be echoed in the clouds, in ridged sand dunes, in whorls of cream dispersing in coffee? Oh, Miss De Witt, in your dumb certainty were you more right than you knew? Is it that way because it *is* so?

She was all at once Genie in kneesocks again, thrust-jawed, resisting what seemed like a lid. Only she wasn't, she was eighteen and Esker by now, adrift from her parents and the old stately anchor of her Adirondack town. For years she had been the strongest force she knew, and she was tired of it, sick from it, sick with an unnamed longing for something larger, something huge and inevitable, whose long arms might cover and hold her completely, as intractable as gravity but more subtle and various, something which would neither shatter nor disintegrate when tested by the full strength of her thrashing skepticism, her railing queries, her exacting probes. She had never fallen in love before. Smitten, she switched majors.

That she met Albert Rose over a photocopy machine was just the sort of ridiculous coincidence she was increasingly willing to notice. A sort of poetry of the invisible. A poetry of repetition, in which nothing is ever new, in which nothing has not been said before, done before, in which every divergence is down a path already paved and mapped. And on some level there was always that feeling with Albert and Esker, from their first prickly encounter.

In college Esker worked part-time as a receptionist in the Office of Student Affairs. Albert had found a position serving as personal lackey to a professor of modern European history, and in this capacity presented himself in front of Esker's desk one day with a stack of articles he'd been sent to duplicate. Esker held the key to the photocopy machine and the log book. Albert gave her a winsomely hangdog look.

"You think that gets you in?"

His pupils shrank to points. "For Chrissakes, what's *your* problem?"

"This machine is for Office of Student Affairs use only."

He sighed gutturally. "I think you might be a little overzealous about your mission here."

"The log gets checked. I'm the one they're going to ask to account for this. Why don't you copy them over at the history department?"

"I already got booted by the sentinel over there. Copyright violations."

"Oh, good. I want that on *my* head."

He assessed her impassively. "At least the other one acted sorry about it."

"I'm sorry." What could she say?

He continued there, long arms weighted down by the stack of papers so that his wrists leaked beyond the cuffs of his blue oxford, and they were wide and flat. The tendons showed fiercely. He appeared to do minor calculations behind his eyes, which were gray and reckoning. His mouth was just a line. Then he returned to the elevator. He waited quite a while for it to come, and held his long blue back straight for the duration.

The next day, when the phone on her desk rang, she prattled by rote, "Good morning, Office of Student Affairs, how may I help you?" and he said, "Hello. I'd like a student affair." In the interim, while she was regrouping, waiting for her brain to fire an appropriate response through, he said, "Oh, lighten up," and hung up the phone. She knew it was him even though his voice wasn't that distinctive.

A week later, they saw each other in the cafeteria and said hi, uncertainly, as if they recalled perhaps once sharing a joke.

Two weeks after that, they ran into each other again, over a keg in a shower stall in some dorm at 1:00 A.M. She was in the stall herself, pumping beer all over her sneakers, filling the plastic cups people shoved forward, and looked up to catch him watching puzzledly, as though struck by the incongruity of her, here.

"Oh, you," she said as wryly as possible.

"No, *you*," he countered.

And she smiled.

"You can do that with your mouth? Smile?"

"Shut up," she said. It got her to laugh. And then they shook beery hands and exchanged names. He was a foot taller, and wearing an awful powder-blue cardigan. They were freshmen.

The thing that made her fall for higher math, more than the oil-slick beauty of the Julia set, more than the rainbow-doily allure of the Mandelbrot set, or the exquisite simplicity of her iterated snowflake, or the levelheaded mysteries of wind-blown wheat, or population growth, or fibrillating hearts—the thing that made her fall so hard was that she'd been wrong. It was the toppling of her certainties that won her, the way, in one fell stroke, ingesting that article in the Escher-like library one day, she'd been diminished, beautifully reduced, relieved, before the promise of something so much greater—not stiflingly greater, like Miss De Witt's tidy set of rules—but something unmastered, uncomprehended, in whose presence she might be controvertible, yielding.

No wonder she had never fallen in love, not once, growing up— never fallen, period, for fear of smashing past the neat, fragile borders of the world that kept her and her family. Esker'd gauged its fragility by the time she was two. What made her parents fearful? She didn't know, only that they assuaged unarticulated fears with dutiful cheer and routine: an ever-constant rotation of meals corresponding to specific days of the week, an ever-constant conversation repeated over orange juice and vitamins each morning, an ever-constant wardrobe so prudently laundered and mended she swore the contents of their closets never altered in all her eighteen years of living at home.

Genie was an only child. Her mother, whom Genie grew up hearing people refer to as delicate, had had a difficult time conceiving; she'd given birth finally at age thirty-nine, named her daughter in an uncharacteristic and unrepeated burst of romantic frivolity, and died of renal failure twenty years later. Her father, whom she never heard referred to as delicate, and who died nevertheless of a heart attack in his early sixties, had held a white-collar job at Boltman Paper Co., and came home most Fridays during Genie's childhood with a pack of samples for her collages: kraft and newsprint, bond and colored construction paper. Sometimes now when she pictures her childhood it's as if their very house had been made of construction paper, with construction-paper tulips lined up in construction-paper flower beds, construction-paper pies her mother pulled from a construction-paper oven, tiny construction-paper smoke curling from her father's construction-paper pipe. Even her parents appear as paper dolls sometimes in her imagination, with Genie the only real, fleshly being on the premises: an alarmingly robust three-dimensional figure giving off body heat and sound, forever in danger of tearing through the façade.

Genie the Giant, her father used to call her, a reference to her supposedly heavy step as she tore through the house. "Slow down, now, easy," his admonition forever followed her, or he would cringe involuntarily as she took the last three steps into the hall in a single bound: "You'll crack the plaster." Her mother forever seated in some dim adjacent room, doing handwork, always ready with a vague smile. They were unfailingly gentle with each other, her parents, softspoken, thoughtful of each other's needs to the point of condescension. As though there were an understanding that no one ought ever to have to bear hurt.

The older Genie became, the more hopelessly, corporeally giant she grew, although by then she'd learned how to mask it, or to compensate, and she tiptoed around the paper boxes of her house and school and all the buildings in town with a mixture of pity and loathing. In reality, she did not cut a particularly imposing figure; she was actually on the small side, and the concoction of genes bequeathed her by an ancestry that included a mixture of Eastern European and Mediterranean ethnicities declared itself in rather muddy fashion: her complexion, her eyes, her hair, her bone structure all sort of a neutral blur. Her conduct, too, was unremarkable; she was reasonably obedient, performed well in school, was respectful toward the institutions of her community.

She sometimes pretended she was a nurse, or anyway that she was disguised as a nurse, someone tidy and soothing, someone trained in the art of smoothing the bedclothes without jarring the body beneath them. It was easy enough and rewarding, in a limited way, to tend to people, to minister to their needs: she made soup and meatloaf and set the table; she gently drew the shades when her mother needed rest; she asked her father about his day; cut elaborate snowflakes from the papers he brought her, and taped these in the windows at Christmastime. Straight through high school, she gave her parents reason to praise her and rely upon her, and she took her satisfaction in never causing any harm.

She didn't learn the story of her namesake until tenth grade, in world lit., and arrived home that afternoon ready to demand an explanation, but her mother, propped at one end of the couch, crocheting more of her endless squares, pleaded ignorance—"I just thought it was beautiful. I thought she was one of the Muses, or something"—then betrayed herself in the next sentence: "Anyway, they all had terrible fates: Clytemnestra, Persephone, Antigone, Io. That doesn't make their names any less beautiful." A sacrificial virgin, sacrificed by her father, for the sake of getting on with war! Yuck, but by far the worst part of the story was Iphigenia's grotesque nobility, her complicity, her self-effacement in deciding not to save herself or let Achilles save her. That spring, playing JV softball, all the girls on the team took to calling each other by their surnames, and Esker dropped her first name altogether after that. Outwardly she still appeared to be the same compliant, beige, thin-voiced girl; inwardly, she promised herself, she was simply biding her time.

The trouble was, having shed Genie, she had no sense of what she might actually become. How could she know without a test, a trial, but how would she ever encounter a fitting test in this construction-paper town? She began to long, like a lovesick creature in a fairy tale, for some force greater than herself, something as vast and patient as the great pine forests all around, but less dispassionate. She wished at once for some great palm she could lean her forehead full upon, and some strong muscle she could wrestle fully against with no fear of hurting. She ached for the relief of a worthy adversary.

Much later, as a high-school teacher, she would catch glimpses of similarly restive students, young women and men who would strike her as familiarly, dangerously unbound, like knightless squires seeking to pit themselves, solo and clueless, against what dragons they could find. Some of these she would see fling themselves into the gaping rapids of drugs and alcohol, and others drift toward the large, vaporous promises of love and sex, and a rare few disappear like shadows into the stern black caves of extreme religious practice. One, attempting a different tack, would try to fly from the Big Room bleachers.

10.

Ann makes Esker a tape.

Ann is in love with Esker. At sixteen she falls in love effortlessly, frequently, at the drop of a hat. She is also in love with (a partial list) (excluding celebrities): Malcolm Choy; Nuncio from Game; a little bit her best friend, Hannah Stolarik; anyone who can whistle with two fingers; anyone who wears beaded fringe; the men who play pickup basketball on West Third Street and Sixth Avenue; Willette and Emil, who are practically her godparents; the traffic cop at Times Plaza who directs cars like a ballet dancer; her second cousin once removed who lives in Paris but spent last Thanksgiving with them; the guy with perpetual five-o'clock shadow who walks his ferret on a leash on the promenade. Her love is absolute and unidirectional, with neither consequences nor accountability, though not without rewards.

Ann spends much of Monday working on the compilation, her wheelchair pulled up to the sleek lighted panels of the stereo system. She writes the play list down in red felt-tip. She wears an old tennis visor with a green plastic bill. She chews gum and pretends she's on the air at a radio station, making up a little patter about the songs and artists as she goes. She speaks *sotto voce,* in a British accent, which she thinks makes her sound like more of an expert. "This next track, Scat" (Scat is the name of the imaginary DJ on whose show she's guesting), "is a recently rediscovered cover of the Velvet Underground's 'What Goes On' by a band that came to popularity in the early eighties, The Feelies. Let's have a listen, shall we? Then we can compare the two." She presses record, rolls back in her chair halfway across the room. Her father is in the kitchen making Indonesian curried vegetable stew for Esker. Every bowl is out.

Ann has not told her father about her mother's call.

"Oh, hello, Alice," she had said into the phone, aware of Denise's banana poised midair, aware of Hannah's hyper-stillness in the easy chair, and she'd felt the instant, corrupting power that comes with being mean. "How long has it been?"

"Ann." Like a lemon—ripe, bright, stung—and Ann could exactly picture her mother biting the corner of her wide bottom lip, closing her wide eyes, regathering resolve. "How is your leg?"

"It's my heels."

"I know, sorry: your heels."

"Fine."

"Well, obviously not fine, but . . . Good. I'm so sorry you fell."

"It wasn't your fault."

A sigh. And then her mother does the thing she's brilliant at. She's too smart, Alice Evers, to sound hurt, to appeal to Ann via sympathy or guilt; she snares her daughter instead with wit, with non-sequitur, with oddities of thought that Ann's curiosity cannot resist. Ann doesn't even know how she manages the transition, but there she is mid-sentence saying, ". . . know that if you dip a daisy in liquid nitrogen it freezes, and you can smash it on the table and it shatters? And it reminded me of that day, after the ice storm that time, when you were ten or eleven and we walked across the Brooklyn Bridge—remember how freezing we were?— and every girder, every wire, on the bridge was encrusted with ice, and we said it looked like a mirror somebody had shattered and that we were walking through it, like Alice? And by the time we got to Chinatown, we said we were on the other side."

Ann remembered. She'd been twelve. They had gone into a restaurant and had hot green tea and cold sesame noodles, and a little bamboo cricket cage hanging outside the restaurant had also been entirely coated with ice, a fairy palace for a musical insect. "Vaguely," said Ann, but in her heart the ice was breaking up and an ache, a homesickness, was trickling beneath the sheer, cracked layer.

"Well, the other reason I'm calling," said Alice (another transitionless moment), and Ann could picture her again—all interesting cheekbones and high color infusing her freckled face, which was otherwise pale as apple flesh—"is I'm thinking of coming out there for the holidays. Or part of the holidays. I have a little break in shooting now until after the New Year."

Alice Evers left home three years ago without putting any name to her departure—not divorce, not separation, not abandonment, not experiment, nothing—and moved to Los Angeles to act in movies. Films. She'd acted in New York, too, in people's living rooms and loft spaces, at PS 22 and La Mama, off-off-Broadway and off-Broadway, and once, for three nights, on Broadway, and when this last venture, despite flopping onstage, was being turned into a film, she followed the camera out west and stayed there, becoming, through a series of diverse roles in four respected-but-little-seen flicks and one box-office success, something of an "indie darling," as more than one article has dubbed her. She has in all this time managed to make it back to Brooklyn for a whopping three—count 'em, three—visits. Ann and Wally have been to L.A. once together, and Ann once solo. Currently, Ann can view her mother's face in a grainy ad that has been running in *The Village Voice* these past few weeks, and on a series of identical posters glued up on construction-site barriers along a sprinkling of downtown streets: in her latest project she is the star, and the only name above the title. Critics have called her "elegantly inscrutable," and "a cross between a gazelle and a Mack truck"; they have lauded her "unapologetic projection of desire" as well as her "fetchingly canny midnight-blue gaze."

"Ann? Are you there?"

"Yes." Bored-sounding.

"Well, say something, goose."

"What?"

A pause. "Say, 'That's nice, Mom.' "

"That's nice, Mom."

"Say, 'Gee, I sure can't wait!' "

Ann sighed. "Yeah, whatever." But a little smile leaked into her voice.

"Say, 'The butter, the butter, the holy margarine—' "

" ' . . . Two black eyes and a jelly nose, and the rest all painted green,' " Ann finished the childhood rhyme: *sucker*. Sucker: one who is easily deceived, a dupe; one who is indiscriminately attracted to something specific. She is a sucker for Alice Evers. "When are you coming?"

"Don't know yet, I haven't called the airlines. I'll see you soooon, though. Kiss your legs for me. Heels, I mean. I miss you."

Ann had hung up and rolled her eyes for the benefit of Hannah and Denise, both of whom are a little starstruck. They have never met Alice Evers, since she left the year before Ann entered The Prospect School.

"How was that?" Hannah had asked.

"I need a smoke." Sometimes they share covert cigarettes in the park across the street from school. Before going back to class, before dodging back inside under that iron bird-creature-thing that hovers over the entrance as though always about to snatch someone and abscond with her, they half mask their breath with green-apple Jolly Ranchers, conflicted over whether to flaunt or to hide the smell. The vile inhalation of gray-white smoke and the sweet-and-sour rush of candied saliva are inextricably linked for Ann, and she wasn't sure what she really craved that minute except for the cold of the balcony. Denise had opened the French doors, and she wheeled herself through them. Hannah produced a pack of filtered lights; all three lent cupped palms to shelter the single match. They'd smoked vigorously, eyes and noses watering in the December breeze, and Ann had been grateful that her friends knew enough not to inquire further about her mother's call.

They could see the promenade from the balcony, and Ann tried to picture meeting Malcolm Choy there, him with his hands in the pockets of his thrift-shop bomber jacket, eyes a little obscured by long black forelock, tilting down to speak to her in her mobile metal throne, smelling of smoke and candy, wiping her nose every other second. She lost heart. "You said he was going to call me anyway," she pointed out when Denise tried to get her to call again.

"Debutante," accused Denise.

"Yeah, that's me."

"She'll call if she wants to," said Hannah.

"Oh go . . . go to a cotillion."

"Wow, that's a really clever insult."

"Shut up." And Denise, laughing at herself, had copied Malcolm's number onto a scrap of paper and used a bit of spit to rub the ink off her own palm.

Now it is Monday, and the scrap of paper has languished in Ann's underwear drawer, and Malcolm Choy has not called. For the moment, she is glad. The Alice Evers front has been quiet, too. Ann looks up from her chair at the portrait over the mantel. Implausibly, out of the jumble of oil and fabric, her face has been fully realized. Emil, the artist, the family friend who'd asked Alice to sit for it, had conveyed something not literally present in her face, something a camera would never have caught. When Ann was little, she used to pretend it was a magic mirror, a portent of her own potential, of the power she herself would someday wield, and she used to address it in whispers peppered with "thee"s and "thou"s. "How are thou doing?" she'd whisper, looking meaningfully into its eyes. Or "Oh, thee, please help me pass the spelling quiz tomorrow!" She'd heard from Catholic friends about making offerings, and went through a stage of leaving things on the mantel: pretzel sticks, silver gum-wrappers, a braid of corn silk. "I dearly hope someday I have cheekbones like thee's."

But today she regards the portrait irreverently, through the green pall of her tennis visor, which renders it the visage of a seasick woman, her mother, Alice, who has left and not come back. "Stay where you belong," she tells it sternly, and after she has spoken considers that this could mean two things. "Stay in L.A.," she clarifies. The navy eyes bore back into hers, at once dumb and knowing.

In the kitchen her father is sautéing onions and chili and garlic and ginger, a kind of olfactory plaid, and chopping up whatever comes next; Ann can hear the knife drumming deft rhythms on the cutting board. She can tell he is happy by the speed of his blade.

The song ends, and she wheels back to the stereo to press pause and cue up the next song: "It's All Right to Cry." Ann snaps her gum and delivers more patter in her British expert's voice: "Now I'd like to play your listeners something from the soundtrack of *Free to Be . . . You and Me*, an early-seventies collaboration by Marlo Thomas and Friends. It became something of an instant classic among the politically correct set, and is still popular in the children's-record market today. Not many people in today's generation will recognize that the artist on this number was a pro-football player, Scat. It quite adds another dimension to the song, I think you'll agree. Let's have a go."

She presses play and pushes off into the room again, arcing into a wheelchair pirouette as she does. The air is interwoven with spices and the growly-earnest crooning of Rosey Grier, and the white lights on the potted grapefruit tree swarm in and out of view as Ann spins herself 360 degrees, and again, and again. She wants her father to wear his jam-colored sweater tonight. She wants to ask Esker about dipping flowers in liquid nitrogen. She wants them to sit around the table for a long, long time, linked and amused and chaste.

11.

At four, the visiting nurse comes and Wally excuses himself to buy fresh bread. "Bye, Pa," says Ann, and it irritates him, the affectation of "Pa"; he doesn't understand what she means by it; it's another thing he doesn't know whether to worry about or not.

Outside, a blast of cold air slams down Pierrepont Street, damp air from the river, and he braces himself against it, shoulders hunched, chin tucked, his old furry shapka pulled low over his ears. Then, consciously, he unbraces himself, untenses his muscles, makes himself lower his shoulders and lift his chin, and the wind sweeps down his neck. Tolerance is something to be cultivated. He tries to conduct himself as though he's in training.

One summer, when Ann was six or seven, they'd been in Amagansett, at Willette and Emil's beach house. That was the summer Alice had sat for her portrait with Emil, and she and Ann had spent the whole month of August out there, and Wally, still working for the city then, had commuted on weekends. And Willette had been visiting her sick grandmother in Jamaica. And anyway, one night Ann had wanted to go swimming after supper, so Wally had taken her down to the beach; it was still light out, what movie people, he has since learned, call the golden hour, and Ann was washed in it, this gold broth, as she ran, in her plain black one-piece, in and out of the green foam-crested waves by herself, like a little bright sylph playing with her pet dragon. She had a great capacity not to need anyone else, and Wally could feel her farness from him, her total immersion in some child's netherworld he could no longer begin to inhabit, and he'd watched her for some time from where he stood up on the beach, a little chilly even clad in long pants and shoes, until, eventually, she'd turned around and caught him smiling beatifically and demanded, "What?"

Wally, caught, suddenly shy, tried to put into words what he'd been feeling. "I just . . . I can't believe I made you." And Ann had shot him a properly grossed-out look and ordered, not unkindly, "Yeah, well, get over it," and dived into a wave. And Wally understood that this was the icing on the cake: not only had he made her, but she had turned out to be her own real person, capable of correcting him, rejecting him, putting him in his place. And if he congratulated himself on having this understanding, at least he had it, at least he is adept at fathoming the world this way: every sad thing, every loss or hurt really a challenge to love that much more, really just another of beauty's many strongholds.

That had been a strange summer, and of course there is no memory of that evening that does not include the knowledge of Alice and Emil back at the house alone together, as they were alone together all summer except for Ann. Wally standing there at water's edge watching her brown limbs flashing dauntlessly in and out of the water, and him smiling through it, through all he knew, willing his head, his heart, to be big enough to take it all in and to hold it. Like holding his finger in a flame.

The memory turns to smoke; he crosses Henry Street. Wally James does not think of himself as a man suffering from a broken heart. He thinks of himself as a man bound to buy bread on a cold Monday. He approaches a Christmas-tree lot smelling of pine and exhaust. The man working in it looks miserable, hunched. The temperature seems to have plunged radically since this morning, and the sky is the dead gray of an old mattress, curbside. "Winter Wonderland" ekes its palsied way out of a dented boom box. As Wally passes, the tree man suddenly smiles at him: an Eastern European smile, stout and mustached and flecked with gold. Wally is almost compelled to offer his hand; he doesn't, but it turns his heart, this man's unexpected gift, and his own ability—he knows this is everything—to be open to it.

He catches sight of his reflection in the window of a parked van. He thinks of himself as a comfortable-looking man. He has enough money and health, and just enough age and girth, to project ease, nurturance, welcome. If he were a flag, his emblem would be the pineapple. If he were a minor Greek deity, he'd be affiliated with the hearth. But his fleeting image in the bottomless mirror of the van window comes back hollow, washed out, and wan, with deep furrows around his nose and across his brow, the shapka framing it all like a black hood. Startled by the image, and subsequently preoccupied with thoughts of morbidity and mortality, Wally bumps into an elderly man carrying several parcels, which scatter to the sidewalk. The man sighs: all the burdens of the world. Wally apologizes, scooping up the parcels, restoring them to the man's arms with deft efficiency. The parcels have been clumsily wrapped, all in the same silver paper stamped with blue dreidels and menorahs; now a few have come partly undone. "Happy Hanukkah," Wally says, pressing his hand to the man's elbow, and watches as the man shuffles on down the block, bent into the wind, bearing his gifts.

The effort. The effort to will love. He is an athlete in training; the heart is a muscle. He sees the man turn in toward an entrance, watches over him until a navy-blue doorman victoriously wrestles the door open against the wind. Wally walks on.

Alice's gift to him, the restaurant, had been so enormous and life-altering, nothing like whatever happy frivolities must be inside those Hanukkah parcels, completely unlike the gift of the Christmas-tree man's sudden gilded smile, but that smile had been like a thread, however frail, binding in some brief, inconsequential way bestower and recipient, whereas Alice's gift had had the opposite, snipping effect: liberating not only Wally from his job in city planning, but herself from the burden of her parents' money, and also, ultimately, herself from Wally.

His mind darts for no reason to Esker's kiss. It was strange to him. This in itself seems strange, since the restaurant business is full of hugs and kisses, and he is well accustomed to receiving the intimate gestures of strangers. Maybe it's because she's Ann's teacher. But Prospect School faculty don't as a rule trouble to maintain the air of professional distance that Wally remembers his own teachers carefully exuding. Maybe it's because she was so prickly from the outset, so almost gruff about bandaging up his cut hand.

He's now far enough from the water that the wind doesn't cut so sharply. He slows his pace. From a low, curvy tree in the tight wedge of yard outside a brownstone, a clove-studded orange twirls on a red ribbon.

He and his sister used to make them as kids, give them as Christmas presents to all their relatives. He still remembers the sore thumb he'd get from pushing the blunt cloves into the tough peel. Everywhere you go, he thinks, he wills himself to think, there are echoes of the familiar. Like signals, carefully planted signposts you have only to read.

When he pictures his childhood home, it's always on a rough mental map, so that he's aware of it existing north of where he currently lives, but he notices now that there's another point on the map, making his own relative location one notch more specific. It has emerged of its own silent accord, again without reason, like a star that's come out in the night sky; a moment ago there was blankness, and now, without fanfare, something definite has taken residence there. It's Esker's childhood home in the Adirondacks, a point north and west. New coordinates. The little globe of the clove-orange spins on its red ribbon.

The bakery he favors is near Parkes Cadman Plaza, and after he has chosen a round brown peasant loaf and some rolls dense with walnuts and raisins, he strolls across the green, the warm paper bag tucked under his arm, crunching the brittle grass, which is studded with little cakes of frozen dog do, candy wrappers, the odd condom, crack vial, and empty minibottle of schnapps. In the waning light, a big kid and a little kid are tossing around a blue foam football. The little kid misses it every time, and has to run to retrieve it. Wally knows their bare hands must be cold, because his are, even shoved in his pockets. He can hear both boys sniffing in that rattly, frozen way. The bread warms his armpit.

It comes to Wally what was unusual about Esker's kiss. It had been exceedingly intentional. The rest of the visit, she'd been somehow oblique, had seemed to deflect everything slightly, even in the midst of all the repartee. But in that moment, he had felt the full, simple intent of her two lips.

He'd responded absurdly with that statement about Ann. It had seemed necessary to change the subject. Not for his sake, for hers. He has the thought that it will be important when she comes for dinner tonight not to scare her.

12.

Esker takes the A to Jay Street–Borough Hall holding wobbling tiger lilies in dun-gloved fists. She's in a terrible mood. The flowers, for one thing: it's completely unlike her to arrive bearing flowers. Her stomach feels all peppery, alive with a curiosity and hope she'd rather be done with. Oh, she is disgusted with her hope. These inane blooms shedding rust on her coat. The lipstick—lipstick!—she put on before she left and now purposefully chews off. The quaky intestinal heat.

She knows what this is. She is not an idiot.

There have been two phone calls since Saturday morning, when Wally bloodied his knuckles knocking on her door.

Saturday evening, him to her: "You're not allergic to anything, are you?" "Ragweed," she'd replied, a moment before she realized he was talking about the menu for Monday night. A beat. "I'll leave that out, then," he'd said, his dry humor singing like an arrow through her slippery heart.

Sunday, her to him: "What you said, about worrying about Ann, what did you mean?"

She had called him at Game, having looked the number up. In the pause she could hear restaurant sounds: music, cutlery, low murmuring crosshatched with high laughter and clinking glass. She'd felt voyeuristic listening, almost prurient. She fancied she could hear, too, the fullness of

Wally's indrawn breath as he thought before replying. When he did speak, his voice seemed stripped, immediate, flat with candor.

"I meant, I think, that I don't understand how she hurt herself."

And there was another pause as Esker thought. She was sitting in her kitchen touching the starfish dish towel, which was hung over the back of a chair. "Me, too. Me, neither. I was thinking about that, too. I don't have any information about it."

"It's nothing I can put my finger on, but . . ."

"Yeah."

Cutlery, gaiety. "I can't talk here."

"Right. I'm sorry. I just wanted to say that I heard what you said the other day and I didn't say back to you that I'd been worrying a little, too. If that gives you anything."

"Thanks for calling."

"She's my favorite student," Esker had blurted then. "I mean ever." And later she'd berated herself for saying that. It didn't matter that she thought it was true; to what end had she said it? What had she been hoping to create between them with those words?

Now, Monday night, Esker emerges from the subway and it's all pretty, in the magical way that moneyed neighborhoods are at Christmastime: lights everywhere, in every single tasteful color, and plenty of tiny whites plotted starrily through the branches of well-tended sidewalk trees. The cold moves quickly through her layers of clothing. She strides down Pierrepont enjoying it, enjoying not resisting the clean force of the wind, but letting it race down her collar and up her sleeves and through her thinnish wool pants. It is already the shortest day of the year, a thought which leaves her feeling oddly bereft.

The doorman knows her. They smile hesitantly at each other. While he phones up, Esker fidgets around the small lobby, embarrassed by the flowers, by the hour. Her awkwardness springs from concerns about neither privacy nor propriety, but from what she believes to be the baldness of this transition, the effortful shift from A to B—in this case, from daughter's tutor to father's dinner guest, so tritely heralded by the bouquet. She brushes at her coat, a fact from childhood registering blandly in her mind: nothing removes pollen stains.

Peering back through the glass doors which just admitted her, Esker sees the decorated street with her own reflection fit over it. The lights that fall within the boundaries of her image make a partial constellation of her body: The Limbless Maiden, it would be called. Right there, next to Orion, see? All fiery head and breast, all thought and feeling, no body, the body nothing but black ether. She finds herself checking for Albert in the glass.

She realizes that when she says "Albert" she doesn't mean Albert; she doesn't even *know* Albert really, not having been in contact with the man in nine years; Albert's ghost is really *her* ghost: the version of Albert that she has invented. Or not her: her brain, some part of her brain she's barely on speaking terms with. But this ghost is derived from a real person; he really existed; *they* existed, Esker and Albert, and the rest of her brain insists on inserting, preserving, as many real details as it can. So the ghost is endowed with a multitude of characteristics not typical of phantasms: body temperature, for instance, and odor (Esker thinks of his scent as Basketball, a fresh, rubbery smell), and a small, persistent sniffle. Often he wears a knit cap, and sometimes he has the pale little beard he'd flirted with that last summer. He is not infrequently humorous, although he rarely speaks, just intimates things with his looks and silences, his appearances and disappearances. Sometimes he yawns; sometimes he rolls his eyes; sometimes he ignores her so coldly and completely that Esker wonders why he bothers to haunt her at all. Or why her brain bothers engineering the haunting; she understands this is really the question.

If he were dead instead of gone, she might have to believe in ghosts, so assertive is his presence, and so seemingly independent, as if generated from a source beyond her own despotic mind. She wishes he *were* dead instead of gone, instead of missing in action. His ghost must be fueled by her latent belief that he will resurface. Those words he'd said, leaving—"I don't know about this." As though it were a question they'd have to get back to. Which she's been waiting to do ever since. Like Penelope at her weaving for seven years, eight years, nine years, ten, only Esker hasn't even been weaving; she's been waiting for Albert so that the pattern may resume itself. As it is supposed to do.

But tonight in the glass there is only her reflection, her and those showy tiger lilies, all lit up green and red and gold by the trick of superimposition. Her and a Cantor dust of lights: growing infinitely more sparse without disappearing altogether. The elevator comes and she boards, heaves shut the old-fashioned gate, and begins to rise at a glacial rate. More pollen shakes loose from the long stamens, as though her hands were shaking, but it's only the vibrations of the motor, of course. Immediately upon stepping out on the fifth floor, she smells the subtle weave of the homemade curry and hopes it's not coming from behind the Jameses' door. "Don't have cooked for me," she thinks, and immediately berates herself, *"Idiot.* You're invited for *supper,"* which is so pitiful she can't help laughing and is therefore still smiling helplessly when Ann opens the door.

Ann has apparently dressed for the occasion, in battleship-gray velour bellbottoms, a silvery-gray ribbed turtleneck, and tiny silver earrings in the shape of Tenniel's hookah-smoking caterpillar. The air casts, a little garish amid the rest of her palette, stick out from her cuffs. "Hey," she says, wheeling backward to make room. Dark silver, like residue of tumultuous weather, stroked across each eyelid tonight.

Wally comes out from the kitchen area in a heathered maroon sweater. It reminds Esker of the way jam would be drawn in a children's book. He smiles at Esker with the quiet, complicit gravity of an old friend, which of course he is not. The hairless top of his head gleams as he takes the flowers from her arms. He has a dish towel slung over one shoulder, and it looks ridiculously nice up there, sort of forgotten, untroubled about. Esker can't get her smile to go away, and in a moment it turns into a laugh.

"What?" says Ann.

She shakes her head. "Nothing. Glad tidings. You look nice."

"It's my mount." Ann pats the wheelchair's metal side as if it were the flank of a horse. "Old Betsy." She neighs.

"What can I get you to drink?" asks Wally, and they all waltz along then, for a bit, to the tune of conventional hospitality, over to the kitchen area for cider and crackers and caponata. Esker bristles, instinctively, at the loveliness of this last item, which she adores—she is determined not to be affected by the idea of anyone's preparing food for her. But she sits on a high stool and finds herself dipping cracker after cracker into the eggplant spread. She can't think of anything she wants to say, and Wally is making peanut salad-dressing, which leaves Ann to talk. This proves no difficulty.

Ann is in rare form tonight, entertaining them with wicked imitations of Prospect School teachers. First she does Buddy, with his bad back, crouched awkwardly as he accompanied her in the ambulance.

With little else besides a few words, winces, smiles, and moans, she captures precisely the duality of his extreme niceness and what Esker would never have quite called his hypochondria.

"Here's Rhada," Ann announces next, and suddenly her features go all Clara Bow and her voice all deadpan-droll as, in heavily dentalized Brooklynese, she intones, "So we're gonna let x equal this sawlt shakah"—which she picks up from the table and shakes vigorously, scattering crystals—"and let m equal the ratio of the radius to the diametah of the peppah. Wit' the absolute value of m nevah to exceed yuh nose. Plawt it. Go."

Then she does Florence, the headmistress: cultured, cultured, cultured, always touching her collarbone, playing vaguely with the vaguely ethnic beads she favors, caressing each syllable, drawing them out nasally, "As I was *say*ing, ladaladalada . . . really a *scath*ingly *brill*iant *art*icle I read the other ladaladalada . . . on the principal capital en*dow*ment funds ladaladalada . . . according to the NASDAQ IQ BMW—" At which point Ann manages to indicate that Florence has inadvertently gotten her fingers stuck fast within her now-tangled strand of beads and cannot yank them loose.

Wally, acquainted with this particular talent of Ann's, is appreciative, but Esker is in fits. "You're a demon," she says, recovering herself. Ann beams. "Oh God, Florence!" Esker smacks her brow. "I was supposed to get back to her about some development-committee thing before the holiday!" Laughing has made her all hot and light, and she fans herself at the collar of her plain white blouse. Then, as if she were at home, she slides off her shoes and folds her legs under her on the stool, a child's pose. It makes her lean forward, and she helps herself to another cracker.

"She gets it from her mother," says Wally, genially, from the stove. There follows an instant stiffening, an almost audible crackling freeze, over in the vicinity of the wheelchair. Ann has gone rigid with terrible composure. All of a sudden: cheekbones. And a neck like a marble column. *Oh! She's going to be a beauty,* Esker realizes with a start.

"Being a demon?" Ann inquires coolly.

"Being a mimic," Wally clarifies, squeezing a lemon half over a pot. He seems unaware of or unconcerned about Ann's mood shift.

Esker looks from one to the other, trying to gauge what has just happened. Has Ann been humiliated? *Clod,* she thinks, experimentally, of Wally.

"Did you ever see her do Willette? A friend of ours," he explains over his shoulder to Esker. "Gorgeous. Jamaican. Set designer. Like six feet." He squeezes the other half and shoots the spent rind into the garbage. "Or Nuncio? You've seen her Nuncio, I'm sure."

"Not that I recall." Ann sounds exquisitely bored.

"Who's Nuncio?"

"My maître d'," says Wally. "A character. You do him, Ann."

"I think you're confusing us. Different repertoires."

"Oh, you could do a good Nuncio."

"Oh, not as good as Alice's." Matching his intonation note for note. Really snotty, actually. Given they have company. Esker is getting irritated with both of them.

"You don't do me, I hope?" she asks.

"No." Ann studies her simply. "You'd be hard."

Esker feels relieved and slighted. "Hard," she assumes, means too nebulous a source material, too lacking in qualities that might be played up.

"Want to go outside with me?" asks Ann.

"What?" Visions of maneuvering the wheelchair into the rickety old elevator, taking off just as they're about to eat.

"Out on the balcony. You can see Governors Island."

Esker glances at Wally, who looks up from bean sprouts to meet her gaze with a complicated brow. He gives her a nod that is almost contained in his eyes. Not a clod.

"We'll eat in five minutes," he says lightly.

Ann, gliding around posts, leads the way to the French doors.

Esker has been feeling, since yesterday's phone call, like a bit of a spy, or a double agent, for, although Wally hasn't asked her to, now she feels responsible for observing Ann more particularly. And Esker, who would make a disastrous spy, follows Ann into the frozen block of night like a tracking shot in a James Bond film, and she thinks Ann must sense it, and at that moment Ann turns and looks at her and Esker bursts out laughing—what on earth is wrong with her tonight? all this uncontrollable laughter—and Ann just looks at her, one of those marvelously impassive faces wise-ass kids know how to level on their elders, and it dissolves Esker all the more; she wants to cup Ann's fine cold chin in her hand and kiss her on the hair.

"I'm sorry. Nothing." Esker whacks herself heartily on the chest a few times.

"You're giddy," says Ann.

"This is an unbelievable view," says Esker, facing riverward. The cold cuts through her blouse and waters her eyes, so the lights of lower Manhattan shimmer and tremble roundly.

"He likes you, incidentally," says Ann.

Esker smiles politely back over her shoulder.

"I'm sorry he brought up my mother. He's very . . . magnanimous about her."

By the careful pronunciation, Esker recognizes it as an SAT word.

"It makes him feel good that he can share her with everybody."

"Share her?"

"Especially now that she's a public figure."

An error in the verb tense, thinks Esker. "Now?"

"Well, with her latest movie, especially."

"What?"

Ann cocks her head. "You didn't know? You've never heard of Alice Evers?"

Esker is literally dumbfounded. She's been walking by movie posters featuring Alice Evers every day for the past month; they've been posted on scaffolding down on Chambers Street, same face after same face after same face. But the image is grainy, and black and white, and she never connected it to the color-drenched, pulsing portrait in the Jameses' living room, nor did she ever connect the name Alice Evers to Ann James; why would she? Especially since she's assumed Ann's mother was dead. Who hangs a portrait of a divorced spouse over the mantel?

"I thought your mother was dead," she admits.

Ann laughs shortly. "Don't you guys have access to all that stuff anyway?"

"What stuff?"

"You know, student records?"

"They're confidential."

Ann scoffs. "It's not like they're under lock and key."

"Actually, I think they are."

"I hate to tell you."

"You mean you've . . . ?"

"It's totally common knowledge. We sneak in the office all the time and read stuff we're not supposed to."

"Like what?"

Ann shrugs. "You know, like if you have a crush on someone."

"What, you have a crush on someone, so you sneak in and read their *grades?*"

"Whatever you can find. Stuff."

Esker feels she ought to be chiding Ann, but the whole situation is too ridiculous, and Ann's bearing so self-assured. *Is* it common knowledge? Maybe she alone has been in the dark. Here she is supposed to be on reconnaissance, and all she's learning is how little she knows. It occurs to her Ann may know more about her than she does about Ann. "You're completely shivering," says Esker, brusquely. "Is that your teeth?" She means the jackhammery noise emanating from Ann's direction. "It's very pretty out here; now let's go back in."

They do, and the warmth and the smell of curry envelop them like shawls, and Wally has lit the candles on the table. Then Esker, still trying to adjust to what feels like a sudden drop in oxygen level, hears, "No fucking way," from Ann and looks up to see a living woman, freckled and honey-maned and handsome in a peacock sweater and blue jeans, standing in front of the bricked fireplace directly beneath her likeness.

13.

Alice is funny, Alice is warm. Alice is both at ease and glamorous. Alice is so happy to see them all—the teacher, who gets thanked, with a solid handshake and a wide-open but rather easily dispensed smile, for doing so much for Ann (as if Alice knows, as if she keeps in regular contact); the husband, who gets asked about work in the most specific detail (has the cook's wife had her baby yet? have people liked the moose burgers?), who gets a hair plucked from his sweater, who gets teased, gently and cleverly, during dessert (as if she has a right to show him affection); and the daughter, of course, the daughter most of all, who barely deigns to meet the mother's eye, who in her fury turns luminous and flickering, like a tissue-paper lantern on a windy night, and who, during dessert, sits biting her water glass so hard it breaks. There is a snap and Ann says, "Oh," and they all look as she picks a piece of glass from her tongue and begins to bleed, slowly, from somewhere inside her mouth and down her chin, like a B-movie teen-vampire chick.

"For heaven's sake!" says her mother.

"Are you all right?" says her father.

Esker hands her the cloth napkin from her lap and inspects the glass. "You're not supposed to use your teeth when you drink," she says quietly. "That's just for eating."

Ann breaks into wild laughter, extravagant laughter, a thing apart from mirth. She presses Esker's napkin into her mouth; from the noises she could almost be choking, but she flaps one hand in an *I'm fine* gesture, and Esker rises with her plate and from this the other grown-ups take their cue ("Sit, sit, I've got it") and begin to clear the table. So the dinner ends.

Now it's later, nine or ten or something, Ann doesn't know, she has no idea, and Esker is gone and so is Wally, having left to help her hail a cab, but that was ages ago, it seems, and Ann is on the red velvet couch and her mother is on the red velvet couch, too, sitting at the other end, with Ann's air casts in her lap, and she's painting the air casts with nail polish, painting snakes and birds on them with Vixen and Pink Grapefruit and Toast and French White.

Ann, whose mouth is fine, just a thin, jagged bolt of metal-tasting cut inside her lip, is telling her mother about Malcolm Choy. "He has those drum muscles," she says. She speaks languidly, as though she has taken some sort of pill. She has become someone else, she is in a play about a girl on a red velvet couch with her mother. The smell of nail polish is like a small dense object, a figurine. "Those drummer forearms," she is saying. "He's part Chinese and part Trinidadian. He's a senior. He's going to RISD next year. His mother's an artist. Like a real big one. She made that paper funeral procession that was on display at Grand Central last year, which you probably never saw. He plays the conga drums, and he's also in this band, The Bernoulli Effect, with these guys from LaGuardia. He was supposed to accompany us for this dance we were doing for Winter Concert, that now I'm out of. He chews cinnamon sticks. It's totally poignant, the way it hangs out of his mouth like a little brown cigarette."

"A Gauloise."

"What?"

"That's what they're called, those little brown French cigarettes."

"Oh. Whatever. He asked for my phone number. His best friend is the shortest kid in the school. Perry. For a science project, they rigged a light in the lobby to flash every time someone flushed a toilet anywhere in the school. A green light. He wears mittens, not gloves. He's always falling asleep in English."

There isn't time to be mad at Alice. Alice is too rare and fleeting. Ann gazes down her leg and surveys the newest denizen of the bestiary there: a sort of hummingbird, long-beaked and vertical in hovering flight.

Her mother the witch, the twisted fairy princess, gives it a Toast-colored eye. She is intent on the project, inhabits it fully. Freckles on her jaw, beside her mouth, all across the topography of her long, strong nose: they subtract a certain possibility of refinement, free her beauty up to be something more than pristine. Even in the low light and shadows of the room she comes off golden. She has not the slightest bit of discomfort in being here.

"You *are* a bad mother," says Ann, letting her head lie back against the arm of the couch. "For the record."

"Sorry."

"How long are you staying?"

"Thursday. Friday, maybe."

"That's it?"

"The food is terrible, and the portions are so small."

"What's that, Chekhov?"

"Woody Allen, I think."

"And then what?"

"And then back to Toronto to finish filming."

"Any sex scenes in this one?"

"Semi."

"Cute leading man?"

"He thinks so. So who is this Esker?"

"My math teacher," says Ann. "I don't really know."

"What's her real name?"

"You mean her first name."

"Yeah."

"I don't know." Ann's not sure why she lies. "It's a secret."

"Rumpelstiltskin."

"Maybe. Will you see Emil while you're here?"

"Willette and Emil, I hope so, yes."

"Oh yes, *Willette* and Emil."

"Yes. Hello? What's with you?"

Ann's voice has been getting smaller and slower; her eyes have closed, and several rounds of breathing come even and peaceful.

"Hello, little faker, why are you feigning sleep?"

Ann ignores her mother, and feels her bare toes kissed. It tickles, and she pulls the leg away.

" 'This sleep is sound indeed!' " declaims Alice, rapping her knuckles on Ann's cast.

A smile asserts itself upon Ann's unwilling lips. "Ow," she mutters crankily, eyes still closed, as though it hurt her heel. She thinks of her father and Esker. Maybe they went walking on the promenade. Maybe they've gone out for a coffee. Abruptly she rouses herself, propping up on her elbows. "Hands off Wally," she warns, pointing at Alice.

"Oh, Ann, how did you ever turn out to be so old?"

"All your fault." She yawns; it is a false yawn that turns real halfway through, and she reclines again, and closes her eyes. "No mystery there." She is far too awake to fall asleep, but wants so badly to sleep, with her mother at the other end of the couch, awake and watching over, and for this to happen sleep will have to come quickly. The velvet is warm against her cheek. Her feet rise and fall with her mother's breath. She plays her tongue over the little cut inside her mouth, and she can't help saying one more thing. "The real question is, how do *you* always manage to land on your *feet*?"

14.

Esker balks at hailing a cab. Wally offers to give her the fare, which nearly gets him belted, and it is by some miracle of restraint, or perhaps some greater miracle of desire, that Esker agrees to let him accompany her home on the subway. Naturally she has to deride his chivalry a little, and he plays along, as though it were a fault, and tells her what Alice has always said about his innkeeper thing, and then her hackles smooth themselves and she offers him a commensurate fault:

"I'm a little pathologically defensive about accepting stuff."

He sees this for the gift it is and is touched, but manages not to show it. "You don't say."

She shoots him a look and says, "Shut up," the greatest intimacy she's afforded him yet, and he smiles, and the train goes under the river and jerks them together and apart.

"So that's your wife," she says after a bit.

He smiles again. It isn't that he is without anger over the circumstance of his marriage. He is both angry and well suited by it, and he knows this, and no one else—not Nuncio, not Willette and Emil, not his family, not Ann—can understand it. Except Alice. The queer circumstance of their parting was their final intimacy, continues to be their final intimacy. In a talk they had right before she left to film that first film, when no one but

Wally understood that she wouldn't be returning in any real sense ever again, Alice had spoken of blueprintlessness.

"Blueprintlessness?"

"It's hard because there's no blueprint for this," she'd said. "That's all."

"What a total crock," he'd said. "That's *all*?" They'd been sitting up in bed, very early Sunday morning, Alice's suitcases, packed the night before, in the corner of the room, Wally pulling at the hair on his wrist.

"Well, no, not *all*. It's hard for other reasons, too. But life is hard. But where there's a blueprint for the thing, for the hard thing, you accept the hardness and don't rail against it, you say, 'That's life.' But this is life, too. And not having a blueprint doesn't make it any less life, or any less possible. Think of "—she snaps her fingers impatiently—"of Findhorn."

"Pardon?"

"*Findhorn.* That farming community in Scotland where they grow giant figs, I don't know, pineapples—*tropical* things in the wrong climate—and no one can give any scientific reason for it."

". . . Yes . . . ?"

"And they have a building there, and architects can't figure out why it doesn't collapse, because it should, according to their specifications, but it doesn't, it stands. Or like bumblebees."

"Alice."

"No! This is a *thing*!"

He had to marvel at what a font of misinformation she was.

"No, yes!" She'd stood up on the bed. She was wearing a T-shirt that didn't come past her hips and nothing else. Wally didn't know Alice to be stupid, but sometimes the only alternative seemed that *he* must be. "Aerodynamically, bumblebees aren't supposed to be able to fly, but they do. Yes, you've heard this. No blueprint. No rationale. They just do."

Sometimes you had to approach Alice like a fascinating article published without any footnotes in an obscure journal: not, perhaps, entirely fabricated, but . . . Wally had cocked his head, weighing the likelihood, but she was immune to skepticism and charged on, her eyes glowing like an hour past dusk, the constellations of her freckles seeming to shift across her face the way they always did when the blood roused beneath them, an optical illusion at which he has never stopped marveling.

She sat again, but at the foot of the bed, away from him. "The fact that this, this split, has no name, no category, isn't inherently bad."

"You mean it's just geography, no big deal."

"I didn't say that. It's not just geography and it is a big deal, but it's not something named, and it's not the end of love."

"What is it, then?"

"I don't know."

"And I have to live with that uncertainty?"

"No. You can divorce me. That would change it into a thing with a name."

"And will name change nature?"

She thought. "Yes."

"So what is its nature now?"

"I don't know. It hasn't happened yet."

Later, when she was in the shower, and thirteen-year-old Ann still asleep in the next room, and the winter morning just beginning to turn chalkily light, his anger gathered itself into a clear shape. He had a glass of orange juice in his hand; he couldn't drink it; it wouldn't go down. He knocked on the bathroom door and entered. "You think by making this something without a name," he said, speaking over the pounding water, trembling with rage, the juice trembling in the glass, "you can turn it into something without pain."

And the shower curtain pushed back and she showed him how little he understood. From inside the spray she looked at him, her face pulpy from crying, her eyes and lips and forehead and cheeks and nose and chin and everything just wasted, spent.

Now, on the subway with Esker, three years later, the smile on his lips is occasioned mainly by her tactless candor—she must be a terrible dancer, he thinks with sudden affection, too heavy-footed and literal—and partly by the knowledge that blueprintlessness *does* suit him, that in the end he found he hadn't needed Alice under certain, proven terms, that in three years he has expanded, quietly and unexpectedly, into someone who likes his life and its surprises. For example, the surprise of this odd woman, in her homely overlayers of dun and tan, rocking along beside him. For a moment, he thinks of her as a cold, biting wind in whose presence he must remember not to hunch his shoulders or tuck his chin.

"So that's your wife," she's said.

"Yes." He responds a beat late.

"The movie star."

"Yes. My wife, the movie star."

"Your wife, the movie star."

They give each other looks absurdly full of bottled humor. Are they laughing at Alice? He is thrilled and alarmed. When Alice, his wife, the movie star, arrived this evening, his first thought—he admits to himself now, in the swaying subway car—was dismay that Esker was there. And for occasioning this dismay he is furious with Alice, whose appeal, whose damned appeal, tarnished though it may be, endures. It makes him a little sick to think of it. It is her most unforgivable trait. He steals a look at Esker beside him. It occurs to him that he would like to stay out noticeably late.

The train is not very crowded. They become absorbed in looking at their fellow passengers. Both Esker and Wally are slouched a little, both with their hands in their pockets, both with their feet extended into the aisle: a posture of hanging out together. Across from them sits a man in his sixties or seventies, black, diminutive, with a watch cap, a decent overcoat, and very good shoes. He has a bouquet of flowers in his lap, nothing fancy, the kind of preselected bunch they sell at corner groceries, and he is reading a tall, thin book with a dark cover, or maybe it's a leather folder with loose sheets inside, and he periodically breaks into smiles as he reads, then tiny frowns, then smiles again, and the smiles are really interesting, various: one full of mischief, one full of surprise, one full of warmth, and so on.

"It's *Chicken Soup for the Golden Soul*," suggests Wally, stealthily, speaking sideways.

"His stash of old love letters," counters Esker, without pause, and Wally feels the delight crash through his ribs: she is in the game.

"It's a cookbook," says Wally after a bit. "Family recipes."

"A screenplay," she returns. And at the next stop, "Doggerel verse."

At Chambers Street they exit through the doors to the left of the man, and simultaneously turn to peer over his shoulder through the window before the train pulls away. It's formulae. Pages and pages of fractions and square roots and cosines and logarithms and absolute values and radicals and equals signs.

They turn to each other on the platform. "Oh," says Wally. "It's the secrets of the universe."

The train roars away and Esker shouts, "Come back!"

Someone in the pedestrian tunnel is playing a lackluster "It Came upon a Midnight Clear." Esker and Wally go upstairs into the cold, both of them surprised by this happiness, which has come out of nowhere, which has grown up between them during the past thirty minutes, since Wally tried to hand Esker two twenties on the sidewalk and she'd said "No thank you" as though she'd been slapped.

It will become a joke between them, Wally sees. Someday, in the future, there will come the perfect moment and he will pull some crumpled bills from his pocket again and extend them to her wordlessly, and she will first freeze and then burst out laughing. He sees this suddenly, prophetically, with the first real and dangerous hope of joy he has had in some time.

15.

Of all things, what do they do? They eat. Esker finds herself hungry. Not just hungry. She searches and cannot come up with the word. Like a space has opened up inside her that commands every bit of her attention. Not pleasurable, not unpleasurable, just a space, an open, commanding space, rare, a climate change. Like a window sash, lifted, and the air outside is a completely different temperature, a completely different quality; you go to it, you thrust your head out the window, you inhale. Like that. So they go to the kitchen. Wally seems amused. Esker tells him it's nothing to do with his cooking, sorry, she just has to eat something, and Wally nods, continues to seem amused, accepts her offer of a piece of toast.

She slices thick slabs of nutty bread, and when they are toasted she butters them unstintingly, and then there are two small glass jars: orange marmalade and blackberry jam, and a knife with a bird on the handle, and she says she is going to have milk, what would he like? He asks for milk.

"I love your daughter," she says.

"I know." They are sitting in the kitchen, such a little room.

"You said you were worried about her."

He nods. "Of course, all parents worry about their children. I don't know if it's more than that. Do you worry about your students?"

"If one seems worrisome." She hears herself saying this in her slightly curt fashion. "I mean, sure. There have been occasions when students have had serious problems, when I've needed to worry about them." She realizes that, although Wally must be about ten years older, and has sixteen years' experience as a parent, whereas she has none, she probably knows teenagers better; certainly she's had more experience with a wider variety of them. She's broken up fistfights, confiscated drugs and alcohol on school grounds, had students reveal they were HIV-positive, pregnant, gay, abused, bulimic, running away, dropping out. She's been on a suicide watch twice. She's seen a student arrested once. Ann, she thinks, will find her way. But in her mind she sees Ann James sprung from the bleachers, her hair streaming up like pale-brown fire as her body falls, and in her mind she sees Ann James with a stripe of blood lengthening down her chin, eyes not the least surprised.

Wally clasps both hands around his cup of milk, as though it were a hot drink. "How do you tell the difference between regular teen angst and the kind that needs intervention?"

"I think sometimes regular teen angst needs intervention."

"How do you know when?"

"I'm a math teacher." Esker opens her palms helplessly to the ceiling. "Have you asked Ann if she wants to talk with somebody?"

"No. Not yet. Right." He sighs and looks at his cup, and drinks some milk, and looks at his milk for a while. When he brings his eyes back to hers, she notices what a plain, ordinary brown they are, and that all their beauty stems from the person behind them. "Can I tell you something?" he asks.

She cocks her brow.

"You haven't eaten your toast."

"You, neither."

Water drips in the sink.

"Ann says your name is Iphigenia."

She nods.

"Do people ever call you Iph?"

Her smile is the first unsmall gesture she's made since she shouted on the subway platform, and it catches him by surprise. "One person did. Mostly it was 'Genie,' growing up."

"Kind of an existential nickname. Not Genie. Iph."

She nods, but the trace-smile lingering across her face has turned inward, private. Also sometimes Albert would call her "Iph-not," and

"What-iph." A luxury, to have your name played with. Like having some-one play with your hair. Like being touched. It feels anachronistic. She shakes her head, almost a shudder. Here she is in her present-day kitchen. There is Wallace James sitting across from her, not eating his toast, look-ing at her, and it becomes urgent to break the quiet. "It's really good jam," Esker hears herself saying, some kind of lame protestation. Wally nods gently. "I felt like toast, but now I don't anymore." An unnecessary explanation. Wally's eyes stay on her, unhurried, lasting. "I think I should kick you out." What is she saying? Why is she saying everything out loud? "Those sound like givens in a theorem. Given: it's really good jam . . ." He still says nothing, and his gaze is the most actively patient thing she has ever seen, and it makes her twist in her chair, and her monologue is growing more shapeless and winged; each utterance from her mouth is like another surprise, so that she wants to say "Oh!" after each word. "It *is* good, I bought them at that tea shop on Bleecker near Sixth Avenue. Do you even like jam? Your sweater looks like jam. I thought that at your house. Did you hear the thing about I think I should kick you out? Also sugar cubes. Are another good thing, I mean. Sugar cubes are like magic food. Like something from a children's story. Especially the kind that come individually wrapped in paper. I've never had a moose burger." Small silence in the kitchen, with only the drips in the sink. "Oh. Now I can't think of anything else to say." Forlorn, she sounds. None of these words has gotten her anyplace she was hoping to go.

"Iphigenia Esker?" He says this as though it's an extraordinary but necessary hurdle to go through.

"My middle name is Julia." She can't look at him.

"Iphigenia Julia Esker?"

"What?"

"Can I kiss you for a minute?"

She considers. He's still sitting across the table. "It kind of seems like a business proposition. A transaction."

"I didn't bring any contracts."

"No."

"Maybe we could negotiate this on a handshake."

"Okay." She sticks her hand out across the table. Wally shakes her hand. He registers no surprise at her excellent grip. Then, for a long time, they don't kiss, and they don't get up and they don't speak and they don't let go of each other's hands.

After a while Esker whispers, "Did you say *for* a minute or *in* a minute?" and Wally's eyes, so plain and smart, register wit, but neither of them stops what they are doing with their hands, which is not a handshake anymore, but something unhurried and unscripted, and unprecedented in her history.

16.

The day after Christmas turns warm, everything to slush, and Ann goes out for the first time; Hannah and Denise wheel her to the promenade. A misleading smell of almost-spring is in the air; the breeze is lace on their faces, and among the roots of a wiry sycamore three purple crocuses peek out as if from behind coy fingers, which Ann finds depressing. "The weather is fucking schizophrenic," she says.

"Give this to me all winter long," says Denise, holding up a hand like she's testifying in church. She got a new shearling coat yesterday, and is wearing it unbuttoned over a green V-neck that is all about her breasts. A fine-looking Rollerblader approaches, wearing shorts and a leather jacket and being towed by two dachsunds, and Denise arches her back automatically. He checks her out as automatically, and then is past, his tantalizing calves growing smaller in the distance.

Hannah lights a cigarette. The solstice-y sunlight is as harsh as a naked lightbulb, and she looks pasty in it, her skin broken out along the jaw, her black eye makeup gone flaky below the lashes, but still Ann finds her strongly beautiful next to Denise's ho-hum sexpot. Her mother has not left town yet. Thursday or Friday has turned into Saturday or Sunday; shooting doesn't resume until after New Year's, but Alice has been charac-teristically vague about whether she'll be needed back in Toronto before then: something about costume fittings, or sound looping, or an interview for a magazine feature.

Christmas had been a dour affair, or anyway a half-assed affair, in a way that Ann can't really put her finger on. A depressingly nice breakfast: sausage and eggs, croissants and melon, Esker's tiger lilies on the table, Bartok on the stereo, Wally in jeans and his really ancient Alvin Ailey sweatshirt, Alice in a torn orange football jersey and sweats. After breakfast were the presents, very subtle and witty and charming presents, all boasting of a certain kind of intimate and hard-won knowledge of one another, all a bit self-congratulatory in their celebration of life; little grinning buffoons, they were, done up in their beautiful papers and real fabric ribbons, Ann thought, even her own: she'd been too well trained by her father's example. She gave her mother a pair of Wonder Woman mugs and cucumber bath soap, and her father a box of fresh figs and a framed black-and-white photo she'd taken of him and Nuncio frowning into a gigantic steaming pot; it had been part of an art project she'd done at school, and the teacher, Buddy, had singled out that image for excessive praise, even for him.

And after presents had come—nothing, a certain laziness, casualness, Alice on her cell phone, talking with movie people, and Wally napping and later assembling ingredients for supper, and the apartment getting very gray very early, and no one *minding* any of this, it seemed—any of it: Wally and Alice as lightly happy to be together as two old friends who stay in touch but get together only once a year. As easy as two old friends who know each other well enough to give the perfect gifts, but not well enough to hurt each other. And all matter-of-fact, no one pretending this was anything it was not: secure, for example; unchanging, for example. Meaningful enough to cause achingly mixed emotions, for example. Ann wished someone would throw a vase, but no one did.

Her present for Esker remained in the top drawer of her dresser. The doctor had authorized her casts to become weight-bearing earlier this week, and she'd been hobbling around the apartment on crutches, fitting through doorways again—hallelujah!—sleeping in her own bed, using the actual toilet instead of the commode. So she was able to secrete the package among her underthings. A flat little rectangle bound with a length of blue ribbon: the compilation tape, completed at last. The best thing is the wrapping paper, which she printed herself off the Internet: a full-color copy of the seahorse tails of the Mandelbrot set.

Ann in her fantasy had imagined seeing Esker Christmas Day; wouldn't Esker pop over, wouldn't her father just call and ask her, impromptu, to come over for Portuguese vegetable soup or something? Her mind had laid it out thus, and so it ought to come to pass, only Ann turned out once again to have confused wishing and willing. The end of the day in real life had dwindled fast to something shallow and poor: soup early, and the radio on, depressing church music—organs and choir—making Ann see scary vaulted ceilings, dimness, towering depictions of ancient transaction frozen in pointy shards of glass. After dinner, Alice had suddenly materialized in a floor-length cashmere coat the color of blue chalk and announced she was going out with Willette. When she kissed Ann on her way out, she smelled of perfume and mints.

And Wally had settled in front of some Christmas concert on public TV, with the newspaper on his lap, too, and glanced from one to the other, pulling absently at the hair on his wrist, and Ann had wanted to scream at him and his complacency, which wasn't really complacency anyway but something bottled and blindered. Complacency: a feeling of contentment, especially when coupled with an unawareness of danger or trouble. If he were dislodged from his chair, he'd have no choice but to look up, the paper sliding from his lap, gravity working him over, and see. See, *see*. Why couldn't he be more like Miss Clavell, wonderful Miss Clavell, who simply knew, who simply woke in the night and *knew* all was not well? Was he truly blind, or pretending blindness for comfort's sake? Ann couldn't tell which; either way it was a betrayal; either way it left her lonely, and she left him to it, his betrayal, and limped off to bed.

Where she lay, far from sleep, on her back instead of on her stomach (which was the first thing she planned to do when the casts came off: go to sleep on her fucking stomach, burrowed into Killycot and her pillow), and she looked at the glow-in-the-dark stars her mother had long ago affixed to the ceiling in the shape not of real constellations but of a snake and a whale and a gryphon. Babyish animals, Ann was used to thinking, because they'd been up there since her babyhood; but it occurred to her now that they really weren't babyish at all. And she had to think it, the loneliest thought: what if no one else felt anything wrong, what if her father really was without sadness and anger, what if her mother really was without guilt and longing, what if it wasn't insincerity they were displaying all over the apartment but a genuine absence of these things? Then what was the matter with them? And whose was all the sadness and anger and guilt and longing Ann felt? And what, oh what, was the matter with her? In her room she chanted a silent plea to the snake, the whale, the gryphon—her babyhood trinity, beginning to peel a bit, in places—*Help me, help me.*

"Can I have one?" she asks Hannah now, on the promenade, and Hannah gets two more cigarettes out of the pack, and the three make a shelter of their bodies to get them lit. Oh, cozy, lovely, thinks Ann. And she loves her friends so much, for being human beings, for being real people in the world who know her, who have shoulders and hair and breath and everything, who are with her at this moment. "Thanks, you guys," she says on the exhale.

"Don't look at me, I'm bumming, too," says Denise, doing a dance. "Oh, and don't look now!"

Ann follows her gaze. Malcolm Choy is coming down the promenade, his long black hair and still-water gait visible in the distance, growing closer.

"You planned this," she accuses Hannah.

"Cross my heart," Hannah denies.

"Right."

"Swear to God. It was Denise."

Denise smiles big and wide at Ann, dances a cocky little hip-hop step in her open shearling coat. She is so damn radiant and sexy. And ambulatory. Damn. Ann looks quickly at her casts, now elaborately patterned in nail polish. What else is she wearing? A coat, obviously, her ice-blue puffy down thing from last year. A hat, for fuck's sake. Knitted and red, like some elementary-school kid's. If she whips it off she'll have socket head. It has to stay. Oh well, it probably matches her nose. She puts out the cigarette and tries to ignore her heart.

Malcolm weaves toward them and closer toward them and there he is, tall, with his lovely lean comic-book muscles and that quiet edge in his face, his bearing. He nods his tranquil hellos, bums a cigarette, keeps his hands in his pockets while Hannah lights it for him.

A warm day in winter, thinks Ann, her head suddenly swirly, and the air smells like sugar. A boat out in the harbor looks like a toy boat, winking, and the water like a mirrored carpet, cracking up. She has a problem with scale for a minute. Malcolm Choy, looming in the foreground, is why she leapt from the bleachers, expecting to float down, expecting time and space to slow and thicken in support of her act. Malcolm Choy, this boy, this boy standing here in front of her blocking the sun, studying the animals on her legs.

"Did you do that?" he asks.

"My mother." Heat invades her; his mother is a painter.

He smiles.

"You know, fooling around."

He smiles. "I like your hat."

She can't think of anything to say to this. Eventually she thinks of "thank you," but it's too late; Hannah and Malcolm and Denise are already talking about something else. Something about Winter Concert and a ladder and some beets. No, beats. No, Beats.

". . . like the Beats," Malcolm is saying, "you know, black turtleneck, beret?"

It turns out Hannah and Malcolm want to do an act somewhat in the style of the Beat Poets, Hannah reciting free verse over Malcolm's congas, only they want to make it a kind of surrealist Happening as well, and that's where Ann comes in: they envision her on a ladder wearing a giant white skirt, lighting matches and letting them drop at odd intervals to the Big Room floor. She'll be the spirit of inspiration and death, they tell her, and Hannah will recite only during the intervals when the flame is going.

"You'll have little bells, too, around your wrists," says Malcolm, and Hannah looks at him in a way that lets Ann know this is news to her. "Or maybe braided into your hair."

His voice travels directly into her chest as he says this, looking at her, thinking about her wrists and her hair, and behind him the glare coming off the December water is so sharp Ann feels like sheets of rare metal are singing to her: very painful and beautiful and too much to bear. She wants a cigarette to cheapen the feeling, to reduce it, circumscribe it. Hannah obliges, and once it's lit and in her fingers, there are a few things Ann wants to know. "A ladder? I'm supposed to climb a ladder?"

Hannah sounds patient. "Winter Concert's in almost four weeks. You said your casts are coming off by then."

Still. "A ladder? Heights? I'm just saying."

"We're getting you back on the horse, Saucepan." Hannah uses her most obscure nickname, etymology as follows: Saucepan from Pan from Anna Panna; also, occasionally, Special Sauce.

"Okay, and fire? You've run this by Buddy? He's fine with it?"

Malcolm and Hannah refer to each other. Malcolm speaks. "We don't want to approach Buddy."

"Because Buddy would basically freak," adds Hannah.

Ann shrug-nods: *Naturally.*

"So at the dress rehearsal you'll use something like confetti," explains Malcolm. "Gold paper or something. Origami. Paper airplanes you could sail into the audience, maybe. Or spoonfuls of water . . . Hey!" He is liking these ideas.

Hannah jumps in. "Then you'll just switch to matches at the performance. It'll be fine; they'll burn out before they hit the floor. And they can't tell us no afterward."

"And whose idea was this?" Ann asks. Hannah's, obviously.

"The Beat part was mine," says Hannah. "The Happening part was Malcolm's."

"Oh," says Ann.

"Yeah, I had this image of you up on the ladder, silent, but controlling the language."

"Oh," says Ann. "You mean like an image of someone up on a ladder?"

"Yeah," says Malcolm.

"Oh."

"Like of you."

"Oh." Kid in a wheelchair, red hat, red nose, red fingers, smoking in the cold sunny light; she's embarrassed, she's grateful, she's dubious; he sees her on a ladder in a long, long skirt?

"I asked for your number, I was going to call and recruit you."

Why me? she thinks. She is almost suspicious. He knows something about her, but is it good or is it bad?

"Where the hell is Denise?" asks Hannah. "That girl is always disappearing."

"Chasing the Rollerblader," ventures Ann.

Denise comes bounding up with a bagful of honey-roasted peanuts from a vendor down the way. She looks like some exotic bird, something gorgeous from the rain forest, in her bright-green V-neck with the ends of her shearling coat flapping out behind her. She looks like one of the animals on Ann's casts. She comes to an almost acrobatic halt in front of them, proffers the paper bag. Honey-steam leaps out at them, and they breathe, to a one: they inhale.

Later, after the peanuts, and with the sun retreating so early, they part. Ann sees their shadows very long before them as her friends wheel her back down Pierrepont; her shadow so broad-based and thinning out at the top, like a radio tower, and the wheels going round and round at her sides, the motion down the frozen street, the buildings rising up around her, their high windows catching the last lozenges of light. . . . She has to close her eyes; for a few minutes she has scale problems again.

17.

It's Sunday at Game, and Alice is there, with Willette and Emil, at table two, the round table in the window, and in the fierce sunlight the whole restaurant looks dusty, but in a golden, rarefied way. Weekend mornings are Wally's favorite times at Game, the times when it feels most like a camp. A cheap metal pitcher of cocoa is delivered to every table upon seating, and the fire cracks and pops audibly (they've discovered which supplier delivers wood with a high sap content), and the brunch menu is absolutely plain: oatmeal, bacon, eggs, toast. Peanut-butter cookies for those who require dessert. Nuncio, that nutcase, dresses for it, disdaining his usual maître d' costume of a ruffled tuxedo shirt for workboots and plaid flannel; he even goes unshaven for that Sunday-morning bear look.

Wally thinks Nuncio was a little chagrined to be dressed that way when Alice & Co. showed up this morning, but he greeted her like the prodigal mother while Wally watched, bemused. Now they are tucked in attractively around their window table, Alice sitting with almost masculine abandon, legs apart, elbows on the table; Willette, with her long throat, gesticulating loosely and languidly; Emil tipped back in his chair, arms folded across his chest, one foot up on the baseboard: at home. Which gives Wally pleasure. Wally with his pineapple coat of arms. It gives pleasure whenever any patrons look that way, not just this group. But it also, for the first time since Alice's arrival last week, stirs in him some sorrow, or some portent of sorrow. She is taking a flight to Toronto later today, and he is not sorry about this, he has even been looking forward to it a little, but still there is some attendant blueness—for what might have been? No, it never might have been. For what never might have been, then.

They are his oldest friends, Emil and Willette, and Alice, too, really, having all met as undergraduates at Amherst College, where they'd basically laughed their way through school. That's how he remembers it: continual belly laughter all around the calendar four years in a row, the real, visceral, helpless variety, so that his stomach muscles were always a little sore. Fanciful, but that's how he remembers it. He doesn't remember the melancholy parts, the stress, the boredom, the cynicism, none of that, not very well. He'd been the odd one out—three artists and Wally, three artists and a poli-sci major—but he'd been indispensable to the group, had brought out their flavors, been the dash of salt to their chocolate, and it suited him to be regarded as something apart, of a different variety. He'd had membership and not membership at the same time. One boot in the circle, one boot out. A thrilling kind of tension.

One night in still-cold spring he and Alice had taken a walk off-campus. They'd wandered onto a golf course, the strange, planned topography of which seemed immense, ludicrous, in the darkness. Without a word, they'd suddenly broken into a run, and the run fast became a race. In his memory, they'd risen and fallen over the course's hills and dips freely, as if half lofted by a preternatural breeze. Alice's hair then had been very long, but in his memory it is six feet long, seven feet, and wavy like a drawing of a brook. When she caught up with him, she'd been mock-angry that he'd beaten her, but beneath that, really angry. She'd stepped carefully on his foot—"Ouch"—and then on the other—"Ouch"—and he'd begun to waltz with her on his feet, like fathers do with their little daughters, and she'd yanked away and hit him not too lightly in the stomach— *"Hey."* And then, after something like a whole minute, she'd gone over and mumbled into his chest, "I'm such a brat."

"Did you say 'bat'?"

"Yeah. I'm such a bat. I have excellent sonar skills."

"I don't think so."

"Oh yeah, I just flew into your chest. Sorry."

He'd had no idea then, or now, what had transpired, what they were talking about, what had happened, but it had made him fill with a prickling, pregnant kind of happiness, like he was being showered with gifts in a language he didn't yet understand.

They had married the week after graduation in a civil ceremony, Alice wearing a handwoven crown of purple clover. Ann was born eight months later, when the Northern Hemisphere had returned to snow and ice and darkness. Wally remembers precisely the way she would stick her strong baby fingers into his mouth and hook them around his bottom teeth like she was hauling in a fish. It was the first time anyone had wanted him so fiercely.

There is something fierce about Esker. He has left two messages on her machine since the night he took her home—what an old-fashioned phrase: "took her home." Since the night she let him ride the subway with her. And kiss her in her kitchen. And only in her kitchen, until she'd turned abruptly standoffish and kicked him out, and he hadn't been hurt or disappointed by this, he'd expected it, perhaps; it even, strangely, gave him a glimmer of hope that he wouldn't have had otherwise, that he wouldn't have had if she'd let the kissing go on and turn to other things. Once coated and hatted and standing before the door, he'd asked, "Is it anything to do with being the parent of a student?"

"Please." She'd scowled. She had put on her gray shmatte-thing and stood not meeting his eyes, twisting the long ratty sleeves over her fingers. "This isn't Victorian England. Nobody cares about that." And he'd grinned, irrepressibly, her very rudeness proof of something that made him feel rich and alert all the long, cold walk to the subway station.

Now Nuncio pulls a chair up to table two and with his fingers helps himself to a piece of roast potato from Alice's plate. Somebody says something; they all laugh. Or so it appears to Wally every single time he looks over at them. In the early days of Game, Alice had Nuncio's job. She was, surprisingly, not very good at it. She missed entirely the fact that Game was a stage, theater in the round, theater with a perforated fourth wall—and consequently she was bored, and patrons felt her boredom as disdain.

Alice had perhaps been not a good risk from the outset. If he were to look at it objectively. She'd been chafing at the bit when he met her; his only mistake was not realizing that this was her constant state, her necessary state: without a bit to chafe on she'd atrophy, she'd wither. Horrible to think that's what he'd been, her bit. But he wasn't anymore, and that was liberating, possibly more liberating for him than for her. Why, then, if it liberates him, does it hurt? It does hurt. Contrary to party line.

He looks over at her, her ridiculously, immensely lovely hair, all man-ner of gold and copper and cinnamon brown mixed together and shining in the bands of sunlight cutting through the window; her face, ever more handsome in its maturity; her hands, bold and declarative as they gesture with her speech, and shake salt, and touch Willette's arm easily in some shared mirth. Her boldness, her declarativeness, these things are all right, are beautiful, as they have always been to him, even as they have made him catch his breath, but her ease is not. Is it only now, in relation to Es-ker's supreme unease, that he sees it? Alice's ease with everything that is not, that should not, be easy corrupts her beauty. This is her ugliness. It is possible to wear things too lightly.

And him, is it his ugliness, too? Ann comes to his thoughts, an image of Ann glowering, heavy about the eyes and mouth. Ann in the doorway before she went to bed last night, with no "good night," then a thunk as her crutches hit the floor, and him in his armchair in the living room, turning the pages of the broadsheet on his lap, enjoying in his stalwart heart the concert on public TV, willfully devoid of hurt, devoid of anger; his gift to his child is his own elegantly developed absence of want, so she can sleep in peace, in comfort, with him steady in the next room; isn't it good, what he has done with Ann? Balanced Alice's exit with his own lack of desire to have it otherwise? Hasn't he met the challenge with grace?

He hears his name. They are talking about him, calling him over: "What's Wally doing?" "Spacing." "Get him to sit." "It's not busy." "Wally!" Alice pats a chair. He is so relieved she's leaving. It's a relief even to think the thought, to allow it, and he smiles at her. Nuncio has risen to see to something in the kitchen; Wally moves to take his space and imme-diately regrets it. His oldest friends: Willette, Emil, Alice. And they have not sat round a table together since Alice left. It's too much the texture of something that has passed out of existence. He can encounter his ghosts in solitude but not in public, not in company, not in this much thick and happy company, whose happiness is so densely knit that nothing unhappy is admissible; he finds it hard to breathe, and the moment he sits the chair gives way with an unhealthy crack that makes everyone in the restaurant stop talking and stare at the wreckage: him, a solid man who's fallen on his bottom.

Emil helps him up, and although the pain in his left hip is bracing, Wally downplays it smoothly; the show must go on—and after a beat conversation resumes, forks are picked up again, glasses set down.

"How bizarre!" says Willette, examining the pieces of splintered wood. Wally is in Emil's chair. Emil borrows an extra from another table. Alice is looking closely at Wally. "Are you all right?" she asks, and he can see she sees he's not, entirely. Nuncio comes out and hefts the broken pieces over his shoulder like a lumberman. "I don't know about this new breakaway-furniture idea of yours," he tells Wally casually. "I never really got how it was supposed to attract customers." "Are you all right?" asks Alice again, and Wally says yeah, and then makes sort of a joke of wincing in pain. He tells Nuncio he'll have a shot of something from the bar. "What?" asks Nuncio. "I don't care," says Wally. He doesn't think it's that bad, but he doesn't want to get up and put weight on it in front of all the diners yet, just in case.

"Ann's about done with the wheelchair, right?" says Emil, his cue to laugh and put them all at their ease, but Wally doesn't laugh. He's had it with that.

18.

$\mathcal{E}$sker is a mess. She's a mess. What happened? Something's gone asunder and she can't forgive herself, she's been going around the apartment all week with her hands clutching the material at her stomach, as if she's literally holding pieces of herself together. All these years of unnamed vigilance, and she let it go, suddenly, last Monday, and now she resembles a crazy person, an abstract painting, all the parts of her anatomy fitting crookedly, gapingly together. She's not eating, eating seems an unlikely proposition, and she has this vague notion that there's no place for the food to go anyway, no *place* within to contain it. Catching glimpses of herself in the bathroom mirror and the tarnished oval glass over the coat rack, she is scared by what she sees: doesn't she actually appear jumbled, undone? Her hair sort of at a canted angle to her head, her eyes at odds with their sockets, her teeth like an ill-advised afterthought.

This has never happened to her before. The last time was different, different circumstances altogether, and she'd had no life of order then to lose; it had been a matter of building one, slowly, where none had existed, drifting through the surreally humid days and nights of that horrible August, in and out of her empty space, with her untethered body, drifting nearly clothesless, mindless, through the vacuous heat. She'd found misfitty bits of furniture people were throwing out; she'd come home from long wanderings sweaty from lugging a broken lamp from Chinatown, a three-legged end table from SoHo, a step stool from Battery Park City. She added these to her milk crates and futon; she bought duct tape and sandpaper and roach poison; she took cooling baths and looked at her iterated snowflake, with its riddle of infinite surface area, taped over the glass. When she thought of Albert, she just dimmed her mind, a good trick; she'd discovered she had a dimmer switch, and she'd turn it down and he would lurk a little, outside the guardrails of her conscious thoughts, like a hopeful ghost, or a surly ghost, or even a hurt and bewildered ghost, but no more than a ghost, which she could dismiss, she could decry, as something aberrant and unrelated to her, something she was not responsible for, and having no legitimate business taking up space inside her mind. In this way she was able to manage it, with him as her incorrigible haunter, and she his unwilling, inconvenienced hauntee.

Then had come September and the beginning of her first semester at The Prospect School. She'd been only four years older than the oldest students, and had for that reason bought two very plain, very conservative skirts, one khaki and one navy, and got her hair cut in what turned out to be a perfectly unflattering style; she'd been going for something reminiscent of Betty Crocker, which, she realized after the fact, happened to be the same general hairdo neighborhood as Miss De Witt. Albert's ghost, like Mary's little lamb, followed her to school some days. At first she fought with him, but there was too much energy in sparring, so she learned just to fire off little oblique disparagements and in this way kept him at bay. Her work kept her busier than she had imagined; there was much order to be brought to planning lessons, interacting with faculty and students, grading assignments, and writing evaluations. She took satisfaction in buying three new notebooks for organizing different aspects of her work; a box of expensive colored pencils and one of plastic-coated paper clips; and a bag of gourmet-flavored jelly beans for a statistics project she created with the eleventh-graders. The months revolved obligingly around the calendar; it was November and then February and then May and then August again. She got through the first year with her dimmer switch intact; she could do any number of years now in the same way, she knew, and she had, she had done this for three and then five and then nine years, a breathtaking, terrifying accomplishment.

She hadn't meant to be shattered when Albert left. As they had both known he would. It would've been less confusing if he'd died or hadn't loved her. That she would have known how to compute. But he didn't die and he did love her. And still he left to marry somebody named Randy Berkowitz, his old high-school girlfriend, and to start a family with her. This was the plan, this had been the plan always, as long as she'd known him, but it had never seemed very plausible to her; the fact that the plan had been in place when they met had made it seem weaker rather than stronger, and when he left to follow through on it, as he consistently reminded her he would, she couldn't, could simply not grasp it: it was like trying to picture a finite universe, or a small-minded God. That he could both love her and choose not to be with her—she could not reconcile these two facts. She tried, because loving him, as she believed she did, seemed to require her understanding how these facts could coexist, but the truth is, she was never able to wrap her brain around it. Her failure to do so became her rationale for why he left: she had failed him—in failing to fathom his choice, she'd failed to love him properly. It was her shame, her limping little brain that hadn't loved him right.

And now, just when she needs him, Albert's ghost has gone missing. All week he hasn't shown his face, not even in her dreams, hasn't so much as smirked knowingly over her shoulder or cleared his silent, transparent throat. She's tried to conjure him and drawn only a blank. All that comes to mind is Wally—Wally, who's really real, who's left two messages on her machine, who makes curry, who kisses, who has a wife. There he is in her mind, like a locket with a faulty latch that keeps springing open. All day his image keeps presenting itself: his solid, unfussy girth; his keen, intelligent mouth; the short, curling wisps around his exposed scalp; his unimpatient eyes. Already, unbidden, a list of things she likes about him has enscripted itself in her mind. She likes the way he keeps silent before responding to something she's said, even if only for a few seconds; he has a way of helping himself to an entirely self-possessed moment of thoughtfulness before speaking. She likes the way his ability to sense humor and his ability to sense sorrow in a moment are not at odds with each other. She likes being startled by what he chooses to say out loud. She likes his voice, which is itself like a thing, an object, and she has saved it on her machine. It reminds her for some reason of a boat. She likes—it gets worse—she likes that he likes greens; no, it's not exactly that; it's that suddenly *she* likes greens because it's one of the things they've talked about, so that, the last time she went shopping and walked past the collards and spinach and kale, she felt tenderness toward them, toward the stupid actual greens, and she bought some and chopped them and sautéed them in butter and garlic and they were so delicious and she felt ashamed, eating them, and threw the rest away. Last night, on the news, they interviewed somebody from the Department of Health about food poisoning and salad bars, and she felt a rapid lunge of affinity for the awkward-looking bureaucrat in his awkward-looking suit, because Wally had told her a funny story about a visit he once got from the health inspector. Not even a story. Two sentences. It's not that she likes everything about him. It's that everything that reminds her of him has suddenly become precious. Horrible, horrible. She is afraid.

Albert, you deserter! She feels bereft without the sour vigil of his ghost. Not bereft, unprotected. Her throat long, exposed, across the temple's marble block. This was her dream last night, and Wally was in it, with a piece of broken glass from her front door in his hand, and his hand was bound up in the starfish towel, and blood was dripping from it, and she'd begun kissing the blood from his hand, which only made him bleed faster.

School vacation makes things worse, because she is without the order of her usual routine. Since her parents died, she has been in the habit of spending Christmas Day with Francie and Arthur Gluck, old friends of her parents who live in Yonkers, but they are in their eighties now, and two weeks ago Arthur had called to say Francie was recovering from hip surgery, and, sorry, sweetheart, we're not quite up to hosting Christmas dinner this year, but we'd love to see you that day for tea anyway, if Francie's feeling a little better by then. Esker had lied and said she'd been invited by someone from work, and when Arthur had said, "Oh, that's good, honey, you have fun, then," his relief was palpable, or at least she had imagined it was. So she has had this intense block of sheer solitude, more time spent unrelievedly alone than she's had since the August she moved in, and the effect of so much solitude is like a metamorphosis; she feels almost as if she's changing into a different creature altogether, a kind of bird, maybe, hollow-boned and not bound to earth. How many more days before she turns to the mirror and sees plumage, a beak, a beady yellow eye?

Wally leaves a third message on Wednesday. The first message, left the Tuesday immediately after they'd seen each other, had been short; he'd obviously expected it would be followed up soon by a real conversation. The second message, left the following Sunday, had been longer. He'd inquired after her Christmas, updated her on Ann's heels (casts off next Saturday if the final X-ray looks good), named a movie he'd like to see, mentioned that Alice was flying out that afternoon. Today's message dwarfs the first: "Is this because I didn't eat the toast?" Pause. "Bye." The little joke undercut by a note of sadness in his voice. And finally it gets through to her that she's being unkind by not calling him back; she hasn't even been capable of thinking of that for the past week, but his voice sounds sad and she hears it, finally, she gets it that he's suffering—*ohhhhh, what a clod she is*—and she's able to come out of her shmatte-wringing stupor long enough to dial the number. She gets Ann.

"Oh," says Ann. "I have a present for you." It sounds like an accusation.

"Really? What?"

"Just something stupid. It took me three days to make it."

Ann made her something. It took her three days. Esker goes cold. What is she doing? What has happened? Where is her dimmer switch, where is her self-control? Where is her starched white apron and her frilled white cap? Where is her neatness, her hospital corners? "Ann James, Ann James," she says, sounding as light and pleasant as she can. "You made me something?"

"Well, it's a stupid thing. I thought I would've had a chance to give it to you by now."

Oh, clod; oh, idiot: Ann is hurt. She's barely begun to be in their lives and already she's letting them down; the only sure way is to back out now, to back out smiling, smoothing her white apron. Esker, you idiot: what were you thinking, what were you thinking? She let herself begin to want something. This is *old*, don't be fooled, this is where corrosion sets in, a little bit of want and the oxidation begins, obscuring the clean lines beneath it, obscuring her nursely duties, knocking loose the frilled paper cap, the pristine raiment tightly buttoned up the back, without which— the frightening sound of buttons scattering across the floor—she will grow monstrous. For a moment she's Genie again, looming large, frozen, over the fragile paper houses of her neighborhood, all manner of destruction ready to ensue at her gentlest tread. She wants to grow very small. She presses the heel of her hand against her brow.

"Esker?"

"Just thinking. Do you want to do math this week?"

"Yes."

They make a date for Saturday, the 2nd. "The second already," says Esker. "A new year."

"Not if you're Chinese," says Ann.

"Well," says Esker. "See you then." And she hangs up and takes off her pilly gray thing and slippers and puts on boots and her coat and her amethyst thistle earrings, which she'd forgotten about but just came across this morning, and she heads uptown, toward the scorpion-tail end of West Fourth, where it starts intersecting other streets.

19.

Ann is afraid to have her casts off. She doesn't realize this until she's sitting in the orthopedist's office with her father on Saturday morning waiting for the X-rays to come back. The orthopedist's name is Irving Mento, which Ann finds in and of itself hilarious; in fact, on the previous visits she's had a hard time not laughing inappropriately in his presence, not strictly because of his name, but because of his bearing, which is so the very soul of uninflected sobriety; he seems to be entirely in the thrall of his own straight-white-male-M.D.-ness. Anyway, the whole effect on Ann was to call forth in her that which is most irreverent, and she sat there on the paper-sheathed examining table with high color in her cheeks, biting the insides of her mouth and breaking into the most awful voiceless, torso-shaking church-giggles whenever his back was turned or his head bent. His hair is thick and black, a little greasy, and lies in impressively rigid order along her skull. After the first visit her father expressed annoyance at her for having been rude, but at the second visit they caught each other's eye during the exam and both nearly lost it.

This time, though, Ann is full of something else, which is not only apprehension about having the casts removed but surprise and embarrassment at realizing she's afraid. The fear has nothing to do with the power saw, which she certainly understands won't hurt. As far as the prospect of putting her weight on her unprotected heels, she does feel a little gingerly, but that's not the root of this fear, either, which is perhaps less fear than foreboding, a kind of primal favoring of the familiar.

Familiar? These four-week-old impostors? She looks down at them, her sullen, ridiculous, blue foot-casings, which have after all been no picnic, no walk (ha-ha) in the park. Why, why would she feel afraid to give them up?

Her father is sitting there looking matronly with her coat and mittens across his lap, paging through an already-much-thumbed copy of *Redbook*. Ann cranes. He's reading a recipe for stuffing. The paint on a patch of wall behind the door has chipped away to gray plaster. Elsewhere there's a framed diploma and an unframed discolored print of green apples in a blue bowl with a butterfly perched on its rim. Not a little sad.

Her stomach is all clutchy-feeling and her hands are ice. Her father turns the page of his magazine, and there's a close-up of Christmas cookies glittering with green-and-red sugar on top. She remembers loving those sprinkles as a kid, as if they were something more special than dyed sugar. Today they look spiteful.

So what is it? Why shrink from getting back on her own two feet? The question itself is uncomfortable, and she resists it, and finds herself facing instead a mental image of her mother applying parrot and viper to her ankles with light, infinite care. And then, like a new slide in the carousel, another image: Esker on the ottoman pulled up next to the couch, drawn in low and close by necessity, her voice low and close as she maps functions, her pencil audible in its friction against the page. And next: Malcolm Choy standing above her, bent, addressing her on her invalid's throne, her child's throne, the metal perch on which her body is so compromised as to be disregarded, inviting her to be a spirit in his act.

A perfunctory knock, and the door opens. Dr. Mento nods at them brusquely—defensively, perhaps, as though he's sensed a baffling disrespect on their previous visits—and clips the X-rays to the light board. "Well, I'm satisfied," he says, and with a ballpoint whisked from the breast pocket of his lab coat, indicates why. Ann, as usual, fails to recognize anything in the jumble of shadow and light that might belong to her own body, but she nods as if she, too, were satisfied. The paper crinkles beneath her. "Your heels have healed nicely," Dr. Mento concludes with a tiny smile, so pathetic and brave of him to offer this pun, given her past rudeness, that Ann feels full of regret and an impulse to take his hand, to let him feel he has ministered meaningfully to her. And to fit her in on a Saturday morning, which he ordinarily reserved for emergencies, simply because her father had said she wanted to make it back to school Monday cast-free—really, he was quite human, after all. He takes her feet and manipulates them around, not smoothly, up onto the table. She adjusts herself a bit; more crackly paper sound; the indignity. Dr. Mento removes the electric saw from its hook on the wall. "This won't hurt at all," he says, switching it on, and the room fills with its whir.

Now she hates him slightly again as he fails to receive or notice her intended warmth. Nor has he displayed any reaction to her mother's art, even now, as he carves away at it, splitting an ostrich in two. Bent over her feet, he's all neat black hair and a faint kitchen smell—baked potato?—and humorlessness. She hates his hands, too white for the black hairs tufting them. She hates his hands touching her shin as he removes the halves of the left cast; she hates how cold they are and also how professional as they move this item, her leg, out of the way. She hates her foot and ankle, looking shrunken and corpse-white and covered with—gross!—dead skin. "I'm molting," she says, repulsed.

"Can you flex?" says Dr. Mento. "And point? Good. And rotate the foot clockwise?"

She moves it around.

"That's counterclockwise," says her father.

She feels, more than looks up to see, her father and Dr. Mento share a smile. *Oh, go stuff a turkey,* she thinks. "The Polish judge gives it a three," Hannah would mumble if Hannah were here, and Ann wishes she were here, all dense and unapologetic in her black-and-red makeup, a buffer between her and the earnest good will of these two men.

"Next," announces Dr. Mento, and starts up the saw again.

At the end of the visit he asks, "Do you want these?" of the casts, and Ann says no. He uses the foot pedal to lift the lid on the garbage can and drops all four pieces in. "Well." He punches out the nib of his pen, scribbles the physical therapist's name on a prescription pad, tears off the sheet, and hands this to her father along with the medical-encounter form to bring out to the desk. "Good luck." And then he does the very decent thing of sticking out his hand not to her father but to Ann, and as she shakes it tears wobble in her eyes and then cascade, and she is crying very messily, appallingly, all pink and splashing behind the quick cage of her fingers. She can feel their alarm, Mento's and her father's, and their utter ineptitude, for something like a whole minute, during which it is simply up to her to try to quash the sobs.

"You all right, then?" asks Dr. Mento the second they seem to sub-side. She nods from behind her hands. "Tears of relief," he suggests summarily, perhaps as much to bolster her father as to pave his own exit. She feels his cold hand pat her shin briefly, and then he is gone, and the last thing she wants is to have to offer her father an explanation for this, which she anyway cannot explain.

"Can we get falafel on the way home?" she says pre-emptively, followed by a great, almost comically rattling sniff, and slides herself carefully off the stupid table onto her feet, which seem tiny, light, distant. She has brought socks and sneakers in a bag, and sits on the floor to put them on. She feels great pity and impatience toward these cold little atrophied appendages and their shriveled skin. "Go ahead," she says, "I'll meet you up front." Her father touches her hair and she manages, just, not to shake off his heavy hand.

"All right, Anatevka, and then we'll go to Mamoun's." He goes to do the copay and she pulls on her socks—she chose her softest ones, duckling-yellow—deliberately over her heels. Then sneakers, and she rises: she is an ordinary girl again, both more powerful and more vulnerable than when she walked in.

Esker arrives punctually at four that afternoon, looking less attractive than usual. Her shapeless hair is somehow more nebulous, her careless clothes are somehow more ill-matched, and there are lavender shadows under her tea-brown eyes. Still in her coat, she takes a little package from her briefcase and hands it to Ann. It's wrapped in aluminum foil, and turns out to be a set of eight colored pencils, art-store ones in sumptuous colors, their pristine tips sharp as arrows.

"Thank you," says Ann. Standing, she's half an inch taller than Esker.

"I have something for your father, too." Another aluminum-foil job, somewhat flatter.

"He's at work."

"I'll just leave it . . ." Esker casts about for a surface. The mantel is the nearest one. "Here." Under the portrait of Alice. "Hey." From across the room she notices. "No more casts."

"I know!" says Ann triumphantly, and bursts into tears. She cries harder and longer than she did this morning. She leans forward into the door for support. Her whole body is like a cloth-and-wire thing, a flimsy object racked by sobs. Esker doesn't seem inconvenienced by it.

"What's going on?" she asks, when Ann finishes.

Ann shrugs. Her forehead is against the doorjamb. "I'm afraid," she says.

Esker steps in closer to hear her. "Of what?"

She rocks her head back and forth. "Nothing."

A pause. Thinking. "Let's go get some hot chocolate," says Esker.

They make their way slowly down Pierrepont, Ann timorous on the dirty chunks of ice that dot the sidewalk. She thinks of an hours-old foal, then of an osteoporotic dowager. Once she begins to slip, and she grabs Esker's arm wildly. The sky above the buildings is that lit-from-within blue, like blue plum-flesh, and the buildings are beginning to be lit up against it. Cigarette smoke and hot-dog vendor smoke and vapor from a Laundromat and vapor from a manhole cover writhe or billow according to their natures. There are other cafés closer and quainter, but Esker keeps walking, beyond the pretty enclave of Ann's immediate neighborhood, threading them through denser throngs of commuters heading for the subway, until eventually, almost reluctantly, Ann thinks, she leads them into a bright, cramped coffee shop opposite Borough Hall. Blue and silver Mylar decorations frame the storefront, and a large cardboard New Year's baby is duct-taped to the wall over the cash register, above a laminated dollar bill. The baby has one tooth and a single yellow curl.

"Two hot chocolates, please," Esker tells the waitress.

"And french fries," adds Ann. The waitress takes their menus. Then Ann braces for Esker to begin questioning her. The radio is playing "I'm On Top of the World." Behind Ann someone says, "Was that his father at the arraignment?" and someone else says, "No, I don't know who that guy was," and someone else says, "Tyrone, I said that's enough syrup." As the sky gets darker outside, the coffee shop takes on a space-station feel, small and bright and buzzing with particular human stuff amid the general immensity of everything in the cold bluish-black beyond. The waitress is wearing white orthopedic shoes and has, who knows, maybe an Armenian accent, and speaks in her own tongue to the fattish man behind the cash register. She makes him laugh, and then she smiles to herself. She walks like a woman who loves her hips, very earth-rooted and mysteriously confident. She is still smiling when she puts down their hot chocolate, and spoons from her apron pocket.

Ann eats the whipped cream and then she says, "I guess you don't need to come anymore, since my casts are off."

Esker acknowledges this, or at least the second half of this statement, her acknowledgment noncommittal.

Ann's cranium keeps flooding with pinkness and light, over and over, in waves. "I feel like helium-girl."

"What do you mean?"

"I don't know. Not like Minnie Mouse–voice or anything, more like one of those balloons in the Thanksgiving Day parade."

"Which one?" asks Esker. "Underdog?"

"What?"

"Underdog. 'Here I come to save the day . . .'" sings Esker.

"That's Mighty Mouse."

Esker looks perplexed. "Then what is the Underdog song? With Sweet Penelope Purebred . . ."

"Before my time."

"So's Mighty Mouse."

"But cable."

Esker nods. "So: you feel like a balloon in the Thanksgiving Day parade."

"Once, when I was little, my parents took me to the parade and one of the guys holding one of the tethers for Piglet had to tie his shoe. They were all stopped, anyway, the way the parade stops, you know, sometimes. And he gave me his tether to hold for him while he tied his shoe. I was little enough that I thought, you know, it was a very big responsibility. I thought if I didn't pull my weight against it it would pretty much lift me up into the sky. I totally remember like digging my heels into the ground, like straining to make myself heavy enough to hold it to earth."

The french fries come. Ann is thorough about the ketchup. When she looks up she says in a small voice, "I'm afraid I don't belong here."

"Here?" asks Esker, patting the tabletop. It's white Formica speckled with gold.

"*Here,*" says Ann, gesturing wide, gesturing toward the storefront, which is now mainly reflective, though pierced with headlights and traffic lights and a red globe light marking the entrance to the subway: satellites and distant planets, confident markers of life elsewhere.

"Where do you belong?" asks Esker.

Ann sighs and bends deep over her hot chocolate. "This is stupid,

stupid, stupid," she whispers. She is suddenly exhausted. It occurs to her maybe she shouldn't have walked so far on her newly castless feet. They feel so small and weary under the table. Her heels, in her mind's eye, are the thinness of shoehorns.

"What did you say?" asks Esker, leaning forward.

"I said my feet hurt," says Ann. She wants to float home.

20.

Wally peels at the aluminum foil and cuts his index finger, a red centimeter. He sucks it and goes back to the gift. It's Sunday, 3:00 A.M. He's just home from work and not tired. The light that lights the Alice portrait had been on when he walked in the door, as it usually is not, and it was because of this that he noticed the flat package on the mantel. It bore a yellow Post-it with *Wally from Esker* on it, and before taking it to the couch he made himself a cup of licorice tea, his regular post-Game, pre-bed ritual. Now, removing the rest of the silver skin from the gift without event, he finds a heavy brown envelope with a tie-shut flap, like interoffice envelopes from days of yore.

He pulls out a large, laminated pamphlet sort of thing: a guide to making paper airplanes. He feels inside the envelope again, but there's nothing else. He rereads the card, if you can call it that: nothing much to deconstruct there. He's not sure whether he feels disappointed or not. Paper airplanes. The pamphlet promises these are the best in the world. All right. He gets a piece of eight-and-a-half-by-eleven.

Three A.M., closer to three-thirty now. He sits at the cherry coffee table, tea near at hand, and folds. There are three varieties. He makes one of each, then hosts a little competition. The Phoenix goes farthest, but there's something about the Nakamura Lock that feels best, the canniness with which it rides the current. The Balcony Bomber's a definite third. Maybe it works better from a balcony.

Nuncio has been cast in a play at the Public. It's not the lead, but it's a major role in a new work by a prominent playwright. He's taking a leave of absence starting next Friday. Wally learned this tonight, less than a week after Alice blew out of town again. It's happened before, Nuncio leaving to do some theater project, but never for off-Broadway. In the past it's been more ephemeral, some showcase or a staged reading or something barely pulled off in a loft space way downtown, or in Greenpoint or something, and he's always come back to Game after a month or two or three, tops, glowing or bitchy or subdued for a time, and then back to normal, sweetly Nuncio again, with his preposterous tuxedo shirts and lightning wit, Wally's first mate and Game's front man.

"So this is it. You're leaving me," said Wally tonight, at the back table, after the restaurant was closed. He'd poured a shot of peppermint schnapps into his cocoa, something he and his high-school friends used to do on snow days in Grange Hill; that was back when parents kept liquor cabinets; he had a sudden, vibrant flash of sitting in a beige Naugahyde chair in Chris Petroni's basement with Jimi Hendrix blaring on the eight-track and an endless game of Ping-Pong in the background.

Nuncio smiled. "We'll see," he said modestly, and Wally knew in that instant that Nuncio wouldn't be back.

"Well, son," he said officiously, clearing his throat, and reached into his back pocket, as if to pull out his wallet. "It's a rough world out there. . . ."

"Don't give me money, you putz," said Nuncio, laughing.

"I was going to give you a condom."

Nuncio gave him the finger.

They each drank. Wally'd forgotten about the schnapps, and it depressed him to taste it, lousing up his cocoa.

"It's terrific, Nuncio. You're going toward what you love."

"I wish I were giving you more notice."

"Yeah, well. Actors."

They were quiet. In the kitchen, mopping, John the dishwasher was singing, with heart, "How Are Things in Glockamorra?" Nuncio and Wally glanced at each other: funny. And Wally's heart sank slowly, so slowly, like a sheet of paper.

Now, 3:40 A.M., Wally drinks from his tea. He feels old and dumb. So what do these paper airplanes mean? Anything? Does he care? What is this, anyway? And what was that, in her kitchen? And again: does he care? She's an unknown quantity, Esker, all hidden and bent in on herself, the opposite of Alice, with her bountiful outward light, the opposite of Nuncio, the opposite of beauty and appetite. She seems purposefully plain, purposefully need-resistant.

She'd come by Game one afternoon earlier in the week with snow on the shoulders of her coat and amethyst earrings dangling from her ears, and it was that feeling of someone from a dream turning up in real life. It had been a bad moment at work: the dishwasher wasn't draining properly and had created a small flood in the kitchen; a plumber was working on it, and Wally had been helping unload a delivery of cheeses. Justine would be in later to do predinner, but it was only three on a Wednesday, a bad time for Esker to materialize. There were, thankfully, no customers at the moment, but Wally, coming through from the kitchen to answer the phone ("No, we don't serve haggis"), caught sight of her pale oval face against the glass, trying to peer in. He jumped. For someone he knows to be so matter-of-fact, she looked remarkably ghostly. He hung up the phone and came around and opened the door, and she wouldn't step inside; she was embarrassed—she'd been in the neighborhood; she didn't know whether he was open; she'd had an errand on Hudson; she was interrupting him—all the while letting the warm air leak out and the cold air leak in, until he took her elbow, almost roughly, and brought her in and shut the door.

"We have a flood in the kitchen," he said. "Hello." He was thinking about what he smelled like; some of the cheeses he'd been unpacking were very strong, and then there was the sewery odor of the backed-up dishwasher.

"A flood," she repeated. "Is that normal?"

He looked at her. The question seemed uncharacteristically silly. Her earrings were swaying a bit, and he found himself paying attention to the way they lightly hit her jawbone. "Well. No."

"I'm sorry to barge in. You go fix your flood."

"No, there's a plumber. What's your errand?"

"Christmas shopping."

"Christmas is over."

"I've been in a fog."

A thousand ways to take that. "Evidently." Silence. Game itself seemed in a fog, all bathed in gray, and the windows steamy a little. Like a stage when the theater is dark. Wally had the fleeting impression that they were actors, he and Esker, here to rehearse something, but what were their lines?

"Anyway, I . . ." She shifted toward the door. "I'll call you back."

"Okay." He held it open for her. "What are your earrings?"

She touched one. "Thistles."

He nodded; she left.

She hadn't called back.

The foil that earlier wrapped the envelope lies crumpled up tight now beside his tea. Wally begins absently to unfold it, careful this time not to get cut. Light pools and darts from its myriad surfaces. He smooths it on the table but it will never return to smooth. Abruptly, referring to the printed instructions, he sets about folding it into a Balcony Bomber, then steps out through the French doors. It's cold, in the bottomless way of predawn. He sends the plane off the balcony. It goes straight for an improbably long time with little loss of altitude, until he loses sight of it.

21.

Ann's compilation tape is incredibly sweet. Esker can't think of the last time anyone made her a mix; she'd sort of forgotten about that rite. That whole thing of passionately needing to foist your favorite music on people you love and desire. It makes her smile. It's a mixture of contemporary stuff and what Esker assumes must be takes from Wally's old stash of albums. Or Alice's. The last song is "Spanish Boots of Spanish Leather." The second to last is "Dancing Queen." The whole compilation is like that, all longing and camp, and it seems reassuringly normal, if not typical, teen fare.

She listens to it all morning before meeting Wally on Sunday. She listens to it like a reminder of who she's there for. They meet at three on Broome Street and have gelato and cappuccino in a nearly empty café. They have no agenda, or they have two agendas, an ostensible one and an unarticulated one, a puppet and an interloper, and they keep swerving back and forth, blindly, between the two, almost from sentence to sentence, so that the whole conversation is disjointed, but the disjointedness has a rhythm to it, a tight syncopation that they nail, so, even as they fail to accomplish anything concrete, they succeed in cakewalking down the shadowy middle aisle with something like panache; Esker feels a heat that her pistachio gelato does not temper; she feels, in Ann's phrase, like helium-girl.

"Ann seemed a little shaky Saturday." The ostensible agenda.

"How so?"

Esker tells him briefly the story of their afternoon, the sudden violent tears, the walk, the french fries and cocoa, the cab ride home in deference to Ann's foolish feet, no math studying after all, and then Ann's quick change of manner as Esker was leaving: she'd become almost wickedly animated, and confided in Esker a plan for her to be involved in Winter Concert after all. She was going to be—what had she called it?—a beatnik angel?—and drop lighted matches from a ladder while Malcolm Choy and Hannah Stolarik did some interpretive drumming and recitation. But please don't tell anyone, she'd begged, you can't tell anyone. Her eyes lit up like pointy little jewels.

Wally listens to all this and pulls at the hair on the back of his wrist. "She started crying at the doctor's that morning. When her casts came off. I think it completely scared the doctor."

"And you?"

"Well, I know her," he starts, but breaks off into a silence that seems contradictory. "That's good about the Winter Concert thing, don't you think?"

Esker shrugs. "I haven't figured out yet whether I'm going to have to say something about the use of fire."

"You could always opt for the prudent but noninterfering tack of standing by with a fire extinguisher."

"They'll think I'm part of the act."

"Under your skirt."

"Then, when Hannah's hair catches fire, I whip it out—*tchhhhhhhh!* like Charlie's Angels."

"Oh, then, forget the extinguisher—you need one of those Super-Soaker water guns."

"I think that's more like Linda Hamilton in *The Terminator.*"

"*Terminator II.*"

"You're well versed."

He nods, modest. "Thank you for the airplanes, by the way."

"I didn't give you any airplanes."

"The instructions. They were actually really neat."

"Neat?"

He colors. "They were actually superior paper airplanes. They flew really well."

And for some reason *she* colors. She scrapes at her gelato, busy. The other agenda, the unarticulated one, is bursting all around them, brilliant soundless explosions pocking the air.

"Are you scared to be here?" asks Wally, so direct it stops her cold.

"I'm afraid I don't belong here." She has déjà-vu when she says this, and then she shudders, although her face feels still very hot.

"Why?"

"I don't know. Because I've never. Been here. Before."

He waits, but she can't think of words to add. "You're afraid I'm not a countryman?" He asks it so gently, as if this were a normal conversation.

"I'm afraid *I'm* not a countryman." This comes out more vehemently than she intended. Then, like punctuation, her spoon breaks; it's only a plastic spoon, but she has snapped it unintentionally, and the force flips her paper gelato cup up and through the air and it lands, right side up, on the next table. They regard it a moment.

"That's better than the Balcony Bomber."

"What?"

"You're leaking."

"What?" She feels like he's suddenly switched dialects.

He looks pointedly at her hand, and she looks down and sees her middle finger is bleeding sort of liberally. The severed edge of the silly little plastic spoon has actually dug away a good flap of skin. How absurd.

"Did you say I'm leaking?"

"I said you're bleeding." He hands her his napkin, hers having apparently taken flight during the fiasco. She wraps it around her finger and squeezes. "We've got to stop meeting like this," he says.

And she scowls: that's right, this is an echo of an earlier moment. It's like a further intimacy, repeating this pattern of cut finger and proffered bandage in reverse. She's as embarrassed as if she engineered it. "What a cheap spoon," she mutters, in some disbelief. She has no idea, no idea: this is terra incognita. But it isn't really; she knows; this is an indication of what's to come: she will break everything. But she doesn't really want to stop being here. But she is going to break everything. A headache arrives suddenly, like a train coming into station, and from the staggering density of it she lifts her gaze and steals a look at Wally opposite.

"Oh. Oh." She says it twice. He's so unexpected.

He appears to be wearing his happiness lightly.

At home that night, when she should be prepping for the first day back at school tomorrow, she tries to summon Albert's ghost. She feels desperate for it. She goes down to the basement of the funny narrow house, where her landlords allotted her a bit of storage space when she first moved in, and where she has virtually never set foot since, in pursuit of a box of old letters she half remembers saving, although it's equally plausible that she threw it out long ago. The basement smells mousy. The banister going down is slightly moist, vaguely spongy to the touch. The vestibule that leads to its two partitioned storage spaces is choked with cardboard boxes overflowing with books. When Esker tries to move one aside, it falls instantly apart and spills its contents, all of which are warped and swollen with water damage. No one will read them again; they ought to have been thrown out, cleaned out of here. She peers at a few, morbidly curious. A 1959 restaurant guide; a James Bond novel circa 1970; a paperback edition of *You Can Quit Smoking Forever*; and something called *The Lilac Handkerchief* with a network of mildew specks greatly obscuring the cover design of a partly clad brunette gazing moodily through a bay window. Odd titles, things she'd never associate with her landlords.

Esker climbs past more boxes of books. She can't help stepping on some, and feels volumes slide and a binding break under her foot. A coat tree in the corner droops with indeterminate garments apparently gone to rot; the dim light shines through sagging splits in some of the once-rich fabric. Again, hard to imagine her faded old landlords in such finery. On impulse, she fingers a mauve silk sleeve, gently, but even so it tears, she feels some seam give, and draws her hand back hastily. A listing shelf beyond the coat tree is crammed with detritus, all of it faulty, none worthy of storage, yet surprisingly suggestive of a more luxurious, indulgent past than Esker would have imagined: a set of electric hair-curlers, a chipped garnet-colored punch bowl with matching little garnet glasses, a mateless stiletto pump, a torn oil painting, a fur muff, a single golf club, a cracked stained-glass lampshade.

It all passes through Esker in the most unpleasant way. She lives in a ghost house. She lives on top of ghosts. Abandoned ghosts, untended ghosts. There's something wrong with this place, and she found it, she chose it. It isn't, as some people have supposed, the charm of the address that's kept her rooted here for nine years, not the delightful enigma of an old wood-frame house tucked amid the weedy lots and warehouses of the far-western edge of lower Manhattan. It's inertia, nothing more, a kind of self-abandonment.

Self. She has always thought of her landlords as selfless, with their below-market rent, their offerings of zucchini and radishes, their tireless little efforts on behalf of peace and justice; and she has thought of their selflessness as something noble and righteous, as something right. But now, in their basement, clotted with what seem to Esker essentially the horrible, hollow grins of skeletons, she thinks of them as selfless in a different sense, as having abdicated self, abdicated claims to punch bowls and golf clubs, to mauve silk and spy novels.

Selfless. "You're so selfless," she remembers someone saying to her back in Delos, back in high school; was it an aunt, a neighbor, a teacher? She'd given up softball, and basketball, and the debate team, and band, one by one, till, her senior year, she wasn't doing anything but coming straight home after school to be there for her mother, or sometimes going straight to the hospital to sit *there* with her mother for an hour or two— because that was the year her mother began to be admitted every few months—before going home to make supper for her father, who'd come home too tired to speak. "You're so selfless." The phrase rings in her mind. And she was, she tried to be, it was the easy thing to be, it was easiest. No, it wasn't an aunt or a neighbor who'd said it. It comes to her now: it was her father, who'd broken his silence to inform her one otherwise undistinguished evening, and she'd responded to his approval with a mute surge of something, not a glow exactly, but a sense of accomplishment. As though it were a good thing. To be selfless. She sees herself in her mind as she surely did not really appear, in white kneesocks and blouse and a khaki wrap-around skirt, her hands folded together below her waist, accepting the compliment silently. She didn't still wear kneesocks in high school, did she? She never owned such a skirt. But the image is fast in her head, frozen like a cameo, the colors of a cameo, with a matching, bland morality.

A fat little spider scuttles up the wall, and Esker starts. She goes around the corner to the storage space she remembers being assigned and is relieved to find it relatively bare—most of what little's in it are the empty packing crates and boxes she used on her move. The fact that she'd apparently thought to save them touches her. She had thought she'd be on her way again shortly. She'd never dreamed nine years would pass without her budging. There they are, still waiting, still in perfectly good condition. Odd: whatever water damage had afflicted her land-lords' boxes of books hadn't occurred in here, in this stall; the cellar floor must be uneven. There, in the back, on a folding table, just a few items: a plastic bin of her college papers; an old rotary telephone she'd once meant to have converted for use with a modern jack; some cleaning sup-plies; her old ironing board (the apartment had a built-in that flipped forward from a nifty little compartment in the wall); and a second, smaller plastic bin containing miscellaneous papers. This last item, with the cleaning supplies balanced on top (might as well), she carries back upstairs with her, out of the mossy mousiness of that dank, disturbing place.

Upstairs, she washes her hands thoroughly, then changes sweatshirts—really, something about the basement's clinging odor disturbs her unnaturally—and makes a cup of strong tea before bringing the plastic bin into the living room and lifting its lid. Esker has a dread of nostal-gia. She's more thrower-outer than pack rat, and most of what the box contains are unsentimental items: school transcripts, a few legal docu-ments relating to her parents' deaths, her paltry résumé from when she'd just graduated, student-loan information. But there, in an unceremoni-ous bundle held together (or actually no longer held together) by a cracked rubber band, is the brief handful of missives—from notes passed in class to letters mailed during vacations—Albert Rose penned to her during their four years of acquaintance. So she managed not to throw these away. She sets about reading them with stoic trepidation.

> *Esker,*
> *Dear Esker,*
> *Dear I.J.E.,*
> *Hello Iph,*
> *Iph-and-When,*

And the later ones with no salutation at all, just immediately into the body of the letter:

> *The idiocy of your last remark has burned in my gut all week, but today I find myself thinking of what you said in different terms.*

Anyway, I no longer want to throttle you and may even (probably) owe you an apology. Are we speaking? Did you go to the concert? Is your cough better? . . .

It is impossible to convey to you the depths of boredom from which I write. I've started something like sixteen letters to you since July and abandoned each for lack of anything to report. This while I know you are living the mad life in The City, holding down sixteen jobs or whatever it was and still managing to hit the clubs every night. The air conditioner broke last week: at last! I thought, a news flash worthy of a letter to Iph! But in the absence of breathably cool air I find myself little able to hoist a pen. I live for the evenings, when Randy gets home from work and we hang out at her mother's and watch HBO, although even after sundown it's still too hot for more than a little halfhearted groping, and anyway, she complains she's too tired after running relay races with the little tyrants at Camp Ramah all day. . . .

Where are you? I can't believe you're not in your dorm right now. If you get this message, come find me. I'll be in the library, you know where, and after that back in my room or in the laundry room. Hurry up and get this note.

In your last letter you said I sounded bitter, and you sounded so repulsed, so wounded and repulsed at this discovery, as though all along you've been suffering under the misconception that I'm a sunny fellow or some crap, and you say I'm being unkind to Randy, well sorry to tell you, lady, but you don't know anything about it, you apparently know way less than the little bit I at once point hoped you'd understood. Anyway if I'm being unkind to anyone it's you and it's embarrassing, for you I mean, if you don't even know that. . . .

You left your watch here last night. Do you want to come over tonight and get it? I have peanut brittle. Love, A.R.

. . . but I swear you are the most mercurial woman I've ever met and I don't mean that as a compliment . . .

*You wanted me to say something about what's going to happen.
I've told you my intentions: same as ever: to live within my faith, to
make a life, as best I can, that's nurtured by, and nurtures, the faith I
was born into, born of and am a part of. But neither you nor I nor
anyone walking around on the crust of this planet can say anything
worth dick about what's going to happen . . .*

It isn't that his words are entirely foreign. In fact, she is surprised by
the extent to which many details come sharply to her: the remark of hers
that had triggered a certain falling out; the specific park bench, under a
swiftly shedding oak tree, where he'd once stood her up; the marzipan
chimp he'd left outside her dorm room door as one night's conciliatory
gesture; the dismal smell of cigarette smoke in his sweater on an early-
spring afternoon; the arid, helpless quality of his anger when she proved,
again and again, ultimately unyielding. Both the topography and the tec-
tonics come seeping back with familiarity, but a distant familiarity, and
the distance functions as a distortion, so that she can't really get purchase
on the words, the feelings running through these notes and letters. They
are familiar and alien at the same time.

Stuck to one envelope is the exoskeleton of some basement insect, a
little black grooved shell. She realizes she doesn't want the letters in her
apartment. She doesn't want them back down in the storage space, either,
festering underneath her body as she eats, reads, works, washes, sleeps.
She doesn't want them inhabiting the space below her floorboards: the decaying carcass of Albert Rose, of her strained idea of him, her shameful
upkeep of his poisonous ghost.

But in fact they are not festering, not decaying; that would suggest
they possessed a bodily, a carnal nature to begin with, whereas they are
only paper and ink, nothing alive, nothing with any life of their own.
And their very inanimateness now strikes her as grotesque, as mocking.
It's been Esker all along manipulating the strings, the wires, jerking into
action the false limbs of Albert's ghost, the illusion of Albert's ghost. And
who is Albert Rose? No one. He doesn't exist anymore, not the man she
knew nine years ago, if she ever knew him then. The real Albert Rose is
disconnected from the letters; he must be a grown-up man now, with a
wife and children and a house and a dog and a briefcase and an IRA and a
lawn mower. And these letters are not tendrils of any living vine; they are

as hollow and meaningless as that vacant bug shell, stuck with macabre tenacity to the envelope there.

And who is the ghost? There must be a ghost. A ghost has been haunting her for nine years. No, not nine, be honest, more. Wasn't it there when she stood in her cameo colors, hands clasped, and flushed to hear herself praised as selfless? Wasn't it there when she came home from school and made the soup and drew the curtains and accepted with the properly calibrated degree of gratitude the endless scraps of paper her father brought home from Boltman Paper Co. and pressed on her, year after year, his gift, his thin gift to her? And all the years she tiptoed and held herself still so as not to crush the paper walls of her paper town, but instead pretended perfectly to believe in their existence as real walls, real houses and streets and shops and churches, pretended to believe they were solid and secure, when all the while she knew if she assumed her corporeal body, her real strength, they would never bear her weight, she would trample them to pieces, their frailties exposed, and then where would she be, after the destruction she caused, where would she be then, after the paper walls were laid flat, after the paper dust cleared? Nowhere.

Oh, she has been a ghost so long.

She doesn't want the letters. She doesn't want them. She doesn't want them. There's a violence in her sudden need to be rid of them. The garbage, obviously. She shoves her feet into slippers and hurries out—the night is frozen in that stinging, purifying way of her childhood winters upstate—and slams the lot into one of the metal trash cans her landlords keep chained along the side of the building.

She goes back inside wondering what she feels, wondering whether she feels nine years lighter.

22.

Once Esker had made Albert take the ferry out to Ellis Island with her. She'd had to drag him along. He wanted to see a movie instead, part of some Werner Herzog retrospective, and she studied him, with his pale face—he was pale every month of the year—sitting in his dorm-issue desk chair with *The Village Voice* in front of him, and said, "No, no, you're coming with me," very bossily, putting on her bossy act.

"I don't know," he said. "*Even Dwarves Started Small* is playing to-day." There was a picture in the *Voice*, a movie still, and it looked dark and weird. Not appropriate for a brilliant April afternoon.

"Sorry, you're not allowed. You'll wind up not going anyway."

"I would, too, go!"

"Yes, well, now you can say that, now that you know you don't have any choice."

"I don't have any choice?"

"Come on," she said impatiently, tapping her foot in the doorway. "Get a warmer coat than that, it'll be windy on the water. Actually, can I wear that sweater?" She grabbed his old root-beer colored one off the bed and put it on over her jacket. It came down mid-thigh on her. Albert put on his coat and they left.

Esker had with her two plastic bags of stale rolls she'd wrangled from a cafeteria worker. "Are we feeding pigeons?" Albert asked when he noticed them. "What a great date you are: immigrants and pigeons."

"This isn't a date, you idiot."

"For some other guy, I mean. What a great date you would *be*."

"Yeah, well. It's not for pigeons, it's for math."

A professor had mentioned some English scientist from the twenties who had studied fluid turbulence by throwing a sack of white parsnips into the Cape Cod Canal.

"That's nice . . . ?" said Albert. "So . . . ? What, your homework is to throw some kind of food into the Hudson?"

"This isn't homework, I just want to see what it looks like."

"Why?"

"Can you picture it? We dump these rolls off the ferry, into the wake. I think I can picture what it would look like, but I want to see how it really looks."

"In order to determine . . . ?"

"Nothing. I have to see it. I have to do it. I can't just imagine it. What good is just imagining something? What good is theoretical . . . *stuff*? If you feel like playing basketball, it's no good staying inside and imagining playing basketball. If you have an itch, it's no good imagining scratching it."

"I don't know. Right now I'm imagining sitting in a nice comfortable seat in a darkened movie theater, with the opening titles just beginning."

"How is it?"

"Pretty good. Ow."

She'd kicked his ankle. By now they were waiting on line for the boat. Sun and wind were making their eyes stream. She could feel him loving who she was.

On the boat she loosed the rolls, and they tumbled down and got knocked up on the white spray and then went bobbing out in various directions, and the gulls cried and swooped and dived, and she couldn't track where the rolls ended up, partly because of the birds and partly because they were soon out of sight in the smashingly bright ripples carried farther and farther away, but she felt great satisfaction, because it had been pretty in a kinetic, exciting way to feel the bread drop off into gravity's pull, and it was an absurd, concrete thing to do that she had wanted to do and had now done; it wasn't about math after all, but about possibility, and she felt lifted up and dizzy in the force of the wind and the oily smell and churning roar of the motor, and happy.

This had been just months before they shut Ellis Island down for the renovation, and the whole place had given the impression of being crumbling. More than that, it was like those ghost stories where you find an abandoned shack in the woods and evidence of its having been left in a hurry: dirty dishes still on the table; a tower, half built, of children's blocks ensconced in cobwebs in the corner. There were rooms with shoes, and suitcases, and books. A ranger had led their small group on a tour of the buildings, a middle-aged white man with a practiced spiel and a great nasal voice that rang out against the cracked walls. Esker kept thinking he was speaking through a megaphone, but he wasn't.

Stories of unimaginable loss and grief, and stories of unimaginable relief and condolence had seeped into every crack and crevice of these buildings. Esker fingered their walls. She was struck particularly by the thought of those who had made it this far only to be turned away, and she came off the tour depressed, but not out of pity for the ghosts of the past. On the contrary, she found herself envying the ghosts, jealous of all who had come through this island, no matter their hardships—even the ones who were finally denied admittance—for their scrappiness and guts, their refusal to participate in their own sacrifice. Their refusal to be accomplices to their own tragedies. She found herself wishing she'd come of such stock, wishing she bore such a legacy, instead of that of her parents and their construction-paper days in Delos, barely lifting their voices, barely lifting their eyes, hewing to vaguely oppressive guidelines they'd long since ceased to see. If tested, she wondered, how would she have fared?

Waiting for the ferry back, she and Albert had walked along a low, crumbling wall by the water, in which floated plastic bags and bottles and a sour-looking yellowish foam. She was beset by a sort of inexplicable rage at what seemed the sadistic hopefulness of the place. There, across the water, catching what was now the late slant of the sun, was the Statue of Liberty, looking beautiful in spite of all the ways her image had been appropriated; Esker was embarrassed to be stirred by the sight; the lady ought to have looked cloying and trite, but she didn't, she looked austerely, achingly beautiful. Absolutely anchored and absolutely . . . well, free. At liberty. And over behind them was the city skyline, taking on a high orangey glow from the afternoon sun suspended over New Jersey. It was a landscape of unattainable strength, a landscape of unattainable possibility. For no one more cruel than for those would-be immigrants who'd been turned away with a chalk mark on a coat, put back on boats, refused. Preposterously, she was aware of feeling contempt toward those imagined gray figures who, barred entry, obeyed the order to sail back out of the harbor. They should have jumped. Over the wall, or overboard. To swim to freedom or to drown.

She fantasized this is what she would have done. It seemed very important to believe she would have had the courage not to comply with rejection or retreat. "Don't you think?" she asked Albert. "Don't you think, knowing me, isn't that what I would've done? I would've jumped and swum back, would've snuck in somehow?"

"I don't know." Big honest shrug. "Maybe. I don't think you probably could've swum that far, to tell you the truth."

"But . . . I mean—don't you think I would have, somehow, *fought* to get in? Wouldn't I have fought?"

"Do you mean do I think you're a rebel?"

"Don't smile at me. Lout. I'm being serious. Never mind. Forget it."

That night, Esker and Albert had sex. It was the first time Esker had ever done that. It spoiled their friendship for some time.

Nearly a year later, when her mother died, Esker went on leave for the rest of the semester and returned to Delos, "to help her father." This was the phrase of neighbors and relatives who, murmuring their approval, provided echoes of all the stultifying praise she'd learned to seek in childhood, and to her vague, her barely registered disgust, she didn't mind, but allowed herself to be comforted by it, even to want it. Without school, without friends, without her mother to care for, the days were even emptier than Esker remembered. The emptiness was validating, a confirmation of something, almost an explanation. The second week, she went through closets, clearing out her mother's things, each garment something Esker remembered well. She was first relieved, then disappointed, to find no surprises. One afternoon, she came across the childhood composition books she'd filled up with numbers, her old compulsive counting in different base systems. These seemed more mysterious than anything she'd found of her mother's, and she stopped packing boxes for Goodwill and spent the rest of the afternoon turning the darkened pages, studying the strange time-warp angles and loops of her twelve-year-old handwriting, inhaling the slightly sweet odor of paper breaking down. She lay back against her mother's tightly made single bed and placed one of the books like a butterfly across her face, her nose tucked into the binding, the wings with their layers and layers of numbers spread across her cheeks, and she fell asleep and into a dream that was like entering the portal of the book, of who she was at twelve, building some kind of ladder to lead out of a thin existence, some kind of escape route cobbled together from escalating numerals and the hope of something tougher and more capacious, less mapped, more complex. . . .

She'd woken with a migraine, something that she'd never had before but which had frequently incapacitated her mother.

She stayed in Delos while the earth came into greenness, tentatively at first and then lushly, extravagantly, and the evenings turned paler and paler in their devastating lavender way, and the blackflies came and the horseflies and the raspberries and the blueberries and the thunder showers and the meteor showers and finally the corn. She and her father had a new lightness between them; they mourned her mother's absence but were relieved of the burden of grieving over her discomfort (no one had ever referred to it as pain), and Genie (he still called her Genie) was more self-possessed in her quietness now; it was less an accommodation to her parents' style and more a state of her own choosing. Conversations that summer, over the dinners she made and they ate on the screened porch, were as slight as ever, but the long periods of silence between them were not oppressive, and stirred no longing. Late at night, when she couldn't sleep, she'd walk amid the tallness of the trees and all the shadows slipping into each other, and she thought she had it, had come into some kind of balance that was the balance of nothing against nothing, void against void. The emptiness she felt in Delos seemed something she could live with, something she could live up to. She felt it filling her, and let it.

Albert wrote. His handwriting looked strange on the envelopes that arrived in their mail basket as implausibly as burning embers somehow making their way to the bottom of the sea. He was convinced she wasn't coming back to school in the fall, and most of his letters were campaigns waged to change her mind; he was alternately witty, abusive, preachy, and tender. She was glad to receive them, but could barely manage to respond. She couldn't really think of anything to say. She sent some postcards. It seemed improbable to her, as she slid them into the blue metal box in front of the bank, that they would ever make their way out of Delos, let alone all the way down to Albert in Manhattan. Nevertheless, she never intended not to return the next semester.

"Goodbye, Dad," she said at August's end, and she rode the train down through the cool ancient body of the mountains and down along the river all the way to its great dirty urban mouth, rocking along the tracks for hundreds of miles, her bones hollow-feeling, swaying compliantly with the train's speed and motion. Yes, she was coming back, sort of. There was something wan and indifferent about the action, too little at stake.

Esker and Albert were eating pierogi at their favorite restaurant on Second Avenue. It was a place where you could get fat cheap: slabs of challah, butter, boiled potatoes and sour cream, blintzes and French toast and syrup, pot cheese, pot roast, kasha and barley. Huge servings. Which, being on student budgets, they felt compelled to finish. They were going to graduate soon, in a matter of months, and a new tension had been coiling tighter between them. It made Esker think of *Robert's Rules of Order:* she felt some kind of imaginary plenary session was coming to an end and at any moment a faceless delegate would stand up and declare, "I call the question!" and then some decision would be forthcoming. It made her want to tunnel and hide, to lose herself among giant trees, to take wing, to vanish. Her stomach felt almost constantly mildly frantic, and her mind out of kilter, slanting. It affected her coloring, and her vocal quality, and her eyes, and what she had very dimly perceived, in the mirror of Albert's response, was that it intensified her appeal, made her more compelling and lovely to him, which in turn made her more giddy and petrified. It was that time of year again of melting slush, coursing sap. Esker thought she might survive the spring if she could just flatten everything, squash it all down.

"Do you want that?" asked Albert. The last latke.

She shook her head, and he helped himself with his fingers, dipping it in applesauce first. She was uncomfortably full and glad of it, the snap of her jeans pressing her stomach. Albert licked a bit of juice from the sauce that was running down the edge of his palm. It was not a smooth move. It made him look like a five-year-old. This was good, safe, this being unbecoming in front of each other. Esker had eaten far too much. She felt like dough. Like a doughboy.

"What's a doughboy?"

"Some kind of soldier."

"Why?"

"Why what?"

"Why are they called doughboys?"

"I don't know."

"Were they like privates?"

"I don't know."

"Was it derogatory?"

"I have no information on the subject."

"It sounds derogatory. Who's paying for this?"

Albert paid this time.

Outside, the sun was setting and the wind was whipping scraps of garbage up the avenue, and Esker spread her arms, and her big floppy cardigan belled out behind her. They were both living off-campus by now, separately, in the East Village. She liked this walking without speaking, this tandem offhandedness, and she liked having to push hard against the wind to get where they were going. Maple seedlings helicoptered through the air. She was playing with the feel of the currents under her arms, slowing her, making the walk more arduous, and she was a doughboy, tenacious, anonymous, crossing the wind-swept plain, chin thrust forward, eyes narrowed, and she was near someone she loved, she did love, someone who had the very good sense or dumb luck not to look at her, not to notice her too well, as she played, as she was safe to play, alone, beside him.

They got to Avenue A, where they were to part, and Albert said, in his voice which was so unmusical, so unresonant, as though there were something always wan and unrooted about him, "Well, good night," and she stopped still and looked at him, and he gave her a sweet, pained sort of smile, and turned away, splitting off north, his tall, coated figure moving with a lilt and a grace that always unnerved her, and she found her throat tight and full. Wildly, aghast, she ran after him, her heart pounding, amazed already at how her heart was about to betray her.

Esker read an article about a mathematician who, while studying six-dimensional figures by mapping their shadows onto two dimensions, recognized the pattern as being similar to the dance honeybees do to tell each other where the pollen is. This, said the mathematician, meant bees could sense the quantum level. The mathematician was a woman.

Esker read the article in the library, and her pulse quickened, and she was thinking, *Oh! Oh! Oh!,* and she was looking around; she wanted to tell everybody, rush up to random people and spread the word that there was something really big going on. She felt as if the universe had signaled it was just about to make good on a promise. She got up, paced past carrels, through stacks, feeling simultaneously held and as though nothing could hold her, and all around her was magnitude, even—no, especially—in the infinitesimal, at the quantum level. She ran her fingers along spines of books, along rippling waves of paper and cloth, and wound up gazing over the railing down to the lobby, with its trompe-l'oeil 3-D spikes seeming to rise up from the floor. (Really, how was that supposed to deter suicides? The way they rose vertiginously to meet you halfway, weren't they actually inviting you to jump? Esker found her palms sweaty on the rail and pulled back.) And, thus duly sobered, with the initial *Oh!*s having worn off, she found her seat and picked up the article again, to try this time actually to understand it, and she couldn't, she couldn't follow any of the math. She was a math major and she couldn't begin to make the leap to understanding what was printed, put forth there on the page; it might've been voodoo, it might've been runes. Pleasure turned to ash in her mouth.

This was the sort of connection she longed to be privy to, longed to be able to recognize, and she couldn't, she wouldn't ever, she knew, be able to see and relate that fluidly. She'd kept waiting for it to happen, all these years of becoming a grown-up and studying hard, kept waiting for her blind and eager mind to rise up, to gain her access to that world of large understanding where nothing could ever be hyperbolic because everything is revealed in all its unfettered expansiveness. Her grades were good, her grades were always good, but what were they good *for?* This question had begun to needle at her, more so as the semesters wore on and she did not experience the illumination she'd never named but had always expected to occur.

And now here it was, at once in her hands and forever ungraspable. Honeybees and quantum math—somehow she'd supposed *she* would be allowed to stumble upon some similar noetic brilliance, some crystalline feat of comprehension, which was to have been her ticket out of her body, her ticket out of all that was small and damaged and damaging. But on that day she had to admit, finally, what she'd been suspecting. Her little mind had betrayed her. She was not and would never be a mathematician. It was as though she'd mistaken herself for someone else. Leaving small Delos, arriving someplace big enough to bear her, she ought to have expanded to her own full size. How cruel to grow big enough only to grasp what you are missing. Better to be Miss De Witt.

Though she had doubled up on courses and studied through the summer in order to earn her degree in four years in spite of her semester off, and though she would graduate in a matter of weeks cum laude, she was ultimately ashamed to pass herself off as a math major; she felt like a charletan, and for penance disallowed herself the fantasy of continuing someday in graduate school. She was lucky to find a teaching position at an independent school, which didn't require certification. She would begin in the fall.

Toward the end of that summer, Albert drove the battered white van he'd recently acquired over to the flat Esker had shared with three other students and helped her load her not substantial belongings into it, and they'd driven—what a hot day it had been, and no air conditioning, of course, in the van, and the air stagnant and swampy—slowly over to the West Side with the sad bulk of her things swaying and clunking behind them as they went over potholes—lousy shock absorbers, of course, in the van—and one of her pictures had broken, a poster-sized reproduction of the Julia set, which she'd framed; the glass had splintered in an intricate web, like a fractal layered over a fractal. She didn't try to salvage the poster, but left it out on the curb.

They'd been having sex all summer. They'd been having ice pops all summer on Albert's fire escape, vast quantities of them: they'd discovered an unusually sour brand of lime that they decided to be fanatical about. And they'd been having pleasantly stupid afternoons of reading the paper all spread out on the floor, and they'd been having sweaty, clean-smelling evenings at the Laundromat and nights of Esker-in-the-bath and Albert-reading-aloud-on-the-toilet, and Esker knew Albert was leaving to get married that fall, but she didn't believe it, because she knew he loved her: surely the one fact must cancel out the other.

Something had happened that summer, which was that she began to grow. Not *out* through her flesh; she'd already settled into what would be her unvarying body weight for years to come; or *up* through her skull; it wasn't the kind of breakthrough grasping of mathematical principles that she had longed for and anticipated for so many years. It was a growing *toward*. And it had everything to do with Albert. She had never imagined anything like this happening, had never wished for it, because she'd never imagined it. It was like a little miracle, a big miracle, and she thought of it concretely, in physical terms. She was growing toward him because she had stopped preventing herself from growing toward him; why this had happened was less clear to her. It might have had to do with faith, if she believed in faith, or hope. And all the while some distant garbled thing deep within her was issuing up what might have been a warning, but it made no sense, it was in a foreign language that had no currency in the light of what Esker had just discovered, which was how wonderful it felt to stop preventing oneself from growing toward someone. Albert didn't seem made out of paper at all; he seemed durable. Big enough. It was like being twenty-two and experiencing her first holiday ever.

And what they wrought began to look more exquisite to her than the Julia and Mandelbrot sets combined. The language she and Albert had invented was as fantastic as any theorem, as intricate as any proof. He knew when to notice her and when to pretend he didn't. He knew when to be tender and he knew when tenderness would have been the end of her, and then he knew to bring her round with little jokes at her expense until she'd rally and lash back. For her part, she knew when to let him talk on and on and when to tell him to shut up, and what question still needed to be asked when he'd thought he was all finished. They knew how to surprise each other. Their misunderstandings were more intimate than other people's understandings. When they had sex, Esker had visions: a broad, low tree dripping with fireflies; a billowing tapestry woven with mythical beasts; white birds zigzagging against a jagged cliff. Was this usual? She reported them to Albert afterward in whispers.

Esker had worn dresses all that summer, cheap flea-market dresses, in pretty cotton fabrics, one like buttercups, and one like an evening sky, and one a pale green printed with tiny brown mushrooms. Her hair got a little long, and her calves got brown and sturdy from the walking she did, alone and with Albert, all over the half-empty city. Even Albert got a little brown, but not very. She made him take off his shoes one day in Central

Park, and his feet were so long and white it made her absurdly sad. He asked what was the matter. She croaked out, "Your feet."

"Yes . . . ?"

"They're so white."

"So . . . ?"

"So I'm never going to see you again."

He considered this. "I wasn't aware you were a graduate of the Hans Christian Andersen School of Logic."

"I am, though." She had tears on her face, which she never had as a rule. In fact, it was the only time Albert ever saw her with them. He asked if he could borrow some money, and then he went over to a vendor and bought her scraped ice with mango syrup, just as if she were a little girl.

When she finished the ice, he borrowed some more money and had her sit for her portrait in charcoal. She didn't want to, but she was in a mode of letting herself be led. The portrait looked something like her, though less unhappy; the artist hadn't captured the day's forlorn quality at all. So the picture was a lie, and Esker didn't like it, and when Albert asked if he could have it to keep, it made her sullen but she wouldn't say why, and he got all bewildered and wounded, and the rest of the afternoon was tense with all their misguided efforts to console each other, although it also made them more tender with each other that night, and they fell asleep in Albert's bed like two animals, like a dog and a cat who are friends.

And the wind through the city all that summer was so warm, so lifting, and so near, so very like the temperature of her own skin.

And the buildings were so tall.

And the sirens so distant and constant.

And what was there to do but surrender, but give one's self up to the course of things unfolding?

But in the end she must have been too much to bear; her desire too large or misguided. It all broke up, and there were wounded. He delivered her to her new place in August and said goodbye—or, no, said, "I don't know about this," his voice all bent and squashed-sounding, and after he left she got up on the island of her bed, under pineapple tin, and she did not want to be welcomed anywhere, she only wanted to sleep and flee and flee.

23.

It's very sunny, the first Monday of the new year. Ann squints up at the iron bird over the entrance, and salutes it with two fingers. Boy Scouts' salute? Brownies'? Who knows. She is glad to be back at school, anyway, back in the real place where her life is, where it's waiting for her to come be in it. This, she feels, is where the real things happen, where they play out in the convergence of all the people she will someday think of as the ones who shaped her.

Ann's first day back at school, she is a minor celebrity, but extremely minor; her return gets a little bit lost in the mass return, since after all everyone has been away the past three weeks. If anything, she has slightly more celebrity status because of her mother's latest picture, released over the holidays, which a few of the kids seem to have seen. It's a period piece; Alice doesn't take off her clothes in this one, but her character gets TB and there's lots of coughing and jaundice. As far as Ann's concerned, is this good publicity or bad publicity? Hard to say. Anyway, not a few Prospect School kids have semifamous parents, so what comments she gets are pretty low-key, urbane, except from Buddy, who confesses, actually blushing, that he cried when Alice's character died.

"And how are your feet, by the way?"

"Oh. Fine. Thanks." It's not her feet, it's her calf muscles, and shin muscles (who knew you had shin muscles?), and tendons or ligaments or whatever those flexible, connective things were that had become less flexible during the weeks she had her casts on.

"So you're doing Winter Concert after all?"

It's after school and they're in the Big Room, Ann and a few other students and Buddy with his clipboard and the fountain pen he wears on an orange silk cord around his neck, waiting for the other participants to show up. Most of the kids already there are hanging out on the floor, lounging against their knapsacks, or lying on their backs with their feet up on the bleachers. Buddy is squatting in front of Ann, the pen going like a pendulum. It's very gym-teachery, thinks Ann, or would be if it were a whistle. Buddy is the least likely gym teacher she could imagine, which makes her smile inappropriately. "What? Oh. I'm not in the dance anymore. I'm supposed to be doing something with Malcolm and Hannah." She says this nonchalantly, but even so gets a wild flipping in her gut, and is it her imagination or do the few other students within earshot seem interested, impressed?

Buddy consults his clipboard. "Do I have this down? What's it called?"

Ann shrugs. "Ask her." She points at Hannah, who has just come in and now slings her behemoth book-bag to the floor. She is wearing a black turtleneck and green fatigues, and her lips are as red as the Red Queen's lips, and her eyes are rimmed in kohl.

"Ask me what?"

"What's the thing called that we're doing?"

"I don't know, you have to ask Malcolm. You have us down, Buddy. I'm positive." She takes his clipboard with offhand imperiousness and locates it. "Choy and Stolarik, right there."

Buddy unscrews his pen from its cap, takes the clipboard back, and writes, saying out loud, "Ampersand James." He screws the pen back on. "Okay, but I need a title soon for the program."

"Aye-aye, Cap'n." Hannah clicks her heels like a good fascist.

"It's called 'Burning Down the House,'" says Ann, but softly, to Buddy's receding back.

Hannah whacks her shoulder. "So," she says, flopping down beside Ann, "how do you feel?"

"Ow." Ann rubs her shoulder.

"Wimp. I mean your feet."

"Oh, my aching feet."

"Wimp." Hannah picks up one of Ann's feet, pulls it into her lap, takes off the sneaker, and begins massaging. Ann lies back against her knapsack. Slowly her foot becomes fluid, viscous, coursing, tree sap. One foot, then the other. Hannah's hands seem like they belong to at least a thirty-year-old; they are that confident, that seasoned. Ann closes her eyes. When she is thirty, will she have more heft? More force of gravity, more force, less flight? Thirty sounds so old. Throat-raspy old, sexy-wise-lines-around-your-eyes-when-you-smile old. Complicated, robust old. Robust like coffee, black and gritty. Un-self-conscious, because . . . because you're old, you're thirty, you've been here, the world knows you. Ann tries to come face to face with her future self, but her future self refuses to be conjured, that enviable imp, evasive, teasing, full of secrets she won't share. All that swims into vision is her mother's portrait, painted when *she* was thirty, suitably complicated and robust with its bold oils and bits of cloth jumbled together to yield, to partially yield, that face.

"Hey, Sleeping Beauty!" Denise's voice.

"She looks so peaceful when she's sleeping." Lamika, one of the fandance girls.

"She's not sleeping." Hannah, of course.

But she is, in a way. Not sleeping, floating. She doesn't have to work not to crack a smile. Most of her is elsewhere. Nuncio once told her about something called lucid dreaming, or, no, it was astral projection. He said it was something you could actually practice. "First just go somewhere nearby. Like try getting to your bedroom door." She never tried it. It sounded not real, more like one of his acting-class exercises. But she feels like she gets it now; it seems totally plausible, totally likely. Up, up she goes. Over the bleachers, way up to the light fixtures, dusty and distant, high over the others, the others with their sad, broken lives. She is not of it. She is peace. She is floating, casting some kind, beneficent rays down upon the rooted, the hurt bodies below.

She tries astrally projecting her body farther, venturing toward the Big Room door and into the hall, but stops, stumped: what's the view from the Big Room doorway? Do the lockers start right away, or does the water fountain come first? And can you see the top of the stairs, or not until you've gone down the hall a bit?

"Yo, Sauce." Hannah dumps Ann's foot off her lap and Ann opens her eyes. She never got off the ground. It's one of those moments like in the doctor's office: an ambush of tears and sobs from nowhere, except this time she manages to swallow them back before they erupt. Control, a tenuous control. Under her fingers, which she touches to her chest, her heart is racing. Her skin feels full, like the moon, like a balloon, expanding.

"Are you okay? You're all red. What happened?" asks Denise, squatting down, peering in. "Did you see that? She just turned like a lobster. What's the matter?"

"My baby brother used to do that right when he's going to throw up," says Lamika. She fans Ann's face with a pleated piece of looseleaf, a rehearsal prop for their dance.

"You going to puke, Ann?"

"Give her your purse."

"Get the fuck away!"

"Not to puke in, you retard, to hyperventilate in."

"You mean to *not* hyperventilate in. Retard." So she's saved, they're laughing, making a joke of it, a dance of it. She marvels; so quickly they act, Lamika and Denise, they know just what to do: a little weird moment becomes a two-step, a shimmy and a shake, no fear, it's swirled up in silvery speed, in the quick-coined insult, fast footwork, dazzle.

"Oh, go stick your head in your purse," says Denise, and snaps her head down with satisfied finality.

"What's going on?" It's Malcolm, towering beautifully above, a conga under each arm.

"Nothing. Ann just had a little mild heart attack."

"I hope not," he says.

"Uh, Buddy, we need another ambulan— Ow!" Denise rubs her shoulder.

"Fool."

"Hannah's hitting everybody today."

Malcolm sits on the floor among them. His drums make small beautiful throat-sounds when he sets them down, gently. Ann lets herself look at a small portion of him. His arm. The elephant's-hair bracelet black around his brown, hairless wrist. How could his wrist be that hairless? He has less hair on his arms than she does. She imagines him waxing. Blasphemous. Banish the thought. He is her imaginary boyfriend. She would like to lick his wrist. She imagines she does. He tastes smooth and faintly woody, like a clarinet reed.

Buddy has been trying to get their attention and they give it to him, finally, the thirty-odd of them gathered here on the Big Room floor, having by now arranged themselves in a pattern suggestive of a narcoleptics' orgy: lots of limbs overlapping, bodies tilted this way and that in positions of languor, prone, splayed, stretched, collapsed. Somebody plays with somebody else's hair; somebody draws on somebody else's sneaker. In the silence they have finally granted Buddy, somebody yawns operatically.

"People," says Buddy, sounding exasperated and fond. He always calls them "people." He's such a teacher. "You've just been on vacation. What did you all do over the break? The triathlon?"

"Decathlon," comes the obligatory response, from a senior boy in the back.

"Okay, I have the order of acts posted by the door. If anybody has a major concern when you read the list, and, I should add, an actual reason for concern, see me no later than the end of today. There's still a little time to juggle acts, but I need a final version ASAP."

"Who's doing a juggling act? That's so lame."

"It is not lame."

"Not if you're juggling, like, chainsaws."

"Who's juggling chainsaws? Is that allowed?"

"Would you guys shut up? He didn't even say that."

"Now, mime. That would be lame."

"Shut *up*."

It goes on like this, all sort of silly and sweet and stupid, Buddy self-important with his clipboard and dangling fountain pen, the kids smart-assed and irreverent, teacher and students humoring each other until finally it's time to break up and rehearse individual acts. Malcolm and his congas get dibsed by Denise and Lamika and the other fan dancers, so he and Hannah and Ann make plans to rehearse their act at Hannah's half-sister's apartment Wednesday night.

In the hallway outside the Big Room, Ann and Hannah see Esker winding her dun scarf around and around her neck, briefcase weighing down her other arm, a comic figure. Ann says hi, and Esker startles and says hi back, sort of blinking, not actually blinking, but giving the impression of blinking. It's the first time in a month that they've seen each other on school grounds. Then Ann says, Well, bye, and so Esker says bye, and goes, and then Hannah turns to Ann and says, "Why are you blushing?"

"I'm not blushing."

"You are *so* blushing."

"Not. Go wait in the car."

They walk toward their lockers.

"I'm not saying she's not hot . . ." says Hannah.

"Fuck you, shut up. Idiot. What? Why do you have that look?"

"I'm not the one with the look. Are you having another mild heart attack?"

"Shut up!" And then, to clear Hannah's head of whatever speculations she's got brewing, Ann lowers her voice and says, aware as she does that she probably should not, "Esker and my father are kind of dating."

24.

So Wally thinks, Enough of this, enough of delicacy and indecision, enough of eliding and eluding, and he takes the train to Chambers Street and walks all those cold, blowing blocks over the frozen grit gone black along the curbs with an almost angry determination, as if he had some right to show up unannounced, and he does, doesn't he, being a person after all, with a heart and a voice and things to say and a life to live, a life that he's in the middle of living, and which is, as they say and he is beginning to understand for himself, short. So. He walks fast up Greenwich, steering clear of patches of black ice, which reveal themselves garishly just as he approaches, reflecting neon signs and traffic lights.

He knocks on her door, mindful this time of striking the wood, not the glass, and exactly in that moment his resolve shrinks. Just like that. Goes from mighty to meager. It's Monday night. For him the weekend, Game being closed on Monday and Tuesday nights during the winter, but for her, he realizes, oh yeah, for her a school night, and her first day back besides. She'll be displeased when she comes to the door. She doesn't come to the door. He can see a light, but some people leave a light on when they're out, but why would she be out on a school night and her first day back besides? And who lives in New York without a buzzer?

He goes to the corner, where a neon shamrock heralds, he guesses, a bar? Yes. A décorless bar, neither shabby nor chic but really, truly, almost Zen-like in its lack of appointments. The interior is actually a degree darker than the streetcorner outside, under its pinkish streetlamp. A black curtain hangs just inside the doorway, to cut down on drafts, presumably, but it seems to suck up light, too, sealing stray bits of street light from the entryway. It's the kind of place Alice would never set foot in. The few people drinking are mostly men, middle-aged, overcoated. There's no music and no TV, but a sportscast is emanating from a radio behind the bar, and it seems possible that everyone's tuned in very intently, and equally possible that no one's paying any attention at all. Wally feels like he's stepped into an allegory. "Got a phone?" he asks. There's no pay phone, but Wally does a bit of explaining and the bartender, a looming, burly, bald guy (of course), slides the regular phone across the bar, then watches while he dials (making sure it stays local, Wally supposes, but envisions a fleeting scenario involving the guy's memorizing the dialing pattern upside down and then embarking on a campaign of harassment that leads to Esker's changing her number, changing her locks, coming home to find gifts of small dead animals on her doorstep . . .).

"Hello?"

"Esker?"

"Yes?"

"It's Wallace James." Why so formal? "I wanted to talk with you."

"Okay."

"I wanted to also see you. While talking with you."

"Oh. Oh, now? Where are you?"

To the bartender: "What's the name of this place?"

"Black Pete's."

"Black Pete's."

"What's Black Pete's?"

"The bar on the corner of your street."

"Really? I never knew it had a name. You're on the corner of my street? Are you asking me to meet you at a bar?"

"No. I just came here to use the phone. Some people don't have buzzers. I'll come back over, okay?"

"No," she says. "No, I'll come there." She hangs up. He has the impression she's amused. Better amused than displeased. Maybe.

He gets a draft and sits. Another middle-aged man in an overcoat. There is nothing to look at, not even a Heimlich-maneuver poster, not even a coaster. The lug of a bartender is polishing pint glasses slowly, with no affect but somehow all of his heart. The other patrons are all either listening or not listening to the rhythmic rise and fall of the sportscast. It's like a bar you'd find along some county road up near Grange Hill in a weatherbeaten wood-frame building. Or in some nondescript developing nation. Or an Ionesco play. Black Pete's, Black Peter, isn't that what Danish kids call Santa Claus? But the shamrock would be Irish. Then someone in the corner behind him—it's so dark inside, Wally failed to notice any life forms in that vicinity—begins to play the accordion. Eastern Europe, then. Or a peasant village in the Alps. Or a David Lynch movie. The game would be more fun if Esker were here. He checks his watch but finds his wrist bare. Quick panic: could it have been removed from his person without his noticing? The bar is actually a den of thieves, a meeting spot for a band of cons, secretly sly and nimble under their burdened, oblivious postures. But no: he left it on his dresser top after showering, which he did before he came, a late-Monday-afternoon shower, not his usual routine, and thus the forgetting to include his watch when he put the rest of his clothes back on.

The truth is, he left home in a rush. Once he decided where to go, it had seemed important not to lose momentum. Also, he lied to Ann about where he was going. Ridiculous. He doesn't do that, but he did, told her he had to meet with a potential new supplier, and then left before she could ask why he'd showered for it. He thinks he lied kind of altruistically, protectively: why should Ann have to bother herself with thoughts about her father and her math teacher's ambiguous, dubious relationship? She has enough on her plate, with the mathski and Winter Concert and physical therapy and being a teenager and everything. But Wally isn't utterly dimwitted about the fact that he was mostly protecting himself.

The accordion music is oddly spellbinding. If this were an allegory, what would the accordion represent? He drinks his darkish beer at a tippy little table, and the music makes him a peasant or a Gypsy with his barrel chest and broad knuckles; he's a farmer, of what? Cabbages. Bulgur. Sorghum. No—he works with horses, he is a horse trader, he pulls back their lips to check their teeth, he holds their hooves upturned between his knees to see whether they are properly shod, he runs expert fingers over their long, flickering muscles and tendons, he carries sugar cubes in his pocket, his secret stash. Or he is a baker, with a coating of flour always upon him like ash, all day long reaching into the oven with a long wooden peel, kneading dough with his thick fists, shaping the daily loaves round and oblong, and the braided loaves for Sundays, and the more exotic, exquisite ones he molds privately after hours, loaves in the shapes of fish and stars, mandolins and angels and women . . .

Is he drunk? He's only had one pint. Probably at Black Pete's they slip something into the drinks. He's not sure whether he phoned Esker ten minutes ago or forty. He is watching the accordion player. Why is there an accordion player? The accordion player looks up and smiles at him. Too surreal. Wally is going to have to leave. He stands up, and there's Esker in the doorway, the black curtain swaying, a thin column of pink street-light leaking in behind her. She comes and sits at his little table, and he sits back down. She hasn't bothered with a coat, she's just run over and is a little rosy and breathless with the cold. She is something else, too, something he never would have expected. Jaunty.

"Hello. I'm in person," she says.

No response.

"Hello. I've met you in a bar," she says.

Nothing.

"Hello. I'm Esker. You called me. There's somebody playing the accordion behind you. What a weird place." She looks over each shoulder. "What a weird place. What are you drinking? Beer?" She gets up and goes to the bar and comes back with two bottles, no glasses. "What did you want to say to me?"

"You're jaunty this evening."

"I cleaned my basement out!"

He lifts his glass. "Whatever gets you going."

She laughs. "What did you want to say to me?"

He searches, comes up empty. "I don't know exactly."

"Slipped your mind."

She's teasing him. Enjoying herself.

The best defense is a good offense: Coach MacPharland, junior-year varsity football. He ribs back. "That must have been some basement."

"Oh, it was."

"Buried treasure? A lost Picasso. Revolutionary War documents."

"You've been watching too much *Antiques Road Show.*"

"What, then?"

"It's what I didn't find."

"Rats?"

"No, actually, I did find those. Or mouse droppings, anyway. I thought I had a ghost. And I—don't."

"You don't."

"I think it was just me."

"You've been haunting yourself?"

She nods, once, almost imperceptibly, as if serious.

"How? Sheets? Rattling chains? Ooooooooh . . ." He makes sound whistle across the top of his beer bottle.

She laughs again. "Never mind. That's not what you took a cab all the way over here on a Monday night to discuss."

"I took the subway."

"I stand corrected. I thought you were a fancy restaurateur."

"I hate that word."

"Well, *that's* a relief."

She's just wearing some kind of sweater over another sweater and pants, and her hair as usual is quite styleless, but she's glowing, somehow, her eyes are like liquid and her spine is straight and pressed forward, her elbows planted unabashedly on the little tabletop; she is self-possessed. And unrelenting.

"What *did* you come all the way over here on a Monday night for, anyway?"

"To talk with you."

Eyebrows up: *So talk.*

So talk. Right. "Well." He rubs his chin. Okay. "I think you're maddening. I think you're difficult and I like you, possibly, and I get the feeling you're going to bolt, or you've bolted. Except not tonight, you've kind of messed up what I wanted to say, because you don't seem remotely bolt-inclined tonight. So I'm flummoxed." He says this last word in quotes, a little ironic protective device.

"I like you, too, possibly."

"All right, then." Then, less combative-sounding: "I see."

And they sip a little, privately, at their beers, and look elsewhere than at each other, and listen to the accordion player, who carries on with his very Old World mix of suffering and gaiety, neither of them knowing now exactly the next step, but Wally acknowledging to himself that it is no longer possible to wear his happiness lightly. It's become more like an anvil. On a rope around his neck. He feels stumbling, bumbling, not without dread.

25.

"*E*sker, may I see you when you have a chance?" It's Florence, sticking her head inside the math-office door. She's got her fund-raising smile on, bright and practiced. Esker figures this is in regard to that development-initiative memo she never got around to answering before vacation—why bother trying to recruit her? Florence knows she'll demur—and replies she'll come down after B-block. Esker has little use for the headmistress, who, as Esker's heard her describe it on more than one occasion, came over into the world of education and human service last year after a long career in the world of high finance because she wanted to "give something back." She prides herself on her natural rapport with the students, which, Esker begrudgingly admits, seems genuine. She's well coiffed—a consummate shade of blond chosen on the basis, Esker imagines, of expert consultation and lengthy deliberation—and well dressed—today in a rather cutting-edge pink-and-fuchsia wool plaid suit—not to mention well connected; thanks to her, the school's endowment now exists in more than token fashion. Ordinarily, Esker's manner toward Florence is just barely shy of rude, but this morning she's in such a good mood that she smiles, even warmly, at her boss, who, Esker thinks, does after all have an earnest, generous heart, and adds, "I won't forget!"—a sort of jab at herself, since she routinely forgets to keep appointments with Florence or to respond to her various little memoranda.

Florence leaves, and Rhada, marking papers with her feet in striped tights up on the slurpy radiator, mutters, "Wear much perfume?" and fans in front of her nose. But Esker doesn't even mind it, today she even almost likes the lingering scent of whatever expensive fragrance the head-mistress feels the need to use, and she only smiles, rather gently, at Rhada, who then demands, getting her Clara Bow eyebrows into full arch, "What's the matter with *you*?"

What's the matter with Esker is she's happy. Baskingly, destabilizingly happy.

In Black Pete's last night, it had gotten progressively stranger, with the dour huddle at the bar increasing as the hour wore on, more men in dark coats drifting in to slump on their stools; the accordion continuing its densely woven music, merry and plaintive, around them; the bartender like some gruff guru drawing and dispensing the beers; and then Wally, over the music, had tried to tell her something about the bar's being an al-legory, and had asked her, if her life were an allegory, what did she think he'd represent, something like that, she hadn't quite made out his words, he'd also said something about horse trading, and baking bread in the shapes of objects, she thought, and then he'd gotten suddenly absolutely pale, even in the assertively dim light of Black Pete's she could see the drama of it, the rapidity with which his face drained of color, the way people say, "He turned white as a sheet," which brought to mind the other cliché, which before she thought about it was out of her mouth, "You look as if you've seen a ghost," and as soon as she said this it filled her with sorrow, an actual slow-seeping ache, like a cold fluid, through her body: her, her! As if she'd painfully named herself aloud. Don't let him see this in her, don't let him see her for a ghost.

He had bolted from the table and toward the entrance, even causing some of the somnolent patrons to look over their shoulders, where he pushed aside the curtain, exiting in a rush of cold air—

And she thought, *I've broken it. I broke it. How did I?* But really she knew, she'd been too much, it was too much to bear, seeing her here, hav-ing her sprint across the street and arriving too jaunty, too free and pleased and ghostless. Too solid and heavy for the paper-thin-ness of life, for their rice-paper connection; she had crushed it; it had crumpled under the full burden of her living weight. As she'd known it would. As she'd al-ways known it would.

But then, grabbing his coat and his funny furry Russian hat, she'd followed him outside, and there he was just getting sick, that's all, retching at the curb. After a moment she stepped up and held his forehead for him. It was burning hot. He heaved a while more.

"You have a fever," she said, after he'd stopped.

"I was afraid you'd think I just couldn't handle my alcohol."

"Yeah. Lightweight."

She helped him across the street, both of them shivering hard by the time they got to her apartment ("It opens so easily for you," he'd kind of marveled, weakly, when she turned her key in the door), and into the bathroom, where he stayed for twenty minutes before she knocked, and called his name, and then pushed the door open, and there he was asleep with his grayish face on the tiny ceramic tiles. She roused him enough to get aspirin into him, and the tiniest bit of chamomile tea before he balked, and then she'd tucked him into her bed in all his clothes but his shoes, which seemed awfully uncomfortable (she did at least want to take off his belt), but she wasn't about to presume. "Sorry, sorry," he kept saying. "I never get sick."

"I can see that."

"Sorry."

"All right, stop that." Esker sat on the floor beside the bed. He lay on his back, his eyes closed. "What about Ann?"

"She'll be sleeping, I don't want to wake her. I'll get up and go home in an hour."

"Sure thing, Attila."

"Or call in the morning."

"You think we need to get you to the hospital or anything?"

"No. I actually feel a little better now." His eyes still closed.

"Do you need anything? Bucket beside you?"

"I'm in your bed!" He lurched up.

She nodded mildly. "You're sick."

He looked for information in her face.

"There's a couch," said Esker. She rose. "There'll be lukewarm tea beside you when you wake up again. Try to drink some."

"I'm so s—" He checked himself, changed it to, "Thank you," and lay down heavily again. A commanding sound from one of the wooden rails that ran under the mattress: not an actual splitting, perhaps, but more than a creak. "I'm always breaking things . . ." he sighed, already half asleep.

"But that's *my* job," whispered Esker. Though she almost could stop believing it. She sank back down on the floor and stayed in the room awhile, not as Florence Nightingale but for her own pleasure, because she seemed to need to listen to his breath, to look at him, sick and peaceful and large in her bed, with her clean covers upon his body, the pineapple-tin ceiling above them both. She dozed, eventually, her head against the wall, and when she opened her eyes his were open, too, and on her. "Where are you going?" he whispered. She thought and thought and had no idea what he meant. Maybe it was the fever. "Nowhere," she said. Then they both fell back asleep, and the next time she woke it was after midnight. She felt his forehead: better. She took off some of her clothes and put herself to bed on the couch.

In the morning, he'd been gone. In the kitchen, on the dark wooden table, this took her breath: he had spelled out her name with spoons.

After B-block, Esker makes her way down the curving staircase to Florence's office, in part of what was once the parlor, so there is a black-and-green marble fireplace behind her desk, and the original brass sconces on either side, refitted now for electric lights. Florence is forever pointing out the restored period details to visitors, so that Esker can hardly walk into her office without hearing in her mind, in Florence's cadences, the guided tour. The Renovation Committee, Florence's pet project, will draw its inspiration from this room. Florence is at her desk, busy with a Mont Blanc fountain pen.

After a moment, Esker knocks on the doorframe. "So what's up?" she asks, trying not to sound brusque. The uncharacteristic burst of tolerance she'd felt for Florence earlier, from the comfortable remove of the math office, is fading fast in the headmistress's actual fastidious lair.

"Oh, Esker." Florence looks up. "Please come in, please have a seat." And then, "Oh, please close the door behind you."

Esker does, gritting her teeth. The airs! She imagines Florence relishes any opportunity to say it.

"You had a good holiday, I trust?"

Esker laughs. "Why do you trust?"

But it fails as humor; Florence looks unnerved.

"It was fine, thanks."

"Good. I'll come right to the point. It has come to my attention that you may have become romantically involved with the parent of a student."

Collapsing, crushing silence.

"Excuse me?"

"Of course, there is no official prohibition on friendships between faculty members and the family members of current students. However, as the senior administrator of this institution, I am responsible for considering the possible adverse ramifications of such a relationship on the well-being of the institution."

Careful, Esker, she cautions herself. Her heart is slamming around inside. She chooses the driest words she can find. "How exactly do you envision a legal, consensual adult 'relationship' might have any 'adverse ramifications' on the well-being of the 'institution'?" Careful, Esker. Stay civil.

"We have to consider, for one, the fact that the parent in question is married."

Floods of hot and cold coursing beneath her skin. Married! Does Florence even realize the terms of their marriage? But again: Careful, don't address it. She wants to rise from her chair and walk out. She wants to take the millefiori paperweight from Florence's desk and send it through the window. Who has been talking to Florence? Not Ann. One of Ann's friends? Some parent? Alice? Has Alice Evers placed a call from her film set? Is Florence thinking about the publicity factor as related to Alice Evers alone, with her demicelebrity status? Or might Alice be in tight with any of the school's larger donors? One of the trustees? Has a trustee placed a call directly? And what might anyone have said? *Is* she romantically involved with Wally? What does that even mean? *Romantically involved.* How do you parse it? What counts? Leaving her appointment book on his coffee table? Eating gelato on Broome Street? Holding his forehead while he throws up? They did kiss, it is true, inescapably. . . . But! She is furious, her mind sputtering in protest, even to be made to go through the exercise of analyzing it, the events and terminology, for Florence's sake, when it's nothing she would do on her own. Who is Florence? Who is this woman in her champagne perm and fuchsia plaid, looking a bit sad as she sits there with her Mont Blanc mini-sceptre, proud but weary guardian of institutional standards and well-being?

"I can see you're upset."

"Florence. I think I need you to help me understand better what is upsetting *you*. Have you been made aware of any concrete harm likely to come to the school as a result of a possible liaison between a parent and teacher?" Anger catapults her speech to a more formal register. But her voice is shaking. Can Florence hear it?

"I can certainly envision concrete, damaging repercussions resulting from public knowledge of a liaison between a married parent and his child's current teacher."

She wants to object to this repeated use of the word "married." *Don't get sidetracked,* she warns herself. *Focus. Don't let that become the issue.* "That's not what I'm asking you." Esker sighs. "It's a little difficult for me to address your concerns without knowing what information, precisely, has been passed on to you, accurately or inaccurately, and without being made aware of its source."

Now Florence sighs, and looks down heavily.

Oh, what an act, thinks Esker, and she hates everything about it, the stilted language, the strategic way she is calculating her own responses, the way they are sitting, the distribution of power: the executive fronted by the fortress of her desk and backed by green-and-black marble, streaky as a fine steak; the employee in her slighter chair, adrift in the middle of this genteel office, which broadcasts a kind of superior claim to morality and righteousness—but of *course*: people installed in offices like this are inherently more fit to interpret ethical guidelines, are by natural law better able to discern, and more likely to protect, the best interests of the community!

"Look, Florence. It's difficult for me to respond specifically when your question is so vague. Basically: who told you what?"

Florence looks up, pained. Oh, how delicate is the skin around her eyes! Oh, how sympathetically pursed the rose-painted lips! "Yesterday afternoon a faculty member overheard Ann James telling another student, in the hallway, that you and her father are dating."

"I see." Esker sits back in the chair and folds her arms across her chest. She feels relieved, as well as annoyed that Florence is wasting her time when she could be preparing for D-block. "This is the whole basis for your concern?"

"Can you tell me whether this is true?"

How much should she say? As little as possible. "I don't know, Florence. I haven't used the word 'dating' since . . . I'm not sure I've ever used the word 'dating,' and I won't presume to guess what your definition of the term would be." Ann said "dating"? Esker wonders if Wally called it that. Now that she knows the relatively innocuous source of Florence's concern, she feels willing to elaborate a little, let Florence feel she's successfully ferreted something out. "I have seen Mr. James on a few occasions outside of school grounds, during which times we have discussed his daughter, my student, as well as other subjects. One of these conversations took place in a café." There. That's the truth. Now Esker can get back to prepping for D-block.

But she has miscalculated somehow, badly. Florence, who ought now to excuse her from this ludicrous interrogation with a little apology about the inappropriateness of having put Esker through it at all, instead folds her hands on her desk and leans forward. Gone are any affectations of sympathy. Esker has a swift, startling image of her removing from the top drawer a revolver and placing it heavily on the desk as preface to her next utterance. "Here are the facts I have to deal with. At least three people in the school community, excluding ourselves, have information that you are romantically linked to the married parent of one of your students. Given the nature of the institution, it is reasonable to assume that that number will grow, if it hasn't already. It is reasonable to assume that this information may come to the attention of members of the broader school community, including benefactors. This ... situation is, yes, largely about perception. Unfortunately, perception matters—is virtually all that matters—in the public arena. In the private arena, too, I would say, but that is not my concern. If I do nothing to address the impropriety, I will be perceived to be condoning it. Such an event, even in this day and age, is likely to reflect badly on the school's reputation, and to impact unfavorably on the school's well-being." Florence pauses and picks up her pen again; Esker's mind transposes the image into the headmistress stroking her gun. "You should know, in the interest of full disclosure, that I have concerns about your commitedness to the school community which predate this development. While your performance in the classroom, as I understand it, is satisfactory, your participation in the full range of faculty responsibilities is, frankly, not up to par. As indicated"—she peruses the open file on her desk—"in your performance review last May."

Esker exhales slowly. Perhaps it sounds like a sigh. Somewhere, dimly, she realizes the sound might come across as insubordinate. She is outraged. That performance review had been Florence's and the dean's show of sulking when Esker had declined to sign up for any of the capital-endowment initiatives implemented last spring. "As I recall, faculty participation on fund-raising committees was voluntary."

Florence closes the file, lays a heavy hand on it, gazes upon Esker with imperial might. "There is the letter of the law. And there is the spirit of the law. And a private-school community is one that functions best with a team that embraces and champions the spirit of the place."

The law? The spirit? Team champions? What the hell is she talking about? It is beyond Esker, who really tries, who concentrates actively, on not smirking.

"I will be talking with a few people in the next day or so regarding the best way to proceed with this. And I ask you, in the meantime, to weigh whether you are truly happy in your position here at The Prospect School. Is there anything you would like to add at this point?"

Esker can see her own blouse moving, faintly, in rhythm with her furiously pounding heart. "Simply that I find it interesting that you have at no point spoken of the well-being of the student."

Florence clears her throat. "Of course, that is another consideration uppermost in my mind."

26.

The idea of him is one thing, and the him of him another. Not better, not worse, but unavoidably another, and Ann can't help feeling inconvenienced at having to deal with it. With him.

Let alone Hannah, kind of leering at them. Waggling her eyebrows. Of course she's not, not really, but Ann suspects she is inside.

It's Wednesday, late afternoon, more like evening, sort of; well, who knows? The sun's down, but in winter how much does that mean? She's lost track of the time.

Hannah's half-sister's apartment is great. It's on Carroll Street, just a few blocks from school, and it's tiny but real: grown-up, hip, all that. Hannah's half-sister is a something or other on Wall Street, but she's constantly taking these monthlong vacations to Europe and Southeast Asia and everything, and she's a photographer, too, and there's all these black-and-white framed prints hung everywhere, and exposed brick, and unusual utensils hanging from hooks and sticking out of gorgeous ceramic bowls in the kitchen. "What's this?" asks Ann, twirling something long and silver and spiral. "Some kind of corkscrew?"

"A pasta server," guesses Malcolm, and they have to make fun of him for a while: "*Pasta* server? Yeah. How would *that* work?"

"I think it's a beater attachment," says Hannah.

Malcolm has extracted another long silver thing—cake slicer?—and he and Ann are having a little swordfight: *clish! clash! ching!* They're sitting on stools pulled up to the counter of the galley kitchen, where they've been snacking on what they could find in the fridge: olives, baby carrots, salsa.

"How about I start reciting from the dictionary *before* Ann lights the first match, and then I just drop it, like thud on the floor, and start going into free verse?" says Hannah.

"You have to do something besides drop it," suggests Malcolm.

"No, dropping is good: thud!" Ann kicks the counter for effect. "And then the congas start."

Malcolm cocks his head: maybe?

"Too forced," says Hannah.

Ann shrugs. She really has no idea what the piece is about, but is perfectly unbothered by this. She thinks it's a given the audience won't, either. Who cares? What a lark! Something beatnik with seniors! And she's a spirit on a ladder with fire, it suits her, it suits her, she'll take the part. She holds the spiral kitchen utensil like a handlebar mustache over her lip. "You must pay the rent"—now placing it like a hair ribbon—"I can't pay the rent! / You must pay the rent / I can't pay the rent!"

Malcolm places his cake slicer horizontally at his Adam's apple. "*I'll* pay the rent."

"My hero! / Curses, foiled again."

"Focus, people," says Hannah, and yawns. "Oh man, I need some real food. Are we doing this, for real? You guys want to stay and eat pizza and really get this figured out?"

"Yeah."

"Sure."

Hannah collects some bills from the other two, and their preferences for toppings, and shrugs on her heavy black leather jacket and goes out. Strategic, thinks Ann, the moment the door closes behind her. She and Malcolm are left. Two. And what happens now? Something unmistakable and concrete? Like do they make statements about digging each other, and then, like, kiss? Is it going to be like that? Horrible, yuck, she hopes not. But neither does she hope for nothing to happen. But what? She can't imagine, can't conceive. She makes her way around the apartment, switching on lights.

Now that she's alone with Malcolm, she can't think of a single thing to say, so naturally she begins to talk: "I love this apartment. Isn't it strange to think of having an apartment and being a grown-up? I mean strange because it's, like, probably going to happen, like not that long from now, either. I mean as opposed to dreaming of other things that'll probably never happen. In a way that's less strange. I hate white walls. They're so respectable. So doctor's-office. I want, like, a tomato vestibule, and a marigold living room. And a dove-gray bedroom. What's dove gray, like a pigeon?" She stops herself, with effort. She has turned on every possible lamp.

Hannah's half-sister's photographs are illuminated all over the walls like silent, stirring portals: a bazaar; some ruins; bananas and firewood on a donkey's back; black girls in white dresses, twirling. Ann wants to jump, but into which one? She and Malcolm fall to perusing them like a couple of strangers in an art gallery. Or like a couple of friends who know each other so well they don't need to look at the pictures together. There's a pale, long-haired dog on its hind legs, its front paws on the arm of an old shepherd in a windy pasture. "The dog looks like an angel," murmurs Malcolm.

Ann comes to his side to see what he means. It doesn't have any wings, but, yes, he's exactly right. "So does the laundry," she says. Another picture: endless white laundry hung in an alley. "A whole flock of angels. Flock?"

"A bevy," suggests Malcolm.

"A gaggle."

"A gaggle of angels." He tests it. He is so mild, he flirts without flirting. He's not flirting. He's being. Will he kiss her now? Will she kiss him? She doesn't want to. She hopes not. Hannah will be disappointed. Too bad. She wants Hannah to come back and be there with them, with the pizza; they can all sit around the steamer trunk Hannah's half-sister uses for a coffee table and eat pizza and be a triangle, amused, linked, chaste.

"Flights," says Malcolm.

"What?"

"It's 'flights of angels.' 'And flights of angels something-something to thy rest.' Right? When Hamlet dies."

"Oh," says Ann, impressed and peeved. "I wasn't trying to think of *that.*"

They have drifted toward the front of the narrow apartment and wind up sitting on the accordion radiator in front of one of the two long windows looking down on Carroll Street. It's snowing again, barely, silver glitter falling around the gas lamps. It's like one of the photographs, only living. Below them: a dog walker. A creeping taxi, searching for an address. Someone who drops her keys, and Ann can hear the sound of the keys hitting the sidewalk, tiny, a miniature sound but perfect, all the way up two flights and through the windowpane. Malcolm huffs on the glass and draws a tic-tac-toe board. Ann goes first. X. He has O's. It's a tie. This has nothing to do with their bodies, with sex. It's all apart. She has no notion of how people go from this to that. It's like a map with a great chunk torn out of the middle. She has no idea. He huffs again on the glass, his breath, the personal object of his breath, condenses into fog, springs into minuscule beads of moisture on the pane, and he draws again with his long blunt finger, and this time he goes first, but he sticks with O's, the letter she in effect assigned him, and she is thinking, How does this become touch, become sex? Not wanting it to, fearing the prospect, loathing it, but thinking it's expected, it's natural, it's culture, it's biology, whatever, something, but isn't it coming, doesn't it have to, isn't there no choice?

"You go."

But now that she's thinking about it, now that she's swept up and tumbled in one of those rolling waves of heightened self-consciousness, she can't bring herself, can't permit herself, to touch the glistening dew of his breath.

"Forfeit." He draws two more O's and a line through the row before wiping it clean with his sleeve.

Ann falls off the radiator.

"Whoa," says Malcolm. He reaches down and they clasp wrists and he pulls her to her feet. "Sit much?"

She laughs. Instead of being embarrassed, she's mock-embarrassed: really it's charming that she fell off the radiator, really it's adorable and funny of her. She is not clear about whether or not she really fell. Did she just will it? How else to account for it? No one falls from a sitting position for no reason, do they? She sits on the couch. She will have a giant hip-bruise in the morning. She's a little worried. And mapless. Where's Hannah? Where's the compass? Should she jump anyway? Should she fall into it? Maybe that's what everyone else does, maybe nobody ever has a map, that's the open secret, they just embark with more confidence. Maybe the trick is you're supposed to pretend you know the way. But the bread-crumbs, where are the breadcrumbs? Eaten. Gobbled up. By flights of wild, bestial angels. Hello hello hello. Wake up, Ann, he's speaking.

Malcolm has asked, "You know what I want to paint?"

She shakes her head. She is reminded that she doesn't know anything about him.

"The beach."

What?

"I've had this idea for a while now, this project, of figuring out a tech-nique for painting sand, like gigantic amounts, a gigantic expanse of it. This was my whole college essay. You'd have to experiment with different binding agents in the paint, maybe, and the application would have to be, you know, drip rather than brush, obviously, but it would be like sidewalk chalk artists, same concept in a way: an impermanent masterpiece. Then you'd get the wind and the tides washing it away, and also sand crabs and seagulls, beach wildlife. You'd have to document it with Polaroids. Over, I don't know, hours? Days? Weeks, even? Erasing it all. This is my thing."

"That was your college essay?" This is the most Ann's ever heard Malcolm Choy speak. He's leaning against the radiator in his tight but not-too-tight jeans and a brown loose-knit sweater, his heavy black middle-part hair hanging straight past his jaw, his almond eyes snapping, and he's gesturing with his hands in a very guy way, very solid, with his elephant-hair bracelet cutting a black, elegant band around the Heath Bar column of his wrist: swoon material through and through. Then he caps it all by drumming something fast and staccato on the radiator.

"That's your thing?"

And he smiles, he even says, "Yep." He knows how to laugh at him-self. "That's my thang."

Is there room for her idea of him and for him, too? Or must one edge the other out, like water displacement? Who knew he had a thing, a thang, such crazy ideas, not the ones she would have made up for him to have? For just one second, she is sad about it; she is forlorn, disconso-late. As if viewed through the wrong end of a telescope, she feels hope-lessly small, irredeemably far away. But, no, that's wrong; she is thrilled, in her stomach, viscerally thrilled, that Malcolm wants to tell her about his beach-mural sand thing, however silly it sounds, with his eyes leap-ing like dark, delighted fish in their almond ponds. But how—she can't help coming back to this one; she's sixteen and a virgin and obviously pathetically goddamn slow to catch on, because she can't grasp it, not even vaguely—how does this relate to sex, to the sex they are supposed to want to have with each other? Does it? Any other person in this room would know the answer to that question—Hannah, Denise, Lamika, you name it—and she has no clue, no sense; the map is still missing its entire middle section, it's been torn right out, and she's left with these two tattered bits, one fluttering in each hand, and no idea how the roads fit together.

She must offer something in return. Perhaps it goes like that, a succession of gifts, of small portals opened up, offered. Progressive bits of the route revealed. What's her best thing?

"Okay, watch this." She springs from the couch, goes back to the galley kitchen, and begins fishing around noisily for supplies: a mug, easy; a fork and spoon, easy; wooden kitchen matches; not there; not there; then to a box of toothpicks, "Okay, I can use you guys, but I still need . . . Matches! Little matches, where are you?" She sings to them. And Malcolm, she can feel him, is on alert, curious, has risen from the radiator and drifted over.

"Does it have to be matches?"

"Yes. Oh, no, because I found the toothpicks. Do you have a lighter?"

"No."

"Hannah will."

But they don't have to wait for Hannah. Malcolm turns on the stove: gas flame, brilliant. Ann sets up her apparatus: fork tines get locked together with the bowl of the spoon, then a toothpick stuck through one of the tines, and balanced—this part is tricky, takes some care, but less than you'd think, there!—balanced on the rim of the mug.

"Whoa," says Malcolm again. He's got this nerd side. So cute. Maybe he thinks this is the whole trick, and it is pretty amazing, the long tippy burden of fork-cum-spoon suspended off the rim of the mug by nothing more than a toothpick, and the counterweight nothing more than a half-inch of the toothpick's tail.

"This isn't it," Ann tells him. She looks around. What can she use for a torch? She rolls a piece of paper towel very tightly, lights the tip in the gas ring, and brings the flame slowly over to the toothpick. She lights the end emerging from the union of cutlery first, and it burns down to the metal and goes out; then, grand finale, she lights the end extending toward the middle of the mug, and it, too, burns as far as the ceramic lip. She drops the rest of the paper towel safely in the sink. A bit of ash falls into the mug. The whole long stainless-steel contraption is now staying sus-pended with *no counterweight*, the dinky stub of toothpick just touching mug and metal, barely, like an optical illusion, but real life.

"Isn't it beautiful? Isn't it excellent?" says Ann, and Malcolm is all over it, smiling and shaking his head, the raven wings of his hair passing forward over the smooth planes of his cheeks, and he's pursing his lips as if to speak, but just emitting these stammery breaths instead.

"That's eerie," he finally pronounces. High tribute. "How does it— Okay, genius, how's it stay up?"

"I don't really understand it," confesses Ann. "I think it was supposed to be something to do with torque and, like, center of gravity."

"Who showed you?"

"Esker." It was Esker's Christmas present to her. Well, Esker hadn't called it that, but she had offered it on the last tutoring session before Christmas, so Ann claimed it as such.

"Cool."

"I know."

Esker has disappeared. Today in class she treated Ann just like any-body else. Not even. With everybody else she was a bit prickly and re-mote, but with Ann she was neutral. *Neutral.* And there was something wrong with her eyes; she had disappeared inside of them, is how Ann thought to put it. And contrary to what Ann told Hannah Monday after-noon in the hall, there hasn't been more than that one dinner between her father and Esker, the dinner of Alice's showing up and Ann's biting the glass, not exactly a hot date. And based on today's overt neutrality—*why?* Wally notwithstanding, why that neutrality toward Ann, who *loves* Esker, isn't it obvious, doesn't she know that, doesn't it count?—there isn't likely to be another. Ann has to concede that the thing between her father and Esker is something she alone conjured, or ultimately failed to conjure.

She gazes at the mug spectacle, sitting there brazenly on the counter. Esker. *Why?* She is through the wrong end of the telescope again, tiny, tiny, cold, forgotten, the sand all cold around her on a small, stinting is-land, a little lump of cold floating land.

"Ann?" says Malcolm Choy, and when he touches a piece of her hair it's first of all so light, the lightest touch, and second of all kind-feeling, nothing like sex, nothing like the video of sex she and Hannah and Denise watched in this very apartment one night, and nothing like the fe-rocious suctiony pretend-soulful activity that goes on pushed up against the metal lockers in between classes at school, but feels instead like someone who might care for her. Oh. He's holding a piece of her hair like a paintbrush, and he uses it—this is so funny and gentle—to pretend-paint her cheek. As if she were a little sandy beach of her own. Then he lets go. So she has room to think only one last sliver of thought on the matter of Esker and Wally before the desire for Malcolm to repeat the gesture closes in and floods it out, like a unit of measure, like water displacement, the simple, base desire for him to lift a piece of her hair again in that light, maddening, monkish way that is just offhand enough that she can still manage to breathe, and her final thought on the matter is: Oh well. With the break over (pun—ha!—vacation as well as her fractured calcanea), the idea of Esker and her father seems less important now, anyway.

27.

It's a slow time of week, Thursday at three, Wally must remind himself that, and also a slow time of year: postholidays, dark and bitter. Today is especially dark, cloudy in the thickest, most suffocating way, layers and layers of dull gray stuff like bandages blocking out not only any sunlight but also the very idea of elsewhere, of beyond. Nothing's actually precipitating, though the threat hangs heavy in the air and has been all day. Wally wishes it would go ahead and let loose, though that would mean a slower night than he already anticipates. Snow would be some relief, some promise of porosity, mutability. He feels strangely sealed in, or sealed off.

Only two customers at the moment, a mother and grown daughter lingering over pumpkin pie and tea. Wally sits behind the bar and reads the paper, but anxiously; he can't get more than a third of the way through an article without looking up, searching out the window for a point of color, or anything, even rain. His eyes keep tricking him into seeing drops, transparent pinstripes against the building across the street, but when he wanders toward the glass he sees nothing's coming down. He can't shake the feeling of isolation, of confinement, that has beset him. It's as though there's a membrane across the sky, a sausage casing.

On a day like today, Game seems shabby and forced, the red velvet curtains too precious, the strings of pomegranate lights garish and overdone, the game on the menu too rich and farfetched. The whole restaurant, the whole conceit, hangs heavy around his neck: a millstone Alice placed there to make him stay put while she left. He lit the fire earlier, when there was a little lunch crowd; it's dwindled to embers. He ought to throw on another log for these women, who have planted themselves by the hearth with their scads of posh shopping bags and their North Jersey accents and that rock on the daughter's left ring finger; they've come into the city to make a day of it; they've got matching gloves, twin pairs of cream cashmere gloves on the table beside them, along with a healthy pink pile of Sweet 'N Low wrappers; they make him immeasurably sad. They themselves strike him as shabby and forced, and dismally unaware of it. They've each been careful to leave a little bit of pumpkin pie on the plate.

Wally returns to the paper. An article about mad-cow disease; lovely. He's only told one person about getting sick Monday night, and that was his seafood supplier. Eighteen hours seems a little long for food poisoning to kick in, which was his rationalization for not telling anyone else, but he's pretty sure it was the mussels he had late Sunday night (early Monday morning), before closing up. Anyway, he was sure enough to trash the rest of that delivery and convince the supplier to credit his account.

"Uh, Wally?" It's John the dishwasher, holding the kitchen door open. "Can you come back here a minute?"

Another flood. Shit. Shit. They're going to have to replace the machine, Wally realizes with a sinking in his gut. The stupid plumber. Wally just got a bill for $390 for the job last week. Or not stupid, crooked. At least he hasn't paid it yet.

"All right, John. Do you think you can work with it until I can get someone over here?"

They're walking around it, hands on hips, a ridiculous pose, as if they know what they're dealing with, either of them, in this big metal monster with its inscrutable mess of pipes and coils. John shrugs. He's an aspiring actor, not a plumber. "I don't know. When's that going to be? I wouldn't want to run her."

Wally takes a step and his shoe squelches. "Let me get on the phone. See if we can stay open tonight." He helps John pile some extra rubber-mesh mats over the worst of the flooding, then heads toward the tiny office off the kitchen. First aspirin, then the Rolodex. His eyes are throbbing. He switches off the overhead fluorescent and turns on the desk lamp. Its halfhearted puddle of light makes him feel even farther away, an outlaw in a hideout, a lost explorer taking refuge in a cave.

After half an hour on the phone with three different plumbers, there seems to be a small, not inexpensive, ray of light. Maybe they won't need to replace it just yet. The guy from last week has agreed to come back and take a look before five. On the other side of the hollow-core door, John's mopping, singing "Do You Know the Way to San Jose?" Wally smiles. The aspirin has made a small difference. He rubs his forehead and can feel the horizontal lines in it; when did they become part of his permanent topography?

Less than two weeks ago, Alice was here, and Nuncio and Willette and Emil. Is that possible? And the house was full and the stage well lit and all the players picking up beautifully on their cues and hitting their marks and waiting for their laughs. . . .

Not really. The trouble is, Wally's so deft at constructing happiness. To whom does he owe it? He is weary of it. Weary, too, of the smell of rancid butter, always faintly present in his office at work.

He spins the Rolodex. That old childhood game of spinning a globe and stopping it with your finger. Where will I live when I grow up? If you landed in the ocean, you were allowed to spin again. Or the desert, or an Eastern-bloc country, or pretty much anywhere else you didn't like. You'd spin and spin until you got Spain or Vancouver or something. He spins the Rolodex again and again until he gets "E." He never filled out a card for Esker. He learned her number too quickly by heart. He checks the clock. Not time yet for her to be home from work.

He had woken in her bed in the small hours of Tuesday morning disoriented, but with a kind of rising elation he couldn't account for until the knowledge of where he was seeped in. Her sheets, her pillow, her blanket, her bed: they were holding him, they smelled nice and plain, like wood and linens, and he felt singularly consoled. A kind of well-being he hadn't experienced in, well, as long as he could remember hung over him, light as a veil or a breeze; it was as though he were being watched over, with the breath of whoever it was stirring a gauzy curtain, something loosely protective, like the cheesecloth his mother used to drape over the playpen of his younger brother to keep out the blackflies, on summer afternoons when she'd put him down for his nap in the yard. Then Wally had woken up a little more and the image dissolved and only the sense of it remained, and he'd gotten up from the bed feeling empty and weak but without nausea. He'd felt for his shoes and laced them blindly, and, remembering what Esker had said, felt for the mug on the bedside table and drunk some cold tea. Little sips, being mindful of his stomach. But his stomach didn't balk. Then there was a lower sort of stirring, and very hastily he realized the complaint had reached a more southerly locale.

A long, long block of time on the toilet. Long enough that his eyes grew accustomed to the dark. First the larger shapes declared themselves—bathtub, sink, hamper, mirror—and then the smaller ones—cake of soap, bathmat, toothbrush cup, candles; she had four candles in variously shaped holders on the ledge next to the tub. He was glad to note that her life was not strictly Spartan. Eventually he was even able to make out the picture she'd taped up over the sole windowpane, an odd geometrical shape that looked like some sort of New Age religious symbol. That seemed doubtful; he wondered at its meaning. But, oh, his quaking bowels. It was awful, aside from his embarrassment and fear that she'd wake up, which were also awful. He'd had food poisoning once before, and it had been worse than this, more violent and scary, with a knot of pain like an actual fist of poison clenching his internal organs, but still. This was bad enough. By the time he felt safe leaving the toilet, he could hear a garbage truck making its rounds outside.

In the living room he'd found Esker cocooned on the couch, her face obscured by a tangle of hair, the shape of her body lost in the lumpiness of one bunched-up and two partially kicked-off afghans. A single hand and wrist lay exposed, palm up, fingers curled. He restrained himself from fixing the covers.

Esker. A name like camouflage, like an ill-fitting trench coat, willfully ugly and obscuring. He wondered what in her life had made it necessary. There was nothing urgent in his musings; in fact, they felt almost luxurious, because he was already in past the trench coat, wasn't he? Admitted. He wanted to tell her something, that he recognized this, that he understood it for a gift.

He brought his mug into the kitchen and slid open the drawer there by the sink, extracted the utensils so quietly, like a magician, and on the kitchen table formed "I P H" in silver.

Happiness clanged like bells along the corridors of his body all the way home, where he'd fallen back into bed, as off-kilter from the dangling promise of things to come as he was exhausted from his battle with whatever bad shellfish he'd ingested. And that had been Tuesday. And Wednesday had followed. No word from her, no response to his two messages since. And that is all right; he is beginning to know what to expect, and of course she would pull her trench coat a little tighter around her now, of course she would try to take on the color of her surroundings, to vanish a little, a reflex. He feels kindly, understanding this. She doesn't even mean to do it, he realizes; she's like some woodland creature, going on instinct, going into a ball or snarling and spitting, pointy-toothed, when she senses danger; unrolling, becoming soft and curious, alert, when she feels safe. And she's feeling safer and safer with him, and he knows what to do now, knows to wait. And if he felt a little less certain of this yesterday than Tuesday, and a little less certain today than yesterday, well, that doesn't mean anything.

He goes back out front. The pumpkin-pie women are just gathering up their things, a protracted affair: their pocketbooks and coats, their matching gloves and embossed velvet scarves, their many shopping bags, each with a tuft of colored tissue protruding, rose, mint, lilac, according to which boutique it came from. "Which street gets us right over to the West Side Highway?" asks the mother.

"Mom, I know where we're going."

"We're not usually this far downtown."

And he's gracious with them, back in his good-innkeeper mode, having dredged up the compassion, the deep empathy which is his trademark. He tells them where to cut over while somehow managing to let the daughter know *he* knows she's undoubtedly an experienced clubber. They're woodland creatures, too, he thinks, in a way, only of a different species from Esker, with different habitats, defensive behaviors, mating rituals, and all the rest. But equally governed by a primary instinct for survival.

And his great gift is understanding this, intuiting it, the creatureness of everyone he meets; he sees past the velvet scarves and cashmere gloves and fur coats to the naked animal within, pathetic and in this beautiful; he knows just how to speak gently, move slowly, let them sniff him, test him, while he holds still and waits. He is confident in this. It always works. He is beneficent, endlessly patient. At last they feel safe; they purr; they lick the salt from his hand.

The plumber arrives, a wiry man with a worried-looking mustache. "Hey, how're you doing, Mr. James, yeah, sorry about that, let me take another look. We're gonna try and get that mess fixed up for you." Deferential, good, though not discreet. Oh well: the gloved women glance at his grimy overall and the back of his jacket—EZ PLUMBING & HEATING CO., INC.—then at the door to the kitchen, then at the plates they've just risen from. An awkward moment.

"So that's West Eleventh?" clarifies the daughter brightly, and they both smile, their turn to be gracious, with freshly lipsticked mouths, before leaving, sailing out, not woodland creatures but sleek yachts, having graced his harbor once, never to visit it again.

"Thank you," he calls after the closing door.

The phone rings. "Game, Wally speaking."

It's Ann: can she sleep over at Hannah's? Thanks. She's in a hurry; yes, she did okay on the history test; no, she hasn't finished her Brit.-lit. paper, but it's not due until next week, she has the whole weekend; yes, she's remembering her physical-therapy appointment this afternoon; she'll go to Hannah's after; goodbye, okay, good*bye,* Dad.

The phone rings again. "Game, Wally speaking."

It's Alice.

"Alice." A rare occurrence. Especially since he's just seen her.

"How are you, Wally?"

"Fine. How are you?"

"No, I didn't mean it like that."

"Like what?"

"Like, 'Hello, how are you—fine, how are you?' "

"Well . . . I'm sorry, what are you saying?"

"No, I just mean, back up. It's actually the reason I called."

"What is?"

"To ask how you're doing. Not—not perfunctorily."

"How *I'm* doing?"

"Yes."

"I'm fine, Alice. I thought you might be asking about Ann."

"Why, is she all right?"

"I don't know."

"Is she walking all right?"

"Yes. The muscles are weak. She's in physical therapy. That's not what I meant."

"What did you mean?"

"Nothing." How did this conversation start? "I just thought you might be wondering about her."

A certain *click click click*. It sounds like she's biting the phone. "But actually, Wally, I've been wondering about you."

He doesn't have time for this. Or space. Or something. Something on the time-space continuum. He flips the Rolodex. "Y." Yancy Hotel and Restaurant Linens. Flip. "P." Jack Potash, his dentist. Flip. "Q." No "Q"s.

"Because, Wally," Alice is saying, "I keep thinking about when the chair broke and everything, and your face, but not just then . . . you seemed . . . really sad . . . and—"

The gall. *The gall.* Clarity gives him vigor. How can someone so bright be such an idiot? "Alice." He explains to her, slowly, not really with rancor, just with the weight of truth, "You don't get to call and say that to me."

"But I—"

Speaking really slowly: "You don't get to ask me how I am. *Except* perfunctorily." It's very, very simple.

"Okay," she says, after some silence. And, "Okay. Bye, Wally."

"Bye, Alice."

The phone rings again. "Game, Wally speaking."

Alice again.

"How are you?" he asks. He is not without humor. In fact, all of a sudden he feels pretty good. It's the clarity, the liberating clarity that comes with anger.

She speaks very fast. "Maybe I don't get to say this, but maybe I do, since I've known you a long time and . . . *love* you, as it were, and I'm going to say this. Please. I know what you do, you make it about everyone else's sadness in the world, you see it in them, and then you get to be Ranger Rick and tend to their poor imaginary broken wings, which is lovely, sort of, not really, but I . . . I . . . I . . . Please. I wish I still got to say this to you, because, I guess, I'm worried, that you're making this thing about Ann . . . that you're using it to divert you from . . . that you won't attend to your own sadness."

Now it's Wally's turn for some silence. "Ranger Rick," he repeats. And then, eventually, with bite, "Don't call back again."

28.

January rain. Esker, home at last, towel-dries her hair. She changes into leggings and wool socks and her coziest, rattiest sweater, and climbs up on the couch, pulling one of her mother's old afghans around her, and still she can't get warm. The damp's gone into her bones, as her mother would have said, preposterously.

Florence has decided to convene a committee to look into the possibility of an inappropriate teacher-parent relationship, said the two-sentence memorandum waiting this morning in a sealed envelope in Esker's box in the faculty room, although it eschewed the singular pronoun in favor of the royal "we." Esker can expect to be contacted by the committee shortly. That's what the second sentence had said. She has no idea how many people will be on the committee, or who they'll be. Presumably she'll find out in advance of being summoned before them. Isn't that how these things go? Are they going to summon Wally, too? Can they do that? It seems absurd; she wants to laugh, but can't. Panic like birds beats at her ribs. Not panic, fury. Isn't that what it's called? Isn't she furious? The whole thing is medieval. Florence, despite all the enlightenment and reason she projects with her decorously appointed office and her genteelly trendy suits and pearls, might as well do her work from a dank stone chamber, clad in chain metal and visored helmet, for all she can be reached.

They will question her about the nature of her relationship with Wally. They will ask her to use and apply the words "dating," "involvement," "romantic." She doesn't want to laugh at all, she wants to throw up. She hates these words, which may be ugly anyway but will certainly be ugly in the mouths of the committee. She ought to have a right to rail against these words, do battle with them, protest them, protest her relationship to them, before Wally if before anyone at all—not before some horrible semicircle of Florence-appointees. She has not dared use these words herself; they have not passed her lips, and now the committee will ask her to claim or renounce them without her ever having had a chance to admit them to the realm of possibility, to hold them there awhile, to see. And now she never will see. She will never have the chance to learn what she might have been capable of, with Wally; what they might have been capable of with each other.

She thinks to quit. Quit her job and she's free. But that's rash, that's shooting herself in the foot, and besides it would be like an admission of wrongdoing. This is crazy. This is Florence's craziness. No; this is what she knew would happen: something bad. She tried to get rid of the ghost in her basement, the ghost in her mind; she has been greedy to want it gone, inhospitable to throw it out; it was hubris to think she could rid herself of it, unreasonable to think she could stop being a ghost, to think she could inhabit her life and want things, things beyond the scope of Delos, with all its measured speech and silences, its well-tempered desires, its kneesocks and right angles and carefully drawn shades, its *care,* its carefulness, above all—and this is the price, not a week later, the damage. One way or another she'll hurt Wally, hurt Ann, whether she wants to or not.

The force of self-loathing is fueling her now. She begins to be less cold. She gets up, shedding the afghan. She goes to the kitchen, then her bedroom, the bathroom, the living room again; she doesn't know where she's going, she simply needs to walk. But this is more like pacing, she feels walled, caged, too enormous and powerful for the space. She gets her coat, stamps her feet into boots, goes out. The rain comes down in icy specks. She cuts over on Spring Street and goes west, toward the highway, sluggish with headlights now, at rush hour, west toward the piers, and the water, black and mobile beneath the perseverating drops, a border. Of course that border's different now from when she moved here, with its fenced jogging path and the landscaping; it's been cultivated, certified now as a place in the city for people to go and enjoy. She prefers it as it was that summer, that August night when she first moved in and last saw Albert, that night she walked and walked along the ragged border between highway and piers, trying and failing to lose herself in that nameless territory. For crying out loud, now it even has a name: Something-or-Other Park.

Her hair is wet again, and there's slush in her boots, but it's not enough. She's still too big for this cage, too powerful for these elements. Let it be a blizzard. Let the river rise into a tidal wave. Let the slushy whoosh of the traffic become a true, drowning roar she could really sing against, screech against. Let there be one thing big enough to assume the burden of her.

She fixes her gaze on the umbral, undulating Hudson—her boundary; she cannot walk farther west—lapping irregularly against the city's pilings, and, like a truly crazy person, smiles suddenly, for the first time relaxes her pace; she is remembering a paper she read in college, "How Long Is the Coast of Britain?" Its thrust had been that all coasts, all borders, are infinitely long. It was written by Benoit Mandelbrot, the "father of fractals," who by then had become her little hero, her college-girl crush, and he'd said, in this paper, that, as your scale of measurement becomes smaller, as you try to get more exact, the coastline becomes more and more curvy—longer—since you'd eventually have to measure around every cove and jetty, every rock and pebble, every jagged groove on the surface of every pebble, and so on forever. It was that "forever" she fell in love with, same as the Mandelbrot–Peano–von Koch snowflake, only this article made her realize you didn't need a specially concocted geometrical shape to find it; it was everywhere; in coastlines and cliffs, but also in the seemingly smooth surface of an apple, whose skin under a microscope would reveal itself as more than a perfect, mathematical curve. It was there in paper, in glass, in her own, asperous skin; anything with surface area was one of infinity's dwellings. She'd even written Mandelbrot a fan letter, as it were, but never mailed it, understanding, perhaps, that she'd rather be in love with an idea than a person.

And it rescues her tonight from her feeling of confinement within her own impossible desires, her own guilt-ridden skin, from her terrible, pacing walk in the icy rain. The idea of infinity counters the idea of confinement, mitigates it at the very least, and though her anger is not lessened her feeling of helplessness is. She is tasting rain; it has slid inside her lips; that's how wet she is, and it's January, cold; what a total idiot. She didn't even put on a hat.

She's been walking uptown this whole time; she's all the way to Charles Street. *Game will be warm and dry.* The sentence comes to her like a given.

Ten minutes later, dry it is. The fire's going, and strings of little lights star the velvet curtain. Lots of customers; the wait staff have to turn sideways, with plates of food held high, to slip through the channels between chairs, and they do it like dancers, a man and a woman, circulating among the close-packed tables. The music on the stereo, turned low, seems to be the Moldau, that building caravan of melody.

Esker stands dripping. She runs a hand through her hair and actually hears drops spatter the glass door behind her.

"Someone will be with you in a moment," says the waiter.

Someone turns out to be Wally, maître d'ing tonight, looking the embodiment of warmth and dryness as he comes through the kitchen door. And registers her with a look. She's beginning to shiver again, the heat of her anger losing out to the winter downpour. A drop of rain descends from her brow and skirts, slowly, the corner of her eye. Wally reaches her, takes her in. "Wet kitten," he pronounces.

"Wet cat."

And he regards her with the efficient, measuring eye of a triage nurse. "Sit at the bar?" he offers.

"No. No."

He is unruffled, reassessing the situation. His eyes fairly click, like abacuses; he is good at this, in his element, a far cry from the food-poisoned, weak thing of Monday night, and Esker wants only to believe that he will know what to do, wants only to be a bedraggled kitten—cat—to his innkeeper tonight. "Come."

She weaves after him soddenly, around pockets of chewing, chatting engagement, follows him back through the kitchen doors, through the sudden fluorescent brightness of the kitchen, over rubbery mats, around gleaming steel counter and industrial sink and range and things—she barely looks up from his feet, her guide—and into a narrow cubicle of space: the office.

"Sit down."

There's one swivel chair on wheels, which is funny, the office being too small for the chair's occupant to wheel anywhere.

"I'm all wet."

"Well, take off your coat."

She does and is less wet underneath. She hands him the coat and sits in his chair. She swivels.

"Wait here." He starts to leave.

"Everything is very bad," she warns him.

He looks at her. He nods. "I'll be back."

He's gone for forever. She swivels back and forth in his chair; she remembers her feet are soaking and takes off her boots and socks; she finds a clean, folded cloth napkin and uses it to towel her hair; she reads the things on the surface of his desk without touching them: bills, business cards, part of the newspaper, a ripped section of yellow legal paper on which is scrawled *ketchup, kale?, orzo* and, next to that, an assortment of doodles, some of which appear to be domestic objects: eyeglasses, a salt shaker?, a gooseneck lamp. Even this doesn't help her to relax.

When he comes back he has a bowl of dark-orange soup and two rolls. He helps clear a place on the desk for the food. "All of a sudden it's jumping out there. Can you wait a little longer?"

She nods. The soup smells unreal, like a dream of soup, like soup as a symbol of bounty in a dream. "What kind of soup is this?"

"Carrot-pear-ginger."

"What does that have to do with game?"

"It complements it."

It's heaven. She eats it slowly, and both rolls, also slowly, and still she finishes before he comes back, but now she is sleepy, and warm from all the heat in the kitchen, and, more than that, lulled by the partly audible banter of the dishwasher and cook, and sometimes the waiter and waitress as they move in and out, with the sound of the kitchen door swinging. Perhaps she could stay here. Not go to work in the morning. Not go home. She could curl up like a cat on some blankets in the corner and stay here, unobtrusive, dozing off and on indefinitely, warmed by the voices of everyone busy and bustling beyond the door, buoyed by the sporadic nearness to Wally whenever he has to come in and do some work at his desk, his back to her. There are some holes in this plan, she realizes, but it'll do for now, more than do. The chair doesn't only swivel and roll;

it tilts, too; really, it's got more ergonomic perks than this humble office would seem to warrant. She tilts back, rests her head against the wall, puts her bare feet up on Wally's desk, closes her eyes. My, these restaurant people work late.

But she cannot sleep, cannot even fool herself into dozing. Tears come down her cheeks, slower than the rain and almost peaceful. She's crying because it's not really a cat she wants to be, its diminutive shape blended in the corner against blankets and such, unobserved, content with the proximal warmth of those moving around her. For all that she might as well be a ghost, a shade passing through rooms unnoticed, sucking drafts of heat from the atmosphere and nothing else. And she doesn't want to pretend anymore that that's what she wants.

His office has no clock. She hasn't worn her watch. It must be midnight or something. When he comes in at last, she hasn't really been asleep, and her eyes fly open and her feet spring off the desk. He sits down on the filing cabinet. "So. What's going on with you?"

She hates to put it into words, to speak the detestable words that tell the story of her encounter with Florence. So she is sullen-seeming as she tells it, looking mostly at the detritus strewn across his desk and not at his face, speaking mostly in a dull voice as though reciting someone else's story, unrelated to her. At the end she says, "I'm sorry."

"You are?"

She can't help laughing. "What do you mean?"

"What do *you* mean?"

"I'm sorry for . . . bringing you into this mess."

He thinks about this. "I don't think you've brought me anywhere I didn't want to go. Or didn't choose to go. And it sounds like the mess is messy for you more than for me."

She acknowledges this with a kind of shrug and hand gesture that are far too casual, and far too resigned, for the situation. "That was such excellent soup," she says, after a moment, hollowly, looking at a pencil.

"What do you plan to do?"

"Say goodbye." She tells the pencil.

"To me?"

She nods.

"And Ann?"

She is a statue. Never mind being a cat in his office; she could just be stone, even better. A paperweight, a figurine, what are those awful things called? A Hummel. She could turn into an ugly little Hummel and adorn one corner of his cluttered desk, and never go in to face Florence or the committee, never have to answer anyone's questions about romance, involvement, love, desire, not even her own.

"I'm not sure—" He breaks off. "Have you spoken with a lawyer?"

"Oh God," says Esker, and lowers her face into both palms.

"Do you need the name of one?"

She is a statue.

"Because it's unclear to me that they actually have any power to regulate this."

She is a statue.

"Or . . . do I have your permission to describe the situation to an attorney and get some feedback?"

"Shh." Her face is still in her hands.

"What?"

She can sense him bending forward to hear.

"Just stop talking," she whispers. And when he begins to touch her, "Don't do that, either." She feels him shift away.

After a moment, with false enthusiasm, "More soup?"

She laughs. She lets her hands fall away to her lap. "I hate you."

"You hate me?"

"No . . . no. I just need a taxi."

"Right. I often get those two confused."

She gives him the finger.

"Come on, let's get you a cab."

She stands up.

"I think you're going to want your shoes and socks on."

She sits back down, dresses her feet. She likes following directions, even such simple ones as these, especially such simple ones as these. It's a relief. Her socks have dried on the radiator, but the boots are still wet inside. She shudders and pulls them on anyway. Stands. He gives her her coat. She puts it on. There. They don't go back through the front of the restaurant, but out the alley door, for which she is grateful. Steam is coming up from a manhole cover, like in a music video. The rain has stopped, and everything is glistening. They start walking toward the avenue. A streetlamp is out; it's very dark. Then a Yellow Cab comes down the street, a reggae-thumping coach, and it swerves to a stop by Wally's upraised hand, and he discharges her into it, says good night.

"Oh, wait!" she cries, and the driver, having begun to roll forward, slams on the brakes. She opens the door, speaks to her friend, who has just turned away. "I have no money."

He has, she notices, even in the darkness of the street, the excellent grace not to smile as he reaches into his pocket for cash.

29.

This is boring. Hannah's making it boring. She's making them talk about the practical details of their performance. She says Winter Concert is a week away and they don't know what the hell they're doing yet. Blah, blah, blah. Ann might fall asleep from boredom if she weren't so awake from Malcolm's presence. He and she are lying at opposite ends of the couch in the faculty room, which they found empty and decided to use for their meeting. Suddenly secrecy seems to have become an important component of their act.

Hannah, in the faculty-room version of an easy chair, which is to say institutional and upright, is talking about Ann's costume, which Ann is supposed to stitch herself from an old ripped parachute she found at the flea market. She'll be in this luminous white nylon stuff from her waist to the floor, twelve feet, and layered over that an old nightgown of Hannah's that is big on her and ruched and Grecian-looking. ("You wore this?" she'd asked. "Oh yes. I picked it out myself," Hannah had replied. "Not.") And she will have, maybe—this is Malcolm's idea, and they're not yet sure they'll put it off—a cluster of white helium balloons tied around her waist and sprouting up behind her, over her head.

"Balloons are so Ringling Brothers," objects Hannah.

"Each balloon will have white feathers glued to it," he counters in his serene way.

"Choy. I have one word for you." Hannah makes her hands into a megaphone. "Logistics."

"It's a visual thing," he insists, undeterred. "Wait'll you see it."

Hannah gives him a look with her heavy, black-rimmed eyes. She has a way of making the whites show under her pupils so that she looks something like a Goth bulldog.

"I'll do it," says Malcolm. "Put that on my list."

"MALCOLM: BALLOONS/FEATHERS," writes Hannah. She alone among all those Ann has met has the extraordinary talent of being able to make the sound of pencil on paper sarcastic. Hannah is in full General Secretary mode. She has brought with her a legal pad, a mechanical pencil, a calculator, a calendar, a cell phone, a pager, an orange, a lipstick called Buck Naked, another called Fuckin' Red, a pack of Marlboro Lights with one bent cigarette in it, some Jolly Ranchers, some tampons, a—

"Hello!" Hannah exclaims, snatching her green army knapsack away from Ann. "Can I get you something?"

"Oh. No. Just prying. I'm done. Actually, I'll have a Jolly Rancher."

Hannah tosses the bag back to Ann, who gets herself a candy.

"Anyone else?"

Hannah and Malcolm both accept, and they all sit there with sweet lumps in their cheeks. The meeting continues, with Hannah playing the role of beleaguered pragmatist to the hilt, and Malcolm rather exploiting the role of incorrigible visionary fruitcake. For her part, Ann finds it delicious to fall into the role of the child, acquiescent, blameless, floating along in the back seat of the car. How delicious, too, that they are meeting in the faculty room; Ann never would have had the balls, but Hannah, finding it unoccupied, set up camp here as though it were her birthright, and Malcolm followed with his natural ascetic grace. There's enough daylight coming through the courtyard window for Hannah to write, though it's gone considerably grayer since they started, but no one gets up to switch on a light, and Ann has a feeling it's because they don't want to be detected.

"So, Ann." Hannah refers to her lists. "You're sewing your skirt-thing, and you're bringing matches and a pan of water." They have decided to place a pan of water at the foot of the ladder for the lit matches to fall into. ("Lest anyone call us irresponsible," Hannah said.) "Malcolm, you're setting up the ladder for Ann. Oh, Ann, you're also buying and putting down glow tape. Okay, Malcolm: ladder for Ann, your drums, whatever you're wearing, you're going to ask your mother if she has that Itty Bitty Book Light, oh yeah, and whatever you want to do about balloons and feathers; you're on your own, sucka, with that one. I'm getting a dictionary, attaché case, slide projector, I'm picking up the slides on Monday, I'm getting the sack of sugar, an extension cord, and my costume from the dry cleaners on Tuesday. Is that everything, guys?"

"Think it's enough?" asks Ann. She is lolling. She is lolling as she has never lolled. Actually, she smoked a little pot this afternoon. Actually, she smoked a little pot this afternoon with Malcolm Choy. A few puffs—tokes. It didn't really do anything. It's just making the watermelon in her mouth so bright.

"Think it's thing-enough?" asks Malcolm. His feet are on the outside. Hers are tucked between the back cushion and his ribs. The balance of light in the room has shifted; gray washes over them obscuringly, like a houndstooth pattern of winter afternoon.

"Yo," says Hannah. "Fuck you."

"Isn't that the name of your lipstick?" queries Ann innocently.

She gets the pencil chucked at her. It stabs her lightly on the cheek, like a pointy fairy-kiss. She smiles.

Their piece for Winter Concert has grown more elaborate and cryptic over the weeks. Now there is a part where Hannah will project slides of text *on* various segments of the audience, and another part where she will tear open a sack of sugar and drag it along the floor to make horizontal lines, and then vertical ones. Ann is still basically clueless about what any of this means, although Malcolm seems to get it. Something about language and logic and processed sugar grids. She knows her part, anyway, which has morphed: now she represents the antithesis of Hannah, who will be wearing a black suit and black-rimmed glasses, austere purveyor of prepared text and grid. Ann is now something like an angel of speechlessness, a goddess of chaos, and every time she drops one of her lighted matches Hannah will go mute, and still, and Malcolm will drum and she will sing, slowly, on an open vowel, "I can't get no satisfaction." Really, it all seems stupid to her, but cool. Stupid but cool.

"That's what we should call this," she says out loud. They still have not given Buddy a name for their act. After making it abundantly clear that, every day they fail to do so, his back pain increases exponentially, he finally told them this morning that it would go in the program as "Unti-tled," upon which Malcolm had begun lobbying for "Not Untitled." Now, too late, Ann tries, "Stupid but Cool."

"That sounds like a jazz standard," says Malcolm, which naturally sets him drumming with his fingers on the wooden part of the couch. The vibration shoots straight through Ann. She is mesmerized. She feels like someone's speaking to her in Morse code, from inside her body.

"Do we really think it's stupid?" says Hannah.

"No, no!" protests Ann. "Yes. But cool!"

"Wicked cool."

"Because I don't want to do it if it's stupid."

"It's not, I was kidding. It's really, really . . . unstupid."

Hannah looks to Malcolm.

"Yes. It's unstupid," he repeats. "And there's our title."

Ann launches the pencil at him like a dart. His hand shoots out and snatches it from the air. Swoon material.

"Actually, I meant it," says Malcolm, tucking the pencil behind his ear. "Kind of Zen, don't you think? 'Unstupid.' "

"Hello, that's my pencil," says Hannah. Ann is not sure her testiness is still all act.

Malcolm holds it out to her. "We love you, Hannah. You are the sun-shine of our lives."

" 'We'? You're speaking for two?" Eyes flick to Ann and back to Malcolm.

"I speak for everybody."

"Aren't you cute."

Malcolm says nothing in reply, and Ann is aware of how bulky Han-nah is in her chair, how black and white and red and heavy. She's aware of being tired of Hannah. Or maybe of Hannah's being tired of them.

"Why are you being a spinster?" asks Ann. "I mean, not a spinster, what's the word? A meter maid. Is that what I mean?"

"A meter maid," repeats Malcolm, and he laughs not quite silently.

Hannah leaves the room.

"Wait, Hannah," says Ann, but Hannah is gone. What the fuck was that? "What just happened?" she says out loud, and Malcolm, male and all, has no comment. Hannah is the one who wanted to set them up in the first place. A minute ago she was the child floating in the back seat lis-tening while the big two created their act, and now she has done something wrong and everything is upended, the whole vehicle has tipped alarmingly; passengers have fallen out. But the most alarming thing is, although she ought to be trotting down the hall after Hannah, being spacily contrite, omitting her cannier sense of what may have just happened, going out on the steps to share that last bent cigarette, which Hannah would light for them under the metal bird, and shivering, letting herself grow cold and shivery on the stone steps, until Hannah makes a protective gesture—although she should be doing those things, she doesn't; she doesn't want to. She doesn't want to: that's the alarming part, the exciting part, realizing she does not, in fact, want to do any of that.

"Aren't you hungry?" she says instead.

"What's in the fridge?" says Malcolm, and they both get up and go to raid the little faculty-room fridge—the balls! Ann is amazed, intoxicated by their temerity; she wants to roll in it, come up all pulsing and mighty—and they are therefore tucked around the corner out of sight when Esker comes in and, without switching on the lights, sinks onto the couch where they have just lain.

Esker is holding a hand over her mouth and staring out the narrow window, which has just begun to take on the deeper glow of evening. For whole seconds in the shadowy corner Ann and Malcolm are garden ornaments, a stone sylph and satyr, with only the whites of their eyes to betray them. Ann realizes their chance to announce their presence without its being something far more awkward and even ominous is fast disappearing. Now is when they must step out from the corner and say sheepish hi's, make some excuse about what they're doing in the faculty room, and bolt. Esker's hand moves up to cover her eyes. Her back looks surprisingly slender, curved like that in its white shirt. You wouldn't know she was a math teacher, thinks Ann. Suddenly Esker throws something—what? something she'd been holding?—at the window, and whatever it was it was solid, because the window cracks with a sound like a shot and Malcolm grabs Ann's wrist and they are out of there.

30.

$\mathcal{H}$anging up the phone after speaking with the dean from The Prospect School, Wally feels more celebratory than he, strictly speaking, ought to. Ann has been caught sneaking out of the faculty room with a boy after school today, both of them apparently high on marijuana. There is also some question of vandalism in the faculty room, a broken window; that matter is being looked into further. Both students are being held at the school until a parent or guardian comes to pick them up, ostensibly because the school is reluctant to send them on public transportation in their current condition, although Wally suspects this show of concern is doubling as a kind of punishment; since no drugs were found, neither student is being suspended. Certainly Ann must be fuming. He imagines her confined to a straight-backed chair in some outer office, wondering whose parent will show up first. Which would be the greater humiliation? To be submitted to the gaze of the boy's mother in these compromised circumstances, or to have her father on display before the boy?

Really, he must stifle a smile as he gets his coat and shapka and informs his staff he needs to head out for a few hours. This is the first time Ann's ever gotten into trouble at school, and he's secretly almost ebullient. Breaking into the faculty room? It reminds him of countless larks from his adolescence in Grange Hill. With a boy? He'd been wondering when Ann would show an interest. Smoking pot? No parent wants his child losing control to drugs, but a bit of experimentation seems like a rite of passage, maybe even a sign of healthy development. On the whole, he's relieved. This seems like evidence of recovery from whatever troublesome state she's been in since her implausible fall from the bleachers six weeks ago.

He catches his reflection in the subway window: he looks portly and amused. Alice might be troubled, he thinks, Alice might go into a flurry, but he knows better, he has the advantage now. A new clarity descended for him with that last round of phone calls; he has hit a new stride. He knows better what he wants, and—somehow even more liberating—what he does not.

By the time he gets to The Prospect School, it's fully dark out, and the building is lit up against the cold like a confident way-station. He pulls open the heavy door and steps inside the beautiful foyer, with its curved stairs and tiled floor. From somewhere else in the building there's the unflappable hum of a vacuum cleaner, and he can hear faint sounds of piano and feet from the Big Room on the second floor, and other than that the place has the great peacefulness of an educational institution after school hours, a feeling of leisure and safety. How fortunate that they are able to send Ann to school in such a place, thinks Wally, as he always does when he visits the building. He believes that in some way the solid comforts of The Prospect School extend to him, also; by proxy, he, too, falls just within bounds of its encompassing embrace.

The school office smells of cleaning fluid and peppermint and appears to be empty. One drawer of one filing cabinet has been left open. "Hello?" says Wally, knocking on the open door. He hears a scrambling, and then Ann peers up from behind the secretary's desk. A candy cane juts from her mouth. She removes it to speak. "Oh, hi." She stands. "My dad's here," she tells someone apparently still behind the desk. She seems disconcertingly cool and poised.

The boy emerges. Not what Wally had pictured. He'd sort of pictured himself in high school: awkward, boyish. There's not much boyish about this boy, except perhaps the smoothness of his fawn-colored skin. He is like an antelope. Like someone in a Gap ad. He is taller than Wally, with chin-length black hair parted in the middle and almond-shaped black eyes that are steady and wide. He's wearing a faded purple shirt and a black bracelet.

"This is Malcolm," says Ann.

Malcolm pulls a curly brown thing—a stick of cinnamon, it looks like—from his mouth and nods. "Hello."

"Hello," says Wally, sternly, he hopes. He has lost his bearing somewhat. "Uh, where's. . . ?" He has forgotten the dean's name. "Am I supposed to see someone before we go?"

Ann shrugs and points with her candy cane. "They're in there." Doors on either side of this office lead to two inner chambers. *Headmistress,* reads the plaque on one. *Dean,* reads the other. Ann has pointed toward the former. "I think they're kind of in the middle of something else."

Wally, Malcolm, and Ann fall silent; he realizes they're all listening. Through the shut door he can make out voices, at least one male and one female, although there is perhaps a third, more muffled voice. No words come intact through the heavy door, but the tension communicates easily. After a minute he is embarrassed to be so obviously eavesdropping in front of and with these two kids. He clears his throat. "Well, I can't wait around." He takes a step toward the door with the intention of knocking, but from within the voices rise in intensity in such a way that he thinks better of it. "So we . . . Shall we go, then?"

"See you tomorrow," says Ann to Malcolm, and then, fluidly, she drops again out of sight behind the desk; Wally hears the sound of papers being gathered; she rises with a manila folder in her hand and deposits it casually into the open drawer of the filing cabinet, which she then slides shut, quietly. She takes two more candy canes from the glass bowl on the secretary's desk and tiptoes to kiss Malcolm briefly on the cheek. To Wally she says, "I just have to go to my locker."

He waits until they are out of the school, on the wide steps, their breath coming out of their mouths in gray clouds, to begin asking her the fatherly questions.

They were in the faculty room to talk about their act for Winter Concert. It was just a private place to meet. Hannah was there, too. Yes, the whole time. She didn't get caught because she'd left a minute before them. Okay, not the whole time, if you want to split hairs. No, Malcolm's not her boyfriend. Anyway, nobody has boyfriends anymore, the expression is passé. He's a friend and he's male. No, they weren't smoking pot. Hannah won't even do drugs. No, she doesn't do drugs, either. She's tried it but didn't really like it. She has no idea if Malcolm has tried pot. Sorry if she doesn't have a complete drug history on all her friends. How should she know why the dean thought they'd been smoking? Maybe the dean is on drugs. No, she didn't break the window. No, Malcolm didn't break the window. No, she doesn't know who broke the window. Maybe the wind; it *is* an old building; everything rattles. Well, fine, she was just saying maybe, how should she know how strong the wind is, it's not like she's a meteorologist for a living. Why should she know anything about the window, the window is none of her business. The file? Well. Nothing. Well, it was just her own file. She'd wanted to see what she'd gotten in French last semester. Okay? Could they please go home now? Okay? Because she was starving.

"Actually, I have to go back to work," says Wally. "Let's get you a cab."

"I don't need it," she says, meaning her calcanea.

"Well, I do," he says, meaning his paternalism.

Ann looks at him full-on for the first time since he arrived to pick her up. She chews her lip a little, but her gaze is whole and sober. The bones of her face have just lately started to declare themselves in a more adult way through the baby softness; they are shifting into an Alice-like comeliness: direct, full of agency. "Sorry they dragged you in," she says. "I don't *really* do drugs." Her blatant equivocation puts them both at ease; it's more welcome than the lie.

"Okay, Anatevka. Stay out of the faculty room."

He puts her in a cab at Grand Army Plaza and gives her a twenty, which makes him feel safe as he watches her pull away.

He calls Game on his cell phone. They're busy, not swamped. No major crises. He says he'll be a few more hours.

He calls Esker. No answer. Just her voice on the machine, which he is used to by now, although it seemed unnecessarily economical at first: "Please leave a message." He doesn't. He wishes she were there, though. He pictures her there, under afghans on the couch, screening her calls, scowling. Funny little bug. Why is he falling in love with her? It doesn't matter; he is, and, what's more, knows it.

He calls Nuncio. Luck: he's still at the theater but just got through rehearsing; they're doing tech stuff; he's off for the rest of the evening. "Where are you, Game?"

"Grand Army Plaza."

"Why?"

"Bad child. Tell you about it later. Where are we meeting?"

"I need to shower. Do you want to just come over?"

"Sure."

"Bring food."

"What kind?"

"I don't care. Pan-Asian."

"What number are you again?" Wally's been over a few times, but he and Nuncio always saw so much of each other at work that they rarely socialized outside of it. Nuncio tells him the address, and Wally heads down to the subway.

Nuncio lives on the top floor of a five-story walk-up in Alphabet City. His roommate is a massage/aromatherapist who keeps a table set up in one room, and the whole place smells as a result like a cross between an apothecary and a rain forest. Nuncio is fresh out of the shower in sweats and a holey T-shirt. His hair is wet and curly. He didn't shave.

"You look like an out-of-work waiter," Wally tells him.

Nuncio, pawing already through the bags Wally has brought, grins. Wally takes off his coat and hat and lays them neatly over the back of the futon frame, and then he touches the top of his head. He looks around. It's such a young-guy apartment. A curtain hangs across one doorway. On the wall there are a couple of framed posters from plays Nuncio has been in, and a rusty robin's-egg-blue metal cream-soda sign.

"Thanks for the Pan-Asian food," says Nuncio, extracting meatball heroes and bags of chips.

"You're welcome."

"Want a beer?"

"Sure."

They eat on the futon with the steamer trunk for a table and the paper bags for plates. Wally's heart is seized by thin coils of longing, wistfulness, for what Nuncio seems to have, which is a kind of freedom. Limitless and fertile ground for the pursuit of happiness. Something about him being so scruffily clean and relaxed; something about the steam coming from the still-hot meatballs as he bites; and the apartment, which is somewhat milk-cratey in its décor, not entirely grown-up—there is about Nuncio the sweet promise of transience. Wally misses that part of his life, although he cannot be sure he ever had it. Being around Nuncio at Game was like being around the essence of possibility; here, in his apartment, the concentration is too pure; it causes Wally to feel hopelessly excluded, dry and monochromatic and lacking. The mantle of his age, Wally supposes: the trick is in wearing it gracefully.

As if they are at the back table drinking their respective cocoa and scotch after closing time, they trade their stories. Nuncio tells Wally about his cast-director-playwright antics, and Wally tells Nuncio about Ann's pot–faculty-room–boy antics. It's not quite like the old days; Wally is conscious that they seem to be regaling each other.

"They don't need you at Game tonight?" asks Nuncio.

Wally shrugs. "I'm thinking about selling it."

Nuncio does eyebrow and jaw things.

Wally shrugs again. "It was always really Alice's."

"You love it. Are you kidding?"

"Well." Wally rubs his jaw. "No."

"What would you do?"

"Open up another place. I never liked the name. I don't even really like game."

"So what would you serve?"

"Well, you know. Pan-Asian food."

Nuncio mimes shooting a chip at Wally. He digests all this some more. "It just isn't the same without me," he announces at last, with a toothsome grin. "So what else is going on?"

"Nothing. Little legal matter."

"Yeah?"

"This teacher of Ann's, she's being threatened with dismissal because we've become sort of involved."

"Really?"

"Yeah."

"Wow, that's awful. Is she nice?"

"Who, the teacher? No. Not remotely."

"I just mean . . . Wow, sorry to hear that. Are you going to fight it?"

Wally shrugs. "It's not mine to fight. I spoke with a lawyer, though. It's a private school, there's no collective-bargaining agreement, she's an employee-at-will, basically they can do whatever they want."

"That sucks. How's Ann handling it all?"

"She doesn't know about it."

"No?"

"Well, she's the one who wanted Esker to come for dinner in the first place, but she doesn't know about the rest."

"Oh."

"So she's fine."

"Okay."

"She is."

"Okay. That's the teacher? Esther?"

"Esker, yeah." Wally crumples up his waxed paper. What had he hoped to gain by telling Nuncio? A solution? Empathy? Camaraderie? Hell. "Maybe you could come by, though, sometime. Give her a little drug talk."

Nuncio looks aghast. "Like what?"

"You know, like: Be careful, drugs are dangerous."

"This is your brain. This is your brain on drugs."

"Exactly. It'll sound better, coming from you."

Nuncio drinks from his beer. "It will? Why?" He might be bewildered or he might be playing bewilderment.

"Never mind." Wally laughs and stands. He's hurt for no good reason. The friendship with Nuncio, he realizes, will fade. "Good to see you."

"You, too."

He gets his hat and touches his bald spot, and then, because he wants something like this to be stated, he turns back and says it. "Because she has a lot of affection for you."

"Oh. Ann?" Nuncio has stood, too. He has his hands up under his armpits.

"You know."

"Oh well. Yeah. Of course." The moment has become unexpectedly awkward. Nuncio is looking shy. His earlobes are red. Wally misses him at Game; it's true, the place isn't the same without him. He pulls on his shapka, suggesting, it occurs to him, a spy in some Cold War novel. He tries to think of something clever to say in a Russian accent, but the wheels are spinning too slowly.

"What'd you say her name was?" Nuncio asks.

"Who?"

"Ann's teacher."

"Esker."

"That's a funny name."

"Yeah." A little surge of pride and affection at the thought of her, and then it ebbs and he feels doubt lapping in its wake. His cell phone rings. It's Game; the dishwasher's flooding again. He sighs, shoves the phone back in his pocket, and walks to the door. "You interested in buying a restaurant cheap?"

"I don't know. Anything wrong with it?"

"It's in mint condition. Tip-top."

"As they say."

"As they say."

Nuncio smiles his easy, crinkly smile, and for a minute they are in it, the old pattern, the warmth and rapport, but that's just what it is, Wally recognizes: an old pattern repeating itself, and nothing more. He touches Nuncio's shoulder for a moment; suddenly this is like farewell, and, perhaps sensing it, Nuncio accompanies him into the hall. After a bit he calls down the central stairwell. "It was good you stopped by. Hey, good luck with that legal matter."

Wally pauses and peers up three flights now at Nuncio's nice, remote face, disembodied and dizzily framed by the spiraling geometry of railings. "Thanks." The coils tighten around his heart as he descends.

31.

*S*he's lost her job. Obviously. Obviously. They haven't said it yet, but it's so obvious. Florence had her come to the office again this afternoon, after school, she'd been warned this time: a letter in her box yesterday, a real letter, not a note, but a completely properly opaque business letter, obviously for the files, everything in the correct place: Prospect School letterhead, addressee's name and address down two spaces and left-aligned, date two more spaces down, then two more spaces and the salutation: full name, and a title. "Dear Ms. I. J. Esker." And then the royal "we." "We wish to inform you . . ." "We trust that you can understand the need for . . ." "Any such involvement would run counter to our fundamental ethical . . ." "We have arranged for the school's lawyer, Mr. Clark Pearson, of McCutchen, Scott, Haverstrom and Fiener, to be present in order to . . ." "We will expect you promptly at . . ."

So she had advance warning, an evening to think, to plan, to take Wally up on his offer of speaking with his lawyer, or at least to call Wally and speak with *him,* but she didn't do any of this. She was afflicted by a kind of partial paralysis. She spent the evening rereading the letter, and ironing what she would wear. A sepia skirt. A white blouse. A sweater the color of buttermilk. She ironed slowly and dumbly. It was all she could do. The iron gave off its baked-potato smell. She smelled it and listened to the metal go over the cloth. She let herself pretend she had the sort of life where you ironed sheets, and she thought, Wouldn't that be a good life, preferable? Taking in ironing. Clean, smooth, hot sheets, all day long. She could be an ironess. How peaceful, how graceful, how devoid of yearning. The heaviness of the iron, the slow drape of the cloth. She could see all the furniture in her apartment cloaked in white.

She played Ann's tape while she ironed. When she finished ironing what she needed to, she looked through her closet for more things to iron, and then she did the afghans that lived on the back of the couch. Her mother never used pure wool but some kind of poly-mix, for which the iron was a little too hot, and it made this dangerously burning yet purifying smell, and Ann's tape played loudly and strangely through the apartment, careering from Liz Phair to Jacques Brel to Janis Joplin, all of it dripping with pathos, or bathos. That was the unifying theme, evidently, pathos or bathos, depending on whether you were in your teens or past them. Against the music she ironed, against her loss, against damage.

The feeling of inevitability was terrible. And the lethargy, like the lethargy that had hollowed out her bones after her mother died, when she'd ridden the train back to the city, back to her life, yes, but without claims on it, committed, resolved, to having no hard-and-fast designs. She'd broken her own unspoken rule, and now the judgment was coming, wearing the terrible, trivial face of Florence, but she could recognize it in spite of that disguise; the judgment was real; Esker would have made it find her one way or another.

She lay awake for nearly ever, and when she finally fell asleep it was the bottomless kind, and so hard, so brutally difficult to scrape herself awake from it in the morning. The morning was cold and dark and the tea steeped too long and was bitter and that was all she wanted for breakfast. She caught herself in the mirror before she left and noticed with some detached interest that it was a Genie costume she'd instinctively chosen, a cameo palette, all prudence and duty.

Classes were classes. She let them work in small groups. They did practice tests: Achievements, Regents, SATs. A tiny handful, of whom Ann was the youngest, did practice mathskis. Her baby-brown hair shone in the classroom's fluorescent lights as she bent over the work. Esker could see her jaw working: gum. In her mind Esker supplied the smell of mint, expelled at regular intervals on each soft breath. She had worked with her own head bent that close to Ann's. Ann chewed with her mouth slightly open, and Esker knew this to be an affectation, not the natural tendency of Ann James but a trying on of a tougher, looser self, an approximation of Denise Escobar and Lamika Pierre and Hannah Stolarik: bigger girls, in a way. She wondered if Ann knew anything of this. Of what she'd done. She wondered if Ann felt betrayed. With her shiny, shiny hair that she washed every day to get ready for school, to get ready for the world, to get ready to meet someone. Ann looked up then, and Esker saw for one half a second, before averting her own gaze, that the girl's face was open and curious to see Esker regarding her. At the end of C-block, Ann seemed to try to approach her, but Esker sensed it well enough in advance and made a fortress of her body language, briskly stuffing papers into briefcase, turning to talk with another student, checking her watch, striding out—a nod at Ann—out into the hall and down, clip clip clip, the polished stairs.

The meeting. Esker was braced for it by the time it came along, thirty minutes after D-block, not enough time to go across the street and take a walk in the park, which is what she badly would have liked to do, slip into the botanical garden, even, and lose herself among the snow-crusted branches, but too much time to sit at her desk doing nothing at all, which is essentially what she did. She arrived neither early nor late, neither smiling nor unsmiling. Florence's "we" for once had not been figurative: there were, in addition to the headmistress, the dean of faculty (a fatuous former history teacher who resembled an aged turkey) and an actually quite pleasant, embarrassed-looking young man whom Esker took to be the lawyer; he was, in fact.

"Attorney Pearson," Florence introduced him.

"Clark Pearson," he called himself, shaking her hand, which for some reason almost made Esker erupt in giggles.

Unfortunately, Clark Pearson had little else to contribute to the proceedings; Florence, in a steel-gray suit shot through with metallic fibers, did the talking, lots more of the same as the other day: the well-being of the school etc., etc., as well as aggressive fishing for explicit details about what was going on between Esker and Wally. ("Please understand that if any of our information is incorrect, now is your opportunity to state so.") The dean did little more than clear his throat significantly every now and then. Esker did not know whether to be furious, exasperated, afraid, or hysterical. She kept wanting to stand on her chair and stamp her foot. Instead, she sat there, one eyebrow arched, her posture growing steadily more noble and elegant as she condescended to listen to their idiot speech.

That was, she supposed, the job after all of lawyers and administrators: to be idiots, to be the idiots of the world.

She found her mind wandering. How little this room was. Not just its dimensions, which did strike her now, for the first time, as cramped, but its aspirations: that meaty slab of marble, the primness of the brass sconces either side of the mantel, the frilled glass cups blooming out of each with their electric chandelier-style lightbulbs burning brightly, their hot little pointy filaments like fingers raised to make a point, to emphasize Florence's point, issued from the pursed pink bud of her mouth as she herself raised a finger, her wrist encircled by a frilly white cuff. . . . Esker blinked hard. Oh, what a little room, she could hardly bear it, and its walls painted the perfect shade of French vanilla, and its chair rail painted lemon, and the dean there with his gray wattle pressed into his neck as he nodded in agreement with the headmistress and shifted in his reproduction cabriole armchair so that it creaked protestingly. . . . Really, I must protest, thought Esker. "Really, I must protest."

As it happened, she said it out loud.

They all looked at her.

You're nothing but a pack of cards, she thought, but checked herself. This was real life. But she couldn't help it; she had, for a moment, not an actual hallucination but a very clear image all the same of Florence and the dean and poor nice Mr. Clark Pearson as collages pasted together from cut-out scraps of construction paper, two-dimensional, all x-and-y-axis, impressive when glimpsed head-on but with no backing, no substance, no standing. And it was perhaps under the influence of what might have been this fleeting delusion or vision that Esker stood up and appeared for a moment to be about to climb up onto the seat of her chair.

She looked oddly bigger than people usually thought of her as being, not so much taller, perhaps, as heightened, and with a stance of fortitude and reckoning, her feet planted apart, her shoulders back and spread to their full width, and she had deep color under her eyes, and her lips were slightly apart. She shook her head as if to clear it, as if at a loss, but in a way less at a loss than she'd been for some time, and, happening to glance down at her brown-and-cream apparel, muttered, apparently to herself, but audibly, and with real, sudden annoyance, "I can't believe I wore this," and then turned her attention back toward the others in the room, and with no less annoyance told them, "This is ridiculous. I am a good teacher. My private life is not your business. My emotional life is not your business. I won't answer any more questions about it. The whole premise of this inquiry is silly. Really. It's silly. I am a good teacher."

She had the impression, as she was delivering this speech, that it was the height of eloquence, and iron-clad in its logic, and irrefutable. And in the seconds after its utterance, the dawning counterimpression that it had been none of these things was sickening, made her feel physically sick, and she sat down again because she had to, because her legs had grown suddenly weak, and her lungs uneasy. The way Clark Pearson looked at the rug after this confirmed it: something funereal and final had seeped into the air; even Florence looked down, tiredly, at the millefiori hemisphere weighting the papers on her desk, and stroked the smooth glass with one finger and said, "You understand that we have no choice but to interpret your response as confirmation of an inappropriate relationship between you and Mr. James?"

Esker made no reply. She understood the term "bristling" in a visceral way she never had before, because every sinew, every cilium, every neuron in her body was erect, tensed with fury and helplessness. She had a flash of Miss De Witt saying, on a peas-and-carroty sigh, "It's that way because it *is* so," and she wanted to say, in a voice thick and passionate, *You're so wrong, you're so wrong,* but what was the point of saying that when they didn't realize their rules were only that, *their* rules, and not some absolute, pre-existing creed it was their mission to interpret and protect? What was the point of saying it when she had no tongue to speak with, when she had been relieved of her tongue at the door, when it had dissolved in the ether of this chamber, where only their language had any currency? Anyway, they would have misunderstood her, would have thought she was denying the existence of a relationship rather than challenging their right to inquire.

And how could she say that, when she knew she'd been too large?

The dean took a stab at reasoning with her. Obviously, he wanted a turn talking. They were sorry for her now; she was an unfortunate; and decent people could but give her one more chance. "If you were able to assure us that you would end the relationship immediately . . ." He glanced at Florence, who picked up the ball halfheartedly.

"Uh . . . we could certainly take that into consideration."

Esker could hear Attorney Pearson shift in his chair. She heard Florence's fingernail tap the paperweight. She heard the school clock heave its minute hand one notch forward.

"Well . . ." Glances among the three. "If you have nothing further to add, that's all. You'll hear from us soon."

She went down the hall without feeling she was walking. Nine years she'd been here. Straight from college, straight from Albert, straight from Delos, this had been her world, her small world, her system, her logic, her algorithm, recursive, self-similar, known. This had been her ironing. She was in the faculty room now, which was dark, and, as far as she knew, empty, and she didn't know why she'd come in, there was the phone but she wouldn't call Wally, not without a tongue, and anyway who was Wally? Certainly no one big enough to bear this, her mess, her weight, her ruinous wake, and they had made her happiness in him a wrong thing; their condemnation was confirmation of her essential mistake in attempting it. And there was a stapler which she picked up, it reminded her of an iron, and she made a little soothing motion of ironing her palm, and she was sitting now on the couch facing the window, and it hurt to make a soothing motion, and she covered her eyes, which were blazing in their sockets, and it hurt. It hurt. And to make it stop she threw the thing, the iron, the stapler, away from her as hard as she could.

32.

The next day, once Ann learns Esker is out sick, she cuts the rest of her classes and takes the subway to Fourteenth Street. This is the stop she uses for Game, but Game is not her destination. Her destination is Esker's, whose address she looked up in the file yesterday evening while waiting for her father to pick her up from the school office. She knows she was a little bit high but not very, and she's *sure* she remembered the number correctly, so it disorients her when she cannot even find the 400 block of Greenwich Avenue; she goes up and down its short length three times, feeling eerier and eerier, and even stops into a Laundromat and borrows their White Pages, but Esker's unlisted. The idea that Esker doesn't actually exist takes hold. She passes through a quick shroud of smoke from a street vendor's hot-pretzel cart. The sun is just spitting blindingly off surfaces: storefronts, windshields, the sunglasses of a cop she asks for directions. He's all shrugs. "This is it, this *is* Greenwich Avenue!" Then a delivery van guy in front of St. Vincent's says, "Maybe you want Greenwich Street." Ohhh. And where the hell is Greenwich Street? She finds it, eventually, it's one of those ones over by the water, where no one ever goes, and she walks down and down past Clarkson, West Houston, King, and Charlton—really, who knew, who knew one of her teachers lived here? This is no-man's-land, edgy. Fitting. And by this time she's really cold and her feet have begun to ache, but it almost fuels her the more.

Along one of those particleboard walls they put in front of construction sites, posters of her mother have been pasted up, and they stop Ann short. Alice Alice Alice Alice, four in a row. In Esker's very neighborhood. How obnoxious. Yet Ann can't help feeling that lift of pride: this public woman, this indie darling, is her private mother, her bloodline, her own. Lame as Alice is, parent-wise, their link has heft, has power, is real. Ann carries traces of Alice's power in her own blood, her own genes. Alice is awful, but Alice is magic. Her current flick is called *Flight*, and the poster shows her aloft, amid clouds. Ann goes up on the balls of her feet. She feels the tension in her not-yet-up-to-speed ankle and calf muscles. It reminds her of what she has to do to kiss Malcolm on the cheek, and she closes her eyes and purses her lips and pecks the air. Then she returns her whole feet to the ground and expels her breath in a white plume. The sky smells like gasoline and a spent Christmas tree someone has put on the curb. Ann goes on tiptoe again and fills her lungs. What is it these days, this feeling? Magic, dangerous. She is on the cusp of invincibility.

Esker's house is past Vandam. It is just that, a house, not an apartment building, and tiny. There's no bell: ridiculous. Ann knocks. She can tell the sound doesn't carry inside. She raps on one of the glass panes. And waits. And raps again. Esker comes to the door and opens it. She looks pained to see Ann.

"Playing hooky," she observes, after a moment. Her voice sounds like she hasn't used it in a long time.

"So are you," says Ann. Her hands are rammed in the pockets of her ice-blue down jacket: the stance of a gunslinger.

Esker holds the door open, and Ann enters.

"How did you know where to find me?" Esker asks, after shutting the door behind them. The apartment is very quiet, very still, and warmed by the sun.

"When you weren't in school, I just thought you'd be home."

"No, I mean, I'm not listed."

"Oh. Remember those unlocked files I told you about?"

"You were serious about that."

"Actually, I'd never done it before, but it gave me the idea."

Esker sits on the couch. Ann stays standing. What an apartment Esker has! It's like something out of a fairy tale, so little and tilty and simple. Nothing looks modern. Whitish sunlight comes streaming in the front windows, a projector beam picking up dust motes and printing bright polyhedra across the wide floorboards, the furniture, a few overlapping afghans, Esker's lap.

"I like your skirt," says Ann. It's crimson jersey, cut very full so it pools out around her when she sits. "You never wear red."

Esker glances at her skirt and sort of nods or something.

"So you want to know what else I found in your file?"

"I have a feeling you're going to tell me."

"A letter to you from Florence."

Esker returns her gaze steadily. She would be a formidable person to have a staring contest with. Formidable: Arousing fear, dread. Inspiring awe, wonder. Difficult to undertake.

"It said there was going to be a meeting with you and a lawyer yesterday afternoon to discuss your relationship with my father."

Another nod. Esker is being even more Eskerish than usual. She's behaving like some naked cross-legged old guy on a mountaintop or something, all wise and quiet and impervious. Ann unzips her jacket. Suddenly she's grown hot, like actually sweaty, with rivulets trickling down her ribs. Also, her ankles are tired. She looks behind her; there is a chair; unbidden, she sits.

"So, um." Oh, this dizziness. She leans way forward, head almost between her knees, like trying-not-to-faint position, like airplane-crash position, and her hair makes a sweeping nylony sound against her sleeves. She picks up her head. "Can't you please just tell me what the fuck is going on? Because I think I should know. Are they firing you?"

The question apparently requires several moments of consideration. "Yes."

"Does Wally know?"

"He knew it had come up as a possibility."

"Is it really going to happen?"

"Yes."

"Is that why you broke the window?"

A pause. "How did you know about that?"

"I was in the faculty room."

Esker starts visibly. Her neck reddens. Then she surprises Ann with this tired, genuine smile. "Personnel files, the faculty room. Is nothing safe from you, Ann?"

It sounds very tender, the way she says this, and saying her name aloud, too. Ann takes off her jacket. "It's really hot." She balls it and puts it on the floor, where it unballs itself like an iridescent caterpillar. "Are you in love with my father?"

Esker laughs, her unnerving, out-of-the-blue bark. Softly, as if to herself, she says, "The sixty-four-thousand-dollar question," and then, differently, "Oh, Ann, I'm sorry. Ann, I'm sorry, I've failed you."

What this does to Ann! Hearing this! She doesn't know, she feels wild, she feels relieved, she feels bitterly angry and clean and young and comforted and shattered. But she feels sane, it makes her feel so sane, to finally hear this from a grownup. She squeezes the arms of the chair. "Why did you?" It comes out hoarsely.

Esker shakes her head. "I didn't mean to. I came where I shouldn't have."

"I *wanted* you and my father to like each other. I *wanted* you to meet."

Esker nods, barely.

"I *did*. Why don't you believe me?"

"I don't disbelieve you, Ann. But wanting it and then having it happen . . . I don't want you to believe you had any control over it." This little bone or muscle is going back and forth in her cheek. A blue vein by her temple is visible, and is wavy. She is so small, Esker, so small and tough.

"I don't want you to lose your job."

"I'm so sorry."

"How do they know?"

"Know?"

"About you and Wally."

"I was careless, I mentioned I was seeing him to another staff member."

"Did you know it was against the rules?"

". . . It wasn't a good idea. I should have known that. It was irresponsible."

"To who?"

"To you." She gets these words out as though they are cutting her mouth.

Ann just sits with this. It is too much. It weighs like 999 pounds. It's in her lap, like this weight, this big black infernal cartoon-drawing lead weight she's never felt before, and it's so so so big and so so sweet, this big black sweet literal weight, pinning her, and all the buoyancy has gone out of her body, all the loft of just minutes ago, when she was rising on her toes and kissing the winter sky in front of the poster of her mother, thinking of Malcolm's hopelessly smooth cheek and all the shrill airy power bubbling uncontainably from her own magical, flawed bloodline—all of this has left her. She has been relieved of something, robbed of something, relieved of something. "You were irresponsible to me?" she echoes.

Esker nods. She is very white.

Little explosions in Ann's head are giving her a headache. She loves Esker so much. "I was just going to tell you something, but I forgot what."

Esker is patient.

"I mean I didn't forget it, but I'm just not going to say it." And Esker must love her, to have said that. Not just loves her, that's easy, but cares for her. That's the thing. The rare, the harder thing. Ann has to go. She has to go. She has to leave. She gets out of her chair, no mean feat when you weigh 999 pounds, and picks up her jacket. "This isn't what I was going to say. It's something else."

Esker nods.

"I want to ask you something. A favor." She gets her arms in her jacket, but the wrong way through, so that the back of the jacket is across her chest, with the silvery blue nylon puffs like armor plating. This is a little play-habit of hers; it's a robot-costume this way, and she can wave her arms in front of her and do "Danger, Will Robinson!" like from *Lost in Space*, and Hannah and Denise always crack up. Esker doesn't know any of this, but it comforts Ann, this reference to play, it distracts her some from the importance of the question: "Will you still come to Winter Concert?"

Esker hesitates. "That might be difficult." From the way she gets up from the couch, Ann can see she must weigh 999 pounds, too. Ann has edged toward the door, but she waits, searching for more. "I'll see," says Esker. And when Ann looks at her again before leaving, "I won't say no."

33.

Wally climbs the steps to The Prospect School with a wave of other parents and students and staff and friends, and enters under the sheltering iron raptor. A formidable mascot, thinks Wally, meant to frighten away anything harmful. The place is abuzz. It smells of cleaning fluid and sweat and all the mingled perfumes of the mothers and the cold coming off people's jackets and the bake-sale items set up on long folding tables at one end of the foyer. Everyone has dressed for the evening. The girls are wearing colored glitter on their eyelids. The boys, in gigantic sneakers, are wearing their most eccentric shirts. They all have a focus, the students, a specific, urgent design: to find so-and-so, to tell this one the message that that one said to tell. Their eyes burn intently through the throng; they are like sleek operatives in some clandestine affair, and when they pick out their targets, they make forceful, graceful beelines—" 'Scuse me, sorry, pardon me"—weaving around all the bulky, murmuring, comparatively purposeless adults.

Wally loves it all, even the crowdedness, even the jostling, the embrace of it all. Such a safe place to be, at school on the night of a performance. Sort of like being hearthside in slippers with a sleeping dog on the rug. There is always a storm outside; the key is the shelter you take from it. It's how he's used to feeling at Game, too, surrounded by voices, the smell of meat gravies, the popping fire, the red velvet curtains hung either side of the plate glass. He is expert at finding this feeling, surrounding himself with it. His smile is genuine as he makes his way through the thickly knotted crowd, inclining his head in greeting toward a few parents he knows, a few teachers, a girl with a nose ring whom he doesn't think he knows but who smiles and says hi to him. Hello, hello, hello, he nods, dodging his shoulders this way and that, until eventually he reaches the bake-sale table, where he buys a cup of tea and a cookie shaped like a violin.

He wonders whether Esker will be here, and can't help craning his neck to scan the room. He knows the situation doesn't look good, not as his lawyer explained it, but he can't believe it won't end up all right. Everyone knows Florence is sort of an ass. And Esker is tough, and Wally will be her best possible champion; it's what he loves to do, what he's born to do, hold other people's hands, nourish and fortify them faultlessly. He's almost excited—he knows it's ignoble—but he's almost excited at the prospect of a long haul, of opposition and of facing it down, hand in hand, with Esker.

He's not worried. Not really worried. He thinks of Nuncio's face at the top of the stairs, charmingly framed by damp black curls, sweet and encouraging: everything comes so easily to Nuncio. And Alice, slipping in and out of worlds as suits her, shedding pixie dust as she comes and goes, turning everything in her path magical for a moment. Why not borrow that, why not *be* like that from now on? Hand in hand, and in their outer hands spears, or wands, for chasing away the Florences, for invoking Godspeed and high winds, and off they go! The sense of the possible fills him up. He hasn't felt like this since Grange Hill, really, since he was a teenager messing around in the breading factory with Chris Petroni and them, climbing along the dead conveyor belts and jumping into the giant metal vats with echoey clangs. He finishes his cookie; the lights have begun to flash on and off, signaling people to make their way up the winding stair into the Big Room.

Metal folding chairs have been arranged on the floor at the edge of the playing space—the ersatz orchestra seats, where most of the adults sit—with the kids filling in the bleachers behind them—ersatz mezzanine and balcony. The seats fill in quickly; soon there is standing room only. Wally chooses a seat at the very top of the bleachers, the better to see Esker should she come in. Also, though he is normally happy to chat with fellow Prospect School parents, he is feeling a certain outlaw/outcast status at the moment, and relishing it.

He consults his program. There it is, at the end of the first act:

Untitled . . . . *Malcolm Choy, Hannah Stolarik, Ann James*

The pieces are not unenjoyable, most of them. He recognizes the fan dance Ann was supposed to have been in, and her friends Denise and Lamika. Witty, really, with electric box fans, and little personal battery-operated fans, and accordion-folded paper fans the dancers actually fold, leaning over and using one another's backs for hard surfaces, as part of the dance. The boy named Malcolm, the one Ann went on tiptoe to kiss outside the dean's office last week, drums for it, and a short white kid named Perry plays the guitar. Both boys seem very serious. Not once do they look over at the dancers. Wally feels warmth for them in their too-obvious show of dedication to the music, and warmth for the girls in their leotards and tights, caught, he imagines, between panic and pride at being so exposed in their various stages of physical development.

The performance drags on. The intervals between numbers are long-ish, with each new act setting up its own equipment or props, and the lights come up while everyone's waiting, and people turn around to chat with their neighbors, and the students up on the bleachers around Wally do the loveliest things with their bodies in the chat time: they twist and lean and lie and lay their heads across laps and get on their knees and steal each other's baseball caps. "Can't get me," taunts a girl on the end, ready to spring from a low step onto the Big Room floor, and, "Of course I can get you," is the dismissive, languid response from the very tall boy whose MetroCard she has apparently stolen. She sticks it between her teeth and makes it flap there with some movement of her jaw. He appears not to look her way, so cool, so bored, and then he lunges with his impossibly long arm; he grabs her wrist, and she forfeits the card with a shriek like a bell: All is well. All is well. Wally presses a hand to his chest. The membrane between fullness and loss is translucent.

And if he sells Game—he hadn't said it out loud before Nuncio's, but it seems true, if sudden, that he wants to sell it—then what will he do? Open another. Open a bed-and-breakfast somewhere. Shelter Island. He pictures Ann there for too-short visits, with a duffel bag full of college clothes and textbooks. He pictures Esker there, barefoot, reading the paper in the kitchen, saying unexpected things to him while he beats eggs and cream with a fork. He pictures an arched doorway off the back with a view of tousled lawn sloping off to water. The possible.

There is Florence, down below, greeting parents and other dignitaries. She's wearing a suit the color of a blood orange, and her hair is swept high and pale gold above it. There is Buddy, the art teacher. Wally remembers him from the hospital: very sweet and worried; Wally had almost felt compelled to comfort *him*. He's busy right now, with that same worried look, speed-walking back behind the playing area with an extension cord in hand. There is the English teacher Ann thinks so little of. There is the nose ring girl. Where is Esker? He wants her here, his ally, his—not protectorate, that's not the word, but his one to protect, and they could smirk at Florence in her blood-orange suit from far above, from twelve feet up or however high these bleachers are.

Has the fact that she's under threat made her dearer to him? He doesn't think so, only that it's made him feel more bound to her, only that it's called upon the part of him that's there to give solace, the part of him that's gallant and steady, the part that's needed, which is the part he is most at home with. Perhaps the part he is most homesick for.

The lights go down before Ann's act, and in that first moment of darkness a slice of yellow is the Big Room door swinging open and shut, and Wally looks and there is the brief figure of Esker, already swallowed again in shadow. He can't be sure it wasn't a mirage. He searches the clumps of people near the door, but in the resumed darkness it is impossible to discern individuals.

The first thing that happens is a blinding light in his eyes. After a moment there is a soft cha-chunk and he's in darkness again, and then another section of the audience is illuminated. The third time, he realizes what it is: a slide projector. And the fourth time, it's been swung around to target the side wall, so now everyone can see that words are being projected, black type, though he can't really make them out. Then the back wall. Slides five and six appear to be random dictionary definitions.

With a sigh, the projector dies, and in the darkness a drumbeat starts. Then more lights come up. Malcolm Choy is drumming with his bare hands, standing over his two tall tapered drums. Now Wally sees it was Hannah who was assaulting everyone with the beam of the slide projector. She is transformed from any Hannah he has ever seen: she is wearing a Wall Streety business suit, and her hair is up in a bun, and she's wearing black-rimmed glasses and regarding the audience with excruciating directness and severity. Even though he knows Ann is in this act, he notices her third. She stands about fourteen feet tall. He has the sense that they are eye to eye with each other, although she wouldn't be able to see him in the darkness of the audience. The audience has grown extremely quiet—his imagination, or is it more quiet than for the other acts?

Ann is wearing a white garment, something like the fusion of a nightgown and a waterfall, the lower portion of which cascades frothily to the floor, entirely covering the ladder or scaffolding on which she must be standing. Her arms are bare. Her face is made up in white, with silver around the eyes and a small red mouth, sort of Noh-esque, Wally thinks, and it's a queer experience viewing his own daughter in what looks like a mask but is, he realizes, her own face, her own unique and subtle bones and flesh and skin beneath the paint. A foot above her head, invisibly attached in a perfect arc, floats a halo of five white-feathered globes. It takes him a second to realize, from the way they lazily shift against one another, that they're helium balloons. For some reason this comes as a relief. There is something so forceful and complete about the tableau these three kids have put together, it's frankly disconcerting. The bob of those balloons breaks the spell enough that he can smile; he can feel warmth for their imperfect attempt.

Hannah removes a great tome from her attaché case and places it on the music stand in front of her. She opens it and with formidable, abrasive confidence, hands clasped behind her back, begins to read in monotone. "Moonbeam. A ray of moonlight. Moonblind. Affected with moon blindness. Moon blindness. Recurrent inflammation of a horse's eyes, often resulting in eventual blindness. Also called mooneye. Mooncalf. 1. A fool. 2. A freak."

Someone giggles and is shushed. The drumming stops. Hannah stops. There are these bells; Malcolm's suddenly got finger cymbals, and they go *shing! shing!*, and the strange angel, Ann, lights a match, holds it, lets it fall. He can hear the audience gasp. He thinks automatically of the authorities; he looks down at the adult heads below, wondering which is Florence's. It strikes him that Hannah in this piece is like the headmistress. The flame drops lightly, almost like a feather. He wonders for a moment—he has never thought of this before—about the weight of fire. He pictures Esker standing by with a fire extinguisher under her skirt. *Was* that Esker who came in at the last minute? Again he scans the standing-room-only cluster under the red-lit exit sign; it is too dark to say. When he looks back at the playing space, the flame is gone. The drumming starts back; Hannah intones. More gobbledygook from the dictionary: Moonchild. Mooneye. Moondog . . . People shift, growing bored

Again: the freeze, the cymbals, the flame. Two flames, this time. Three, four, falling one after another with little pause. By what law of physics do they seem to float? Three go out in the air; one gets smothered against the material of the epic skirt.

Back to the recitative and the drumming. This time, though, Ann overlaps, softly at first, singing something, no words, just "oh," very slowly, three rising notes and then back down for the fourth. She continues, so unearthly and dulcet, this wordless singing, and Wally is annoyed when someone in the audience giggles, but then comes more laughter, soft and appreciative, and finally he gets the tune; it's "Satisfaction," and he has this sense of uplift. Oh! Is this supposed to be funny? The whole thing is some teenage joke; no wonder he doesn't get it. How relieved he is that it's not supposed to be serious.

Malcolm keeps drumming, but with greater fervor, and Hannah keeps to her task, with greater volume, and something surely unplanned begins to happen: the kids in the bleachers start to sing along with Ann, using the actual words, and then some wiseguy holds up a lighter like he's at a concert, and almost immediately maybe a dozen other lighters are raised, and Ann begins to light and shed more matches, in rapid succession—musn't the book be used up by now?—until they are falling all over her skirt like drowning lightning bugs, these hot pointy lights, falling and extinguishing themselves, but as more and more of them fleck the front of her at once, isn't one likely to catch, aren't they beginning to accumulate, still burning? And then, as if it were the only natural next thing, Ann steps out—surely he sees this, not a fall, not a panicky loss of balance, but a calm, deliberate, even slow-motion stepping away from the ladder. Her eyes gleam very bright, but then Wally realizes it's the silver makeup on her lids, and he can't even tell whether her eyes are open, and then, as her body descends through the air, the skirt-thing, which seems in fact to *be* a parachute, mushroom-clouds up and around her body so that she's hidden from view.

And for just a moment, in the stillness and sudden silence that follow, the thing he feels is clearly pride, the proudness of being associated with her, this magical angel girl who's brought down the house; how special she is, more special than he would ever want to be, but, oh, the association with her confers just enough on him that he can taste it without being of it. This lasts only a moment, and then the wrongness crashes against him like a sheet of metal, informed by the cries of a few girls in the audience and the rush of a few bodies toward that heap of slippery, pearly material and the belated switching on of the lights—but he will remember it later, it will remain disturbingly indelible, that kernel of pride.

The people around her are Malcolm and Hannah and Buddy and Esker. Being at the very top of the bleachers, and being that the bleachers are thoroughly crammed with kids, Wally sees that his quickest way down is to lower himself over the back, but it's too high, really much too high; maybe if he were a teenager. Instead, he has to squeeze himself halfway down the bleachers first, stepping over and occasionally on kids' hands and feet, "Sorry, excuse me," and they are so nice and helpful and cordial and they bend out of his way and their hands reach out to steady him as he loses his balance a couple of times, and then he is close enough to the ground that he can lower himself off the side, and this big gangsta-rap kid wearing a do rag just reaches out and holds his hand as he does, so he has something to take his weight, and he is embarrassed to feel his eyes prick with tears at all their native kindness.

And as he moves now through the crowd on the floor, gently and firmly threading past chairs and shoes and pocketbooks, trying to hold off fear as he makes his way toward the playing space, toward Ann, toward Esker, both of whom will need his help, he is only like a wave responding to the moon, he is homing, returning to what he knows best.

34.

It's so warm inside the hospital.

Hannah and Malcolm slouch in the waiting room's orange bucket seats with their twin chewed-rimmed Styrofoam cups, watching Court TV on the high-mounted monitor, looking reassuringly bored. They're lumpy in their coats still. Malcolm seems to be nearly nodding off. Esker, standing away from them, glances over frequently; the sight of them is a kind of ballast. She envies both how easily they have taken up residence here, and how easily they could get up and go if they wanted. After a while, Hannah does get up and disappear, but returns shortly with her hair loosed from its bun—she is still wearing the business suit that was her costume—and a box of Junior Mints in hand. She shakes a lot of the contents into Malcolm's upturned palm, and then they both return their focus to the program: a sullen-looking woman on the witness stand. They swallow their chocolates, eyes trained on the screen, innocent and disinterested.

The swinging doors open. Cold air snaps forth like a sheet, and another emergency rolls in on a gurney. Esker takes a step back. She is unable to sit. She has had coffee, too; Malcolm and Hannah, unbidden, had brought her a cup when they got theirs, having tracked and isolated the coffee shop within minutes of arriving at the ER. Their ability to as-similate almost instantly and so unconcernedly to these environs is bewildering; she doesn't quite know whether she finds it touching or cynical. She had walked over here with them, to Methodist, ten blocks from the school, the three of them plodding quietly in the silence left behind by the ambulance. Wally had ridden ahead in its shrill white capsule with Ann.

Behind her, for Esker is looking out through the dark glass revolving doors, looking again at her own reflection cut up and layered over by the lights and lighted objects on the other side of the glass, she can hear the sounds, general and specific at once, of the others gathered in the ER, sounds of the distressed, the bored, the cheery, the urgent. Conversations in Creole, Mandarin, Spanish, Farsi. A family leaves, trailing a powder-blue balloon. Two cops go out, laughing. A woman wearing a stethoscope around her neck and a lab coat printed with a nursery pattern—pastel teddy bears, Esker thinks—rushes in hugging herself: "It's fucking freezing tonight!" A fat man with blank eyes set in his face like currants in a bun. An elderly woman with calves like walking sticks. Someone holding blood-soaked newspaper to the side of his face. A child with a great cheekful of bubble gum.

Esker attends to them mentally in all their specificity; in her mind she pauses over each one, takes each one in with equanimity and regard. But she is anonymous, unknown to them, a figure standing by the door. This is safest. She is already in retreat. They are so beautiful and fragile in their specificity, frail as paper, and she is so large—the old fear, the secret truth—now, for a moment, she sees the hot geometry of her college library floor, beckoning and forbidding at once, so confusing—*jump, don't jump*—and she is so tall and heavy and pointy and wild, it's true; she may crush whatever she touches, so she stands very still; she is resolved. With a kind of pity, a cool benevolence, she stands still, she is a sentinel, sentient only in a general way, a desireless way, selfless.

She'd come tonight late on purpose, and hidden out for part of it in the faculty room, just down the hall from the Big Room; it had been empty; she hadn't switched on a light. The great crack she'd made in the windowpane shone interestingly in Park Slope's ambient nighttime lights. It was jewellike, a motherlode of diamonds she'd exposed. Another item now for the Renovation Committee. She lurked about outside the Big Room doors when she sensed the first act was nearly over, and slipped inside just as Ann's piece was beginning. She could have come on time and held her head high. But she was here tonight for no one but Ann. It would have cost her to have to smile at or converse with anyone from the school community. And why had she come? Not to stand by with a fire extinguisher under her skirt, not exactly. But in a way, yes. Ann had asked her, and she felt uncommonly obligated, uncommonly needed.

After Ann had sailed off and down like that, and the lights had come up, and Esker had found herself almost instantly on the floor sorting through the slippery fabric heaped around the girl, who was still unconscious at that point, she wondered just what she'd been needed for, and how she had managed to fail Ann again. "Don't move her," someone had said sharply, though Esker hadn't been going to. It was Florence, standing behind her, and the look she gave Esker was so shriveling and so cold with blame, and it dovetailed so smoothly with everything Esker most feared about herself, that she nearly scrambled to her feet and ran away, but then Ann stirred; Ann was looking at Esker. She didn't have the slightest look of pain or fright, only the strange enchanted quality that was a product of all the silver-and-white makeup, and she smiled at Esker and said simply, "You came."

And now she has the thought that maybe she did provide the thing Ann needed her for: to bear witness to what she would do.

She did bear witness, and she bears responsibility, of this she is certain; it is the heaviest weight. She asked too much, and things broke. It is so simple. It's like arithmetic. She dared a thing, she dared to want, and in the school's condemnation and Ann's fall lie the proof: it was too great; the equation could not balance. So: Retreat. Cut losses. Lift off. Again she thinks, with despair and longing, of the peculiar peace of the emptiness after her mother's death in Delos, her vacuous hometown, the long vacant summer, the summer devoid of wants or wishes, the great selfless safety and promise of naught, of null, the immense and perfect *nothing* from which she has strayed. Twice. "You're so selfless," they praised her, and she pulled up her kneesocks and pulled down the shades, and when she neglected to do this, neglected to be this, she was too much to bear, and she and Albert got wrecked beneath the weight of her, and now Wally and Ann. (Is it true? Is it that simple? Arithmetic of the sort Miss De Witt would endorse? *You don't believe that for a minute, Esker,* something says, but she won't have it, won't listen; what if it's just her cunning heart?)

It is eleven already, and then eleven-thirty. Winter Concert will have long finished. There are fewer empty seats now than when they first arrived. Malcolm has dozed off. Hannah, beside him, lifts her fingers in a small wave to Esker from across the room. Esker goes to sit beside her.

When Wally finally comes, near midnight, it's with a theatrical shrug. It's a shrug for their benefit, Esker can see that much. He's got one of those hospitals-are-so-annoying expressions on his face, and he yawns and cracks his knuckles as he stops before their seats. Hannah wakes Malcolm by knocking her shoe against his. His chin comes up with a start.

"You guys should go home," Wally tells the kids. "She seems fine. It's just hospital policy, once you come in, they have to run five thousand tests before they let you go. She's fine, though. She's had a Popsicle. You guys should get some sleep."

Hannah and Malcolm look at each other. "Okay, Mr. J. Tell her I'll call her tomorrow," says Hannah.

"Same," says Malcolm gravely. "Take care."

Wally smiles. The kids slowly get their jackets on and pass through the revolving door. In the light outside, Esker can see their breath hover like empty speech balloons by their mouths for a second before they slip out of sight arm in arm like some ancient married couple. A marvel. Babies. How do they do that?

Wally takes Hannah's vacated chair. "They did a CAT scan," he says. "There's no bleeding. The doctor saw no signs of neurological deficiencies, no what they call focal signs, no head trauma or anything."

Esker is looking at him. He's looking ahead, speaking distractedly. His manner changed as soon as the kids left, relaxed into something more agitated, more frightened. He looks tired. The skin around his eyes, the gray in the sparse brown curls above his ear. These things look precious to her, even now. She swallows.

"Did you see the way she fell?" he asks.

"What do you mean?"

"Were you looking? When she fell?"

She nods.

"Did you think she was conscious when she fell?"

She nods.

"She says she wasn't. She says she fainted."

"The lights must have been hot. And that costume. And she'd been standing still for a while. You know how people faint in churches and things, when they're standing for a long time with their knees locked."

"It looked to me like she stepped off the ladder."

"Yes. Yes."

"The doctor asked her how she fell and she said she didn't remember."

"What tests do they still want to run?"

He licks his lips. He looks elsewhere than at her. "Psychiatric."

"Okay."

"It's the second time in less than two months she's here because of a fall."

"I know."

"They didn't see any reason to call a neurologist."

"All right."

"We're waiting for a psych consult."

"I understand."

He nods. He's seeming not to know what to do with his hands. Esker restrains herself from taking them.

"Do you think she would like to see me?" she asks.

"She still has all her silver makeup on. She's sleeping at the moment. They gave her something."

"To make her sleep?"

"She was shaking a lot." Holding his own voice steady with obvious effort. "I wonder if I should call Alice now or in the morning."

After a little, Esker says, "Do you want coffee?"

He turns to her, looks at her for the first time full in the eyes. "I *hoped* you'd come. I thought you would. I kept looking at the door."

"Ann asked me to."

"I just had a feeling I was going to see you."

"I care about Ann. I always will."

"We'll fight this."

"This? You mean whatever's going on with Ann."

"The Florence thing."

"Oh."

"I mean, of course, we're going to take care of . . . what Ann needs . . . help. But I was talking about the Florence thing. I wanted to tell you that. We're going to fight it."

"I mailed in my resignation."

He looks at her.

"This morning."

"Oh."

Now he is looking at her with much too much love. He has misread the meaning of her statement.

"Wally. Also—I need to say goodbye to you."

The radical shift in his face. The struggle to understand her. He takes her hand, and, yes, it is a good touch he has, full of ken, she's not immune. But this is necessary, what she's about to do. She's taking the reins away from her heart. Sacrifice is purifying, isn't it? Freeing.

"I care about Ann. I'd like to be in contact with her. I want to stay a friend, an adult friend of hers."

"But not of mine."

"I can't."

He squints. The awful effort to control his face. "If you were telling me that in order to keep your job you needed to say goodbye . . . If . . . If you were saying you wanted to keep your job . . ."

She shakes her head. "I won't stay at The Prospect School on those terms."

"Then I don't understand."

"I just need to say goodbye to you. I shouldn't've . . ."

"What?"

She retrieves her hand as gently as possible. "Attempted this."

"What?"

"This. This."

"So." He takes his breath. "All you have to do to keep your job is not have . . . a relationship with me. And you resigned your job. And now you're saying goodbye to me." He searches her face.

"Yes."

"Because . . . ?"

This is the last time she will hurt someone. This is her largest possible act. This is the way she must tell it to herself in order to get out the door.

"Have courage, Esker."

"This is my courage." Knowing she's lying.

He shakes his head, stares at her as though she were the most infuriating student, oppositional, willfully dense in spite of testing bright. "Why," says Wally, and she has never heard him sound angry before, "why would you choose to be lonely? Why would you elect to be complicit in your own unhappiness?"

Nostalgia fills her mouth like cotton. His words go through her with the echo of the familiar. If only he knew; they are a kind of beacon, they are almost welcome. She is almost eager.

"How do you know," says Esker, "I'm lonely?" As she bends through clouded vision to gather her gloves, her coat, her scarf, her hat, a blind bundle, the words rise of their own accord: "I don't know about this." The old words, Albert's hex, his innocent taunt, now passed through her lips, involuntarily and unimpeachably true. She utters them with her mouth close to the wool, so low as to be barely audible even to herself.

When she leaves, one glass compartment of the revolving door admitting her body, then discharging it into the night as the door swings round again, free of her, the pain is so great it is like a burn. She wants nothing, not even air, to touch her skin. But air is touching her skin. The thing to do is keep walking. She walks and walks for a long time, waiting for the gift not to feel it.